MISSING

BOOKS BY K.L. SLATER

Safe With Me

Blink

Liar

The Mistake

The Visitor

The Secret

Closer

Finding Grace

The Silent Ones

Single

Little Whispers

The Girl She Wanted

The Marriage

The Evidence

The Widow

MISSING
K.L. SLATER

bookouture

Published by Bookouture in 2022

An imprint of Storyfire Ltd.
Carmelite House
50 Victoria Embankment
London EC4Y 0DZ

www.bookouture.com

ISBN: 978-1-80314-240-1
eBook ISBN: 978-1-80314-241-8

To Francesca Kim, my beautiful girl x

PROLOGUE

1993

The disused warehouse was massive, but Jimmy was trapped in a tiny room within it.

Earlier, he'd climbed in through a broken window and looked around. The old metal machinery was still intact. It ran in lines up and down the vast floorspace. Some had been broken into bits by vandals, others had metal pieces stripped from them, but all towered above him like dinosaur skeletons.

Jimmy had been in the place about ten minutes when he'd heard shuffling noises and a funny strangled noise like someone had coughed and tried to cover it up. He'd run further inside the wide-open space of the warehouse and seen a door standing open over on the far wall.

When he'd got closer, he'd spotted an old sign hanging lopsided on it. Jimmy was the best reader in his class, if you didn't count the new boy. He'd held the sign straight so he could see it properly and pieced the sounds together. He'd said slowly to himself: 'Re-frig-er-ation unit.' Everyone knew it was dangerous to hide in a fridge in case the door shut by accident and you got trapped.

Jimmy had pushed the sign hard to watch it whizz round on itself and it had flown off, clattering to the concrete floor. He'd looked around in panic, watching and listening for movement but all was still. He'd stuck his head through the gap and squinted into the gloomy unit. There was no fridge in there.

The shuffling sound had seemed like it was getting closer. Jimmy had stepped inside the unit and waited for his eyes to adjust. There were no windows in here. The room was very dusty, bare shelves all around it and rusty metal hooks hanging from the ceiling. The door had been weirdly thick and heavy when Jimmy had pulled it to behind him, leaving just a tiny gap.

People at school said the warehouse was haunted by two burning women. Once a food manufacturing plant, lots of people had died here ten years ago when there was a fire and a big explosion. Nigel Burley in Year 6 had said he'd seen the two women in the Easter holidays last year. Everyone had sat quietly in a corner of the playground, listening as he'd told how they'd rushed past him screaming, their hair smoking, the flesh melting from their faces. Nigel had told them he'd thought they were real people until they both ran through a solid wall and disappeared, leaving nothing behind.

So Jimmy had held his breath when the shuffling sound had drawn closer and he'd bit his knuckles to stop himself crying out. If the burning women pulled open the door, he would put his head down like a Spanish bull and charge forward. Ghosts weren't real, they were like fog. You could walk right through them.

He'd heard heavy breathing and then the door had begun to open. Jimmy had caught a scream in his throat and balled his fists ready to run. Then the door had been pushed hard from the outside, like someone had their shoulder against it. When it had closed with a clunk, the space was plunged into pitch black.

When Jimmy had heard the big metal handle being turned on the outside and a cough, he'd known then it wasn't the burning women who had trapped him inside. It was a real person.

'Hey!' he'd shouted into the soupy darkness, and kicked hard on the solid metal from the inside. 'Open the door! Let me out!'

He'd banged with his fists until his hands hurt, but the door didn't open. He'd heard the footsteps moving quickly away and then everything fell silent.

Someone had played a nasty trick on him, but it wasn't funny because he'd been stuck in here for ages now and he couldn't see a thing unless he pressed his watch. Then he could see his hand and a small circle of nothingness around it.

It had supposed to be fun, coming out here on his own. Josie had packed him some jam sandwiches while Mum was still in bed and made up some orange cordial in an old water bottle. Josie had given him the rucksack with the picnic and said, 'You get going, little brother.' She'd always called him that. 'I'll meet you up by the old railway tracks.'

At the exact same time he'd left the house, he'd seen Samuel Barlow coming out of his own front gate.

'Hey, Jimmy. Where you off to?'

Jimmy had looked up at his mum's open bedroom window, worried Samuel's shouting might wake her and she'd bang on the glass and order him back inside. 'None of your business,' Jimmy had replied, hooking his rucksack further on to his shoulders.

Samuel had grinned and leaned on the gatepost. 'Where's your Josie at?'

'She's busy.' Jimmy had frowned as he'd walked past their

neighbour. 'She said she doesn't want to see you today, so just leave her alone.'

Quick as a flash, Samuel had grabbed him in a headlock, pressing his face so close that Jimmy could smell his stinking breath. Jimmy bent his knees and slipped out before he could get a good hold. Samuel lunged forward to cuff his ear, but Jimmy had dodged him, nimble as a boxer. Josie hadn't said anything of the sort, but Samuel wasn't to know. Jimmy was sick to death of him, always hanging around, watching his sister's every move. Josie didn't like going out in the garden any more because of him.

Jimmy had run the length of the street until he'd turned the corner, relieved when Samuel didn't follow him.

But now he was stuck in this room, he wished he'd said Samuel could come along with him. He was nineteen and big and strong. He might have been able to open the door.

Jimmy shivered and huddled closer into the corner. He hoped the burning women didn't pay him a visit now he couldn't get away.

If Josie was here, she'd know what to do. His big sister was tough and hardly ever cried. Last month, Josie had hidden Mum's bottles so she wouldn't get drunk before going to Jimmy's parents' evening. Mum had ripped the kitchen cupboards to pieces looking for them and when she'd found one, she'd cracked it over Josie's head. She'd cried that time, but then anybody would.

Jimmy felt confident that Josie would come looking for him soon. She would find whoever had locked him in here and batter them senseless.

He started to feel a bit funny. His chest was sort of tight, and he couldn't seem to get enough air inside, even when he took a big breath. It was strange because he hadn't been running or jumping or anything like that. He'd just been sitting here, not moving at all.

He closed his eyes and he started to half-dream, like he did sometimes just before he fell to sleep at night. He looked at his watch but he couldn't work out how long he'd been here. He'd forgotten where his sister was, and he couldn't remember if he should be at school or back home for his tea.

Jimmy drifted in and out for what seemed like a long, long time and then, just as he started to slide down a dark tunnel, Josie came and sat next to him. She felt warm against the cold skin of his arm. She slid her arm around his shoulder and whispered in his ear like she always did when Mum started shouting. 'Everything's going to be alright, little brother.'

He forced his heavy eyelids open to smile at her. But the darkness rushed at him and he realised that Josie wasn't there. He shivered and wrapped his arms tighter around himself. The air around him felt like cotton wool and his breaths came in tiny little gasps.

He wouldn't come here next time on his own, he thought. He would stay outside, by the railway tracks... that's what Josie had said... that's wha...

He wouldn't... come here...

Jimmy thought about splashing in the water in the garden with his sister. The way the sunshine lit up her face and her eyes sparkled and got rid of all the sadness.

And after that, there were no more thoughts.

ONE

JOSIE

2019

I locked up the café, loaded my laptop into the boot of the car and set off for the school run. I glanced at my watch. I should just make it. It was rare for me to finish in time to pick up my eight-year-old daughter, Ivy, but I'd pulled all the stops out to do so today.

I reversed out of my parking space and drove by the café, taking in the façade as I passed. My pride and joy that had taken over my life. I'd started Delicious Desserts about two years ago when Terry and I sold the house and got divorced.

I'd always dreamed of opening a café, but wanted something different to the usual coffee shop. I fancied something with a twist and it was Sheena, a fellow waitress at the restaurant I worked at part-time back then, who suggested a dessert café with a menu consisting only of drinks and sweet treats.

Growing up, I'd always enjoyed baking and her suggestion really resonated. For the first time in my life I didn't dither, didn't spend weeks debating the pros and cons. Instead, I'd enrolled on a food hygiene course and taken the plunge, renting the premises of a small greasy-spoon type café that had closed just a ten-minute drive from my bedsit.

My credit score wasn't in the best shape thanks to my meagre earnings. I knew I wouldn't qualify for a bank loan so I took a chance and used the small amount that was my share of the house sale once our joint debts were paid. I used the two thousand pounds to pay the rental deposit and buy some chalk paint for the scratched grey chairs and tables the previous tenants had left after their moonlight flit. There was just enough to get a sign made and have some menus printed.

I got to school just a couple of minutes before the bell rang to signal the end of the day. I rushed over to the group of parents I usually stood with, and their conversation broke up as, yet again, everyone turned to watch my last-minute arrival.

'Nice of you to join us!' my friend and Ivy's childminder, Fiona, teased and I pressed my chest, feigning breathlessness. A few of the other mums standing in the group laughed. I knew they liked to get there early to secure their place in front of the classroom doors that opened out on to the playground. I was known affectionately as the mum who was always rushing around, always late and I laughed along with them: the capable parents. Underneath, inferiority nibbled away at the edges of me.

'I had an appointment in town and ran into an accident on the bypass on the way back.' I blew air up on to my hot face and slipped off my lightweight jacket.

I noticed the conversation I'd interrupted did not resume and I thought I caught a couple of furtive glances sent my way.

'Is everything OK?' I whispered to Fiona. 'People seem to have gone a bit quiet.'

'Fine! Everything's fine,' she whispered back, looking up at the sky. Then she raised her voice again. 'Nice day, isn't it? Dull but warm.'

That kicked off a new discussion among everyone about the

dilemma of getting the kids to play in the garden for some fresh air, instead of them vegging in front of the TV or begging for the PlayStation.

I soon found myself, as usual, observing the conversation but not really taking part. It wasn't that people were unfriendly, it was just an unspoken difference I felt between me and them. I was the only single mum in the group and the only one who wasn't free to join in with all the clubs, groups, and activities that I knew filled Fiona's day. Nevertheless, I often got invites and I was included in a school mums' WhatsApp group, which was so well-used I'd had to mute notifications.

Jimmy had died twenty-six years ago. Lots of the people – adults – who'd been around at that time had either died themselves or moved away. Still, folks don't easily forget a tragedy like that in a small town like Hucknall. It passes through the generations like an ill wind and, so long as I stick around here, I'll forever be the murdered boy's sister.

'Nobody thinks of you in that way,' Fiona had said dismissively when I'd told her how I felt. 'You're just a school mum, like any one of us.'

Maybe she was right. Maybe being the odd one out was something I imagined. Since Jimmy's death when I was thirteen, I'd become an expert at pushing the past away. Now, I tried only to think about the future. It had worked for me so far and spared me from the awful memories.

Parents stepped forward as the classroom doors opened and the children began to pour out on to the playground. The adult chatter was instantly drowned out with squealing and shouting as the kids exploded across the warm tarmac with pent-up energy, their small, warm bodies darting in different directions.

I spotted Ivy and waved. Darcy – her best friend and Fiona's daughter – shot out and headed straight over to us. 'We both got a sticker, Mummy!' she cried out. 'I got one for collecting the worksheets in this morning and—'

'I got one for handing out the milk!' Ivy blurted to me.

'What clever girls we have.' I grinned at Fiona. 'I reckon this calls for a treat.'

'Yes! Yes! Yes!' the girls chanted in unison.

'Can we go to the milkshake parlour?' Darcy asked hopefully and Ivy's face brightened at the suggestion. They looked first at me and then at Fiona.

'Hmm, I don't know. Milkshake... before tea?' Fiona raised an eyebrow. 'What do you think, Josie?'

'Maybe just this once, seeing as there were *two* stickers involved,' I said to much whooping and jumping around from the girls.

The girls bounded off towards the school gates and Fiona turned to me. 'Well, that was a popular decision. I wanted to have a quick chat to you about something.' She noticed my expression. 'Nothing to worry about. It's just... well, we can chat when we get there.'

TWO

The milkshake parlour was bustling with parents and kids who'd come straight from the school run like us, teenagers and a couple of older people. Fiona looked around. 'I guess a lot of different people like milkshake.'

I stood on my tiptoes. 'There's a couple getting up from that table at the back. Take the girls over and I'll get the drinks in.' We usually took turns anyway, and it was my shout.

The queue moved quickly, and I carried the tray of tall frothy drinks over to the table, managing to dodge a rampaging toddler and an assistance Labrador I only saw and stepped over at the last second. 'So, we've got two strawberry milkshakes for the girls, a banana one for you, Fiona, and a lemonade for me.' I set out the drinks and popped the tray under the table.

'Lemonade because you don't like milkshake!' Fiona exclaimed in mock horror, as she always did. 'What's wrong with you, Josie? Everybody on the planet loves milkshake, for goodness' sake.'

'Everybody but Mummy!' Ivy said smartly as she sucked at her straw, and we all laughed.

The girls were soon huddled together over my phone, playing Crossy Road.

'So,' I said, taking a sip of my drink, 'what did you want a chat about?'

Fiona glanced across at the girls. 'It's a bit of an awkward one,' she said, stirring her straw around in the viscous yellow liquid. 'I wasn't going to say anything and then... well, Dave said I should tell you because if you hear it from someone else, it will be worse.'

'Gosh,' I said faintly.

'I don't want you to be worried.' She sighed. 'The last thing I want is to needlessly upset you or—'

'Just tell me.' I put my lemonade down and looked at her. 'What is it?'

Her deliberations were making me nervous. Maybe something had happened at school involving Ivy, or possibly she'd heard someone badmouthing the café.

'Well, I can't be sure there's any truth in it. It could be just a rumour, a bit of gossip. Although anybody saying something like this must be sick.'

I glanced at Ivy, who had just whooped in delight at an explosion of colour on the screen. She'd seemed happy enough at school all week, hadn't shown any signs of distress or being troubled. 'Go on then,' I whispered.

'One of the women at school... James's mum. You know her?' She paused to check I knew who she meant, and I nodded. I'd spoken to the woman briefly now and then. 'Well, her sister lives in Ravensdale.'

I knew Ravensdale, an area of Mansfield, a large market town nearly ten miles from here. The back of my neck prickled as I recalled my childhood home there.

Fiona stole a glance at the girls and then said in an even lower voice, 'Well, her sister knows Maggie Barlow, who, apparently, told the lady in the corner shop that her son, Samuel, is coming home soon.'

'No, that can't be right,' I said, blowing out air. 'He's got another five years to do.'

'Really? Oh, that's a relief! I mean, we don't want someone like him on the loose, even if it is a good way from here.'

It was 9.6 miles. A fifty-minute bus trip. A twenty-minute cab ride.

I always knew exactly how far I was from my past, and it was never far enough.

'He's got another five years to do before he's out,' I murmured again.

Fiona bit her lip and frowned. 'It couldn't be he's got parole though, could it?'

People might know my brother had been murdered, but Fiona was one of the rare people I'd spoken to about what had actually happened to Jimmy. I'd been honest about my dread of still being in the area when Samuel got out in a few years' time. Land's End wouldn't be far enough, I knew that. But I'd envisaged putting even more distance between him and us than we'd have right now if he returned to live in Ravensdale with his mother. I'd always thought I had plenty of time.

'I suppose it's always possible, but I seriously doubt it,' I said, sucking at my straw to disguise my frozen face. 'He's already had three parole appeals turned down that I know of. The judge recommended he should serve all the sentence.'

Fiona gave a wide smile and clapped her hand to her chest. 'Oh, thank God for that! I've never been so glad to hear I got it wrong.' She nodded to my glass. 'How's the lemonade?'

'It's really good.' I put down my glass, the lemons sour on my tongue.

Already moving on, Fiona opened her calendar on her phone. 'So, have you remembered it's Sanjeet's birthday party tomorrow afternoon? We have to drop the girls at the leisure centre reception at three. Then I wondered if you fancied a drive out to the retail park, I need...'

I tuned out her voice as my thoughts turned to Maggie Barlow. After trying to contact me unsuccessfully for a few years after Samuel received his sentence, she'd faded into obscurity. She knew nothing about me and I knew nothing about her. I'd always stayed away from social media anyway, paranoid about putting any personal details online.

She didn't know where I lived, about the café and didn't even know I had a daughter. I wanted to keep it that way. Even so, about three years ago, fate found a way of intervening to keep that tenuous link alive.

I'd been travelling home after a confectionery course. It had been a hot day and I remembered I'd promised Ivy barbecued burgers for tea so I'd called into a supermarket in Mansfield. I barely registered the stooped back of what looked like an elderly lady next to me at the freezer, but she turned so we were facing each other. I couldn't process who it was for a moment, but when I did, I turned on my heel and quickly walked the other way.

'Josie! Josie!' Maggie had called, hobbling up behind me. I had on a sleeveless top and my skin felt scalded when she touched me on my bare shoulder. 'Just a quick word, please. It won't take up much of your time.'

I turned round and hissed, 'Leave me alone. I'm not interested in anything you've got to say.'

I'd been shocked, how, close up, her once smooth skin was etched with deep creases and marionette lines that ran from the corners of her mouth down to her chin. She could only be in her mid-sixties, but looked so much older than her years.

She'd looked at me pleadingly and I'd had to force away memories of her enduring kindness to me as a child. The times she'd taken me from the street and in, out of the rain. The hours I'd spent in her small kitchen while she'd showed me how to make all the different kinds of pastry, feather-light Victoria sponges and the crumbliest butter shortbread that melted on my tongue. She'd even let me sleep there night after night while my mother had lain comatose in bed after Jimmy's death, sometimes for days on end.

But none of that counted now, after what she did.

THREE

Twenty-five years ago

The Mansfield Guardian
21st February 1994

MOTHER LIED TO COVER FOR SON AFTER MURDER OF SCHOOLBOY

The mother of the man accused of murdering schoolboy Jimmy Bennett last year has been jailed for eight months, after lying to police in an effort to protect him.

Margaret Barlow, who lives at the same address as her son, had claimed Samuel Barlow was at home in bed, recovering from a viral infection for three days, and could not have been responsible for the child's death.

Barlow was nineteen when he allegedly intentionally imprisoned the eight-year-old schoolboy in a sealed refrigeration unit of a disused food manufacturing plant, on the outskirts of Mansfield. The child's body was recovered three days after his disappearance following a major search operation. He was found to have died through suffocation.

As a result of Margaret Barlow's false account, police changed the focus of their investigation before returning to question Barlow a few days later.

The senior investigation officer, DI Don Mitchell from Nottinghamshire Police, said: 'It is never acceptable to lie to protect somebody who has committed a crime. Even if that person is a family member, it is still a criminal offence. Sadly, we will never know if Jimmy Bennett's life might have been saved if the investigation had been allowed to follow its initial course.'

Margaret Barlow denied perverting the course of justice but was convicted following a short trial. The forty-one-year-old was sentenced to eight months in jail at Nottingham Crown Court.

Samuel Barlow has denied murder. The trial continues.

FOUR

MAGGIE

2019

Outside the milkshake parlour, Maggie stood, safely tucked away at the very edge of the large front window. She peered through the muddle of busy tables until she caught a glimpse of Josie's little group, huddled at the back.

Maggie had used her free bus pass for years to get from Ravensdale to the school in Hucknall where Josie's daughter had started primary school and was now a Year Four pupil. She'd follow Josie and the girl at a safe distance. Her favourite thing was when they'd stop off at the park and Maggie could loiter on the pavement at the other side of the hedge, even catching snatches of their conversation as they fed the ducks.

She'd found out so much that way, by just watching and listening. She'd learned Ivy's best friend was called Darcy. She knew all the child's favourite Disney films, that she loved Taylor Swift's music and that she'd recently gone off cheese sandwiches. It was a major part of Maggie's life, keeping alive a secret, invisible thread between the three of them. It didn't matter Josie was completely unaware of Maggie's presence. She felt like their guardian angel. Always watching, always sending her love and hoping for the chance to make up for what happened all those years ago.

Maggie knew where they lived and she knew about Josie's sweet treats café. She'd even been in there for coffee and cake last year when she'd overheard Josie tell little Ivy she was taking a rare day off.

But the school was the one sure place Maggie knew she'd find them together, although more recently, Josie only made the school run a couple of times a week. The rest of the time, Ivy had been collected by her childminder.

Maggie sometimes followed anyway and had seen Josie playing in the childminder's garden with the other small children whose parents worked seemingly never-ending hours. Too busy to do the school run, or take their children out during school holidays. When they came to collect, Maggie wanted to call out to them how precious this time with their children was before the years slipped by, never to be recovered.

Maggie took another half-step closer to the parlour's window. She couldn't be too careful. If Josie spotted her watching, she'd have the police on to her faster than Maggie could think up a good excuse why she might be there. *Stalking*, they called it these days, but that was a horrible word. Stalkers wanted to do their subjects harm, whereas Maggie only wanted to satisfy herself that Josie and Ivy were both well and living a happy life. She kept a notebook full of all the details she might otherwise forget, including the name of the care home where Pauline Bennett, Josie's mother, was now living, Magnolia Fields. It was a lovely name for a care home. Particularly one where a ruthless, cruel woman like Pauline resided.

In many ways, Josie looked just the same as she had then, back when she'd been a neglected little girl who'd badly needed Maggie's help. The same wide, brown eyes that looked constantly surprised. Smooth, olive skin and a tense, stretched mouth. Maggie knew, if she got close enough, she'd be able to spot the two-inch scar that ran from her left temple to her hair-line. Inflicted by her drunk of a mother, it had faded over the years, but it would never go. Not completely.

Maggie's gaze drifted to the pretty child sitting next to Josie. Her daughter, Ivy. The girl had those same brown eyes and smooth skin but also dark glossy hair that Josie kept in a simple bob style. The hair must have come from her father's side.

Maggie had done her best for Josie as a child, had tried to protect her from her mother's neglect and even Samuel's obses-sion with her. Sadly, Maggie had been unable to help little Jimmy, but you couldn't save the world, could you? Not on your own.

In lots of ways, things had been easier back then because Maggie had thought she'd been able to control Samuel to a large extent. Regrettably, that was no longer the case.

Maggie studied the child's delicate profile. The snub nose, the way she sipped her drink and laughed with her friend as they played their game. So vulnerable, so innocent and not a care in the world.

Despite her initial relief when she'd heard the parole board's decision, seeing Josie and her dear child today had made Maggie's stomach churn.

It was no surprise that prison changed people. A thirty-year sentence was one hell of a long time for both the inmate and their family. It was easy to imagine people were just the same person they used to be, easy to idealise how life might be when they returned home. But now, Maggie had to face the facts. Samuel, during the twenty-five years he had served, had changed beyond recognition.

Her regular visits to HMP Wakefield had proven she'd be welcoming a hardened, cynical middle-aged man – who had kept himself very fit in there – back home. Over the years,

Maggie had witnessed the changes in him. First subtle, then more pronounced.

She'd visited twice a month without fail, apart from a handful of times she'd been unable to travel because of bad weather or illness. She'd recognised the distance growing between them but had felt that was normal, under the circumstances.

It was easy for Samuel to play the part of a repentant man to the powers that be while he was still inside, but once he was out, the mask would lift and Maggie was fearful of what might appear there.

What her sixty-minute visits hadn't given air to was the writhing fury and bitterness that filled her son. Call it a mother's intuition, but she had felt it for every minute she'd spent in his presence.

As a child, he'd saved the worst of his vitriol for the other children at school and the Bennett family. Maggie had made so many mistakes during her life. Mistakes that still visited her in the early hours when she'd get up, make a cup of tea and watch the sun rise from the kitchen window.

The worst torture being the certainty of how things might have turned out differently if she'd faced up to her son's deviance instead of defending him, protecting him.

And the lies... she'd told so, so many lies. What could she do now to make amends? Perhaps there was some way to warn Josie to keep vigilant and safe without alarming her.

She stole one last glance into the parlour, her heart swelling with regret for the girl she had never stopped caring about. Then Maggie turned and walked away, cutting a lonely figure as she weaved through couples and the families, all far too busy with their own lives to register her presence at all.

FIVE

JOSIE

The next morning, I made Ivy a quick bowl of cereal before we set off to the wholesaler. We had regular deliveries to the café but I'd really upped the baking output recently and we often ran low on critical supplies.

Six months ago, I was invited to tender for a contract with Brew – a new national chain of bean-to-cup coffee shops – and to my delight, my bid was successful. Delicious Desserts would supply them with fresh daily flapjacks and biscuits to sell in their outlets.

The contract had the potential to transform my year-end figures from strictly small fry to an impressive turnover. If successful, the CEO of Brew had intimated they'd be looking to potentially roll out the contract to their other branches in the Midlands.

I saw it as a way of building a successful future and life for myself and my daughter and so it was important to me to make it a roaring success.

'Why do we have to always do boring stuff on Saturdays?' Ivy grumbled as I locked the front door. 'I'll miss all my favourite TV programmes because of this. You promised we could go to the seaside again, but we haven't been for aaages!'

I felt like Ivy's punchbag, and deservedly so. Everything she said was true.

'You're right, sweetie, and I'm sorry,' I said as I reversed off the drive. 'It won't be for long, but I've explained about the Brew contract. Once I get that running properly, we'll be back to normal.'

Up until now, I'd been strict about taking weekends off. Sheena was saving for a deposit for a house with her partner, Warren, and she'd willingly taken on more hours when we won the Brew contract. I'd structured the staff rota so the café could run perfectly well without me and once, when I had a staffing problem, I simply stuck a notice to the door apologising for closure due to unforeseen circumstances. But generally, the pressure had increased more than I'd expected and at times I'd found myself impossibly stretched between running a business and being a mother. There were so many things on my to-do list, including a visit to see Mum, which I was way overdue on.

'I hate that stupid contract!' Ivy jutted out her bottom lip and stared petulantly out of the passenger window.

'I agree it's a nuisance, but it's going to give us a better life if it's successful.'

She looked at me. 'I don't want a better life, Mummy. I like this one.'

'I know, I do too but... we can move to a new area and get a lovely house with a nice big garden and—'

'I don't want to leave this house. I like it here, with Darcy and my other friends at school. And what about Daddy?' Her bottom lip jutted defiantly.

Daddy. Who was forever promising the earth and consistently delivering next to nothing.

I stopped at a red light and turned towards her, smoothing down the ponytail she'd hastily pulled together herself before we left. 'We could get a house in the countryside where Daddy can visit. You could go horse riding at the weekends, and we'll have a big enough garden to keep a few hens.' Ivy loved hens and dreamed of collecting her own eggs for breakfast.

'Sophie and Emily in my class go for horse riding and *they* live around here.' She thought for a moment. 'I do like hens, but I want to be friends with Darcy more.'

I sighed. As usual I'd made a mess of things and Ivy had brought me bang down to earth by pointing out people mattered more than things. But I couldn't tell her the truth. I couldn't tell her why I'd always felt a constant pull to get further and further away from the past. That I feared for her safety in a few years' time when Barlow was released. At least, I hoped and prayed Fiona had heard false gossip and I *had* still got a few years. But maybe it was a sign, to remind me that years roll by quicker than we think. That when Barlow is finally released, Ivy will still only be thirteen. A beautiful teenager who wants to be out with her friends and craving her freedom. I shuddered at the thought of how that would feel. Wanting to keep her in to protect her but battling her natural need to pull away from her over-protective mother.

The wholesaler was in Kirkby, a small town about a fifteen-minute drive from Hucknall. A big warehouse on an industrial park that stocked the catering-sized packs of butter and flour I seemed to get through with lightning speed.

I parked up and, as soon as we got inside, Ivy changed her tune completely. 'Oh, Mummy, I forgot... I really like it here!' She scampered ahead as I flashed my trade card in the foyer and grabbed a trolley. The nice thing about this place was I could give her a free rein to move around on her own, as everyone in here was a member and it wasn't open to the public.

'Look what I found!' Ivy came running up with a pack of a dozen Fruit Shoots in her favourite flavour.

'Pop them in the trolley,' I said. 'That'll keep you and Darcy in drinks for a bit.' She dropped them in before running off again.

I watched her turn the corner and someone called out behind me. At least I thought I heard my name. I turned quickly but there was no one there. Then a group of young staff members appeared from around the corner, laughing and joking and obviously off on their break. I realised I must have misheard.

I wondered if there would ever be a time I felt settled and safe enough somewhere that I wouldn't jump at noises, or feel like someone was watching me. I lived in hope we'd get to that day but Fiona mentioning the gossip she'd heard had made me jumpier than ever.

When I had the trolley fully loaded with everything I needed to tide me over until our next delivery, I called out to Ivy. When there was no response, I walked to the end of the aisle and looked down the main thoroughfare. Nothing. I walked slowly past the end of each aisle and, eventually, I found her on the confectionery aisle.

'Ivy, come on, time to go.'

She ran towards me carrying an outsize bag of Haribo jellies.

I shook my head. 'Too much sugar there for a small girl.' I'd bought her a bag before and, once it was open, she constantly hassled me for 'another one, another one'. She groaned, but knowing she was beaten, she dumped the bag back on a shelf before running down to me. We headed for the tills, Ivy happily chattering on about this and that.

Outside, the car park had filled up since our arrival. It was about one-third full of vehicles and vans now and there were people walking to and from their cars, a handful who had brought their kids along like me.

While Ivy ran up and down a grassy bank in front of the car, I finished loading my purchases and wheeled the trolley back to the nearest bay.

'Back in the car now,' I called to her and opened the passenger door.

Instead of getting in, she rushed to the front of the car and reached up. 'What's this?'

She grabbed something that had been wedged under the windscreen. Some kind of flyer. I glanced at the cars parked closest but there was nothing under their wiper blades.

Inside the car, I looked at the piece of paper. The words had been written neatly in a black marker pen.

CHANGE IS COMING. KEEP YOUR DAUGHTER SAFE.
FROM A CONCERNED FRIEND X

Something squirmed in my belly as Fiona's words came back.

Maggie Barlow has been telling anyone who'll listen that her son is getting out of prison soon.

I leaned over the seat and dropped the paper into the back of the car. My throat felt scratchy and dry.

'What does it say, Mummy?'

'Just a silly note someone dropped,' I said and produced a Fruit Shoot. 'As you've been so good, you can have one of these on the way back.'

Ivy reached for it, beaming, the flyer instantly forgotten.

Who could have written such a note? I wanted to discount it, but it had mentioned a daughter. And there was a kiss at the end of the message. It was as if someone had definitely written it to me.

A concerned friend... could it be someone at school who'd

heard the gossip about Barlow too? It wasn't threatening in itself but it made my blood run cold by what it inferred. That soon, I'd need to keep my daughter safe. Why? Because Samuel Barlow was being released?

Once we were on the move, I put my seat heater on. Strangely, I felt cold despite it being a warm day. I hoped I wasn't sickening for something.

'Can we have Taylor on, Mummy?'

'Good idea.' I gave her my phone and she found her favourite playlist and effortlessly hooked it up to the car's Bluetooth.

I took a deep breath and zoned out.

Maggie Barlow's face flashed into my mind and I blinked it away again. I hadn't heard from Maggie for years now. There's no way she could know we used that wholesaler, and she wouldn't warn me because her loyalties lay with her son. She'd made that crystal clear when Jimmy died.

Ivy's sweet voice filled the car as she sang along to 'Shake It Off'.

I couldn't just ignore the gossip and now the flyer. I decided that, when I got home, I'd make a phone call and find out the truth about Samuel Barlow. I just hoped and prayed I got the truth I wanted to hear.

I turned the car into one of the two permit spaces behind Delicious Desserts and, as soon as I had parked up, started emptying the boot.

'I'll help, too,' Ivy insisted, pulling at cellophane, and causing butter packs to fall out.

'You carry these,' I said, giving her a few packs. 'That's a big help, thank you.'

I watched as she walked carefully towards the back door of the café. I felt bad dragging her in here on a weekend, but she actually enjoyed being useful and she loved being involved.

My heart used to lift when I came to the café every day. After scrimping while working multiple jobs to try to get by after the divorce, I'd started this business and it became successful quite quickly.

But then, about ten months ago, my regular customers began to drop off, and I realised the novelty of a dessert-only café was waning. Profits quickly reduced and I barely slept more than two or three hours at a time, racking my brains to think of a solution. Everything I had was tied up in the business.

I had to make it work, so when I won the contract, I threw everything I had at it. I took on extra staff and, for what seemed like an eternity, we baked half-a-dozen varieties of biscuits and fruit flapjacks from dawn until dusk, on top of catering for our customers in the café. Every day counted and each tray of perfect bakes I slid out of the oven represented, to me, a step closer to a positive future for me and my girl.

However, given time, the new contract turned out to be bittersweet. Although it was rescuing the business from almost certain closure, it made for a poor family life with zero work-life balance. I was turning myself inside out on a continual basis to fulfil the demands of the supply contract.

I'd just about managed it until now, but disaster had struck in the last couple of weeks. My usual temporary pool of students had suddenly depleted. Some had dropped like flies with a virus that was going round, others had finished studies and had abruptly moved back home without serving notice.

Sheena had been worth her weight in gold and dealt with all the supplies orders and deliveries now, as well as front of house duties, but she wasn't a baker. For now, I was just about struggling on.

In the main kitchen, I watched as – under Sheena's supervision – Ivy slathered whipped cream like a pro on to our signature home-made waffles.

'You've had ten minutes' practice and you're already a better baker than your mummy!' Sheena joked and Ivy beamed, bristling with pride.

'You're not wrong!' I washed my hands then began to grease the large baking tray ready for the lemon and ginger biscuits we were making next. 'She's definitely my star baker of the week.'

Ivy's smooth brow furrowed as she focused on covering every millimetre of the waffle with cream.

'See, you have to make sure it's spread out all over the waffle, Mummy,' she said, repeating Sheena's earlier instructions.

Tendrils of guilt stretched up inside me. It was so nice to spend a bit of time with Ivy, even if I'd had to bring her into work today to do so.

Sheena waved a hand in front of my face and frowned. 'Are you OK, Josie? I mean, I know you *said* you're OK but... are you sure?'

'I'm sure!' I said lightly.

She hesitated. 'Terry hasn't been causing any more trouble, has he?'

'Haven't heard from Terry for the best part of a month,' I said shortly. I didn't want to start a conversation about Ivy's father in front of her. Despite constantly promising to be a better father, Terry continuously let Ivy down. 'If I seem distracted, it's probably because I'm just running through everything I've got to do in my head. That's all.'

She smiled, relieved. 'I know, I know. There's just so much to think about, isn't there? If you can sign Monday's order, I'll get that off.' She slid a sheet in front of me and handed me a pen. 'I've briefed the two new starters on everything so hopefully you won't feel too overwhelmed.'

I'd not even thought about the two new starters. Thank goodness somebody had.

'Can you just watch Ivy for a sec?' I said to Sheena and went out the back to our refrigerated lockup in the small yard where we kept most of our chilled stock. I stacked a couple of industrial-sized blocks of butter to carry through and then stood, with my back against the wall, willing my fluttery heartbeat to settle down.

My mood had changed since finding the flyer on my windscreen, but I had to get a grip or Ivy would pick up on my nervousness. I felt sure after a few phone calls I'd be able to put my mind at rest that Barlow would remain behind bars where he belonged.

But, of course, that's what I thought before everything went so badly wrong.

SIX

NOTTINGHAMSHIRE POLICE

DI Helena Price scanned the weekly case overview on her computer screen. A jolly whistle – a bit too jaunty for eight o'clock on a Monday morning, it had to be said – reached her ears. She looked up from her desk and warmed a little at the gratifying sight of Detective Sergeant Kane Brewster advancing towards her with takeout coffee.

'Thanks, Brewster.' She took the paper cup gratefully. 'I think I might've keeled over if I drank much more of that bitter sludge from the station machine.'

'I thought you'd appreciate it, boss,' Brewster said, pleased. He put down his own cup and untucked the foolscap folder from under his arm. He held it in the air before placing it on to the desk. 'I got that file you asked for.'

Helena looked at the folder. 'Anything interesting in there we should know about?'

Brewster removed the lid to his cup to take a sip of coffee.

'You can drink it with the lid still on, you know.'

'Huh?'

'You can leave the lid on and drink your coffee through that little hole in the top.' Helena took a swig of her own to demonstrate it.

'You know, I learn something from you every single day, boss,' he said wryly, sipping directly from the cup.

Helena frowned and glanced at the folder. 'So, Samuel Barlow's managed to get parole after all and he's out on Friday. Do I need a quick recap before I speak to his victim's sister, Josie Bennett?'

Brewster pulled the corners of his mouth down. 'Think you've already got a pretty good overview of the case. Twenty-six years ago, eight-year-old Jimmy Bennett went missing after leaving home to have a picnic near a disused railway. His older sister, Josie, was meant to be looking after him, but she was involved in a hit-and-run accident.'

'She ended up in hospital?'

Brewster nodded. 'The notes say she was unconscious for some time and had amnesia when she first came round. A full-scale police operation swiftly followed, as you might expect, but there were no leads. Nothing.'

'It took three days to find him?'

'Yes. He'd been locked in a sealed refrigeration unit in a derelict warehouse located just a twenty-minute walk from home.'

Helena winced. 'Was he found alive?'

'The ambulance arrived within fifteen minutes, but he'd already gone. Asphyxiation.'

Helena bit her lip. It was impossible to even begin to imagine the suffering and pain the child had endured at the hands of a monster who would soon be a free man mixing among the unsuspecting public. Like everyone else, it was times like this she wondered what was in the parole board members' heads.

'And what's little Jimmy Bennett's family situation now?'

'There's his sister, Josie Bennett, as you know. There was a bit of an age gap between the two of them. Josie is five years older than Jimmy. She was thirteen when he was murdered by Barlow. Their mother, Pauline Bennett, is in a nursing home suffering with advanced early-onset dementia.'

Helena blinked. 'I understand the Bennett family knew Samuel Barlow well.'

'That's right. Says here that Barlow was their neighbour. His own dad died when he was just a young lad and his mother, Margaret Barlow, brought him up on her own. As mother and son they were very close, apparently.'

'Close enough for her to lie through her teeth for him, by all accounts.'

Brewster nodded. 'She lied under oath. Gave Samuel a cast-iron alibi for the period Jimmy was missing. The tragedy is, they might've found the kid in time if she hadn't put them off the scent.' Brewster opened the file and flicked through a few sheets before pulling one out and reading from it. 'Maggie served four months of an eight-month sentence for perverting the course of justice.'

'And she's maintained her close relationship with her son during his sentence?'

'Yup.' Brewster plucked out another sheet. 'Weekly visits, letters. She spent the first couple of years campaigning for his release but gave that up when there was no support and she realised he hadn't got a hope in hell of getting out. I checked with the probation service, and they've confirmed Barlow has given his mother's address as his destination on release.'

'Same house, same town as they used to live,' Helena remarked.

'That's right. About ten miles away from Hucknall, where Josie Bennett now lives.'

'OK, well, let's hope their paths don't have cause to cross. Although she's never going to get over the death of her brother, Josie has hopefully moved on with her life.' Helena picked up her cup and took a swig of coffee before scribbling a note on her desk jotter. 'So, it's just a straightforward early release call I need to make?'

'Yes. There's just...' Brewster hesitated.

Helena put down her pen. 'What is it?'

'Probably nothing. Just a detail that I thought was a bit strange when I read the case notes.'

'Spit it out, Brewster.'

'The road they lived on was a close-knit community back then. A couple of the neighbours said Samuel Barlow had a bit of an obsession with the Bennetts. With Josie particularly.'

'With Josie, not Jimmy?' Helena frowned.

'Hmm. Rumour was, he attacked Jimmy when he was a baby because he was jealous of him being close to Josie, although Maggie denied it. He was a bad 'un from the start, it seems.'

'As they so often are,' Helena sighed. She gathered up her paperwork. 'Thanks for the overview, Brewster. I'll call Josie Bennett now and tell her the bad news.'

SEVEN

SAMUEL

He dropped down to the cold, hard floor and performed ten one-armed press-ups each side, before standing up again and doing twenty-five squats.

From as far back as he could remember, people had told Samuel he was bad. When he was a child, his father had remarked, 'On the inside, where no one can see, you are rotten.'

Samuel had never forgotten that and, in a strange way, had sort of liked it. The thought he had a secret, something hidden from others.

His first memory was cutting off all a little girl's long hair at pre-school and handing another boy the scissors when he spotted the teacher approaching. Sitting back and watching the boy get punished had given Samuel his first thrill. At nine years old, he'd pushed an old lady over in the street when she'd spotted him throwing stones at a shop window. Her bones had crumbled like powdered chalk. He'd sat down on the pavement next to her and watched as she mewed in pain.

He'd always enjoyed feeling the power of inflicting such acts on others. He found himself in trouble so many times in his early teens he began to almost feel a responsibility to do the wrong thing. It was as if the people around him expected nothing less. So, Samuel had willingly obliged. He'd fearlessly pushed the boundaries of bad behaviour and it had eventually led him here. To hell.

He looked around his bleak cell now with its stark white walls and stale air. He'd lived in this space for over half his life. Twenty-five years of relentless waiting until his chance came around again.

He had relived virtually every minute of the two-week trial – that took place before Mr Justice Curtis – for what felt like thousands of times. He'd never forget the austere court surroundings. All that wood, the hard seating under an impossibly high ceiling and the cold... he could recall shivering despite wearing several layers. Every pair of eyes – from the jury to the press and family in the spectators' gallery – fell on him as he was led to the dock to state his full name and enter a plea of Not Guilty.

For the first time he understood why some defendants smirked or smiled as they stood in the dock. It was a reaction, pure and simple. A way of silently answering the angry glares, the belittling sneers... it was the only thing you had left. The ability to bait and appal the onlookers and the rubberneckers who had already cast him as a monster.

So he'd smiled at the section of press, at the court artist and finally, as the ultimate act of rebellion, he'd smiled at the judge in his silly wig and pantomime outfit as if to say, 'Do your worst because I don't care.' Then he'd caught the eye of his mother, and of Josie Bennett and her witch of a mother, Pauline, and the smirk had slid from his face.

After a two-week trial and a jury made up mainly of women who looked at him like he was nothing more than a maggot, the judge's final words had come and seared themselves on his mind forever.

'Samuel Reginald Barlow, you have been found guilty of the

murder of James Bennett on the fourteenth of April nineteen ninety-three. You will be detained until your sentencing, which will take place here, at Nottingham Crown Court. Until that time you will be detained at Her Majesty's Pleasure at HMP Nottingham.'

His first thought had been he was glad he was sitting down. His head had swum with confusion as the jeers and whistles and clapping came from the spectators' gallery and the judge called for order.

Two months later, he was led into court again and given a thirty-year jail sentence. Everything around him had slowed. The judge's voice had drawled low and long. Samuel had looked up and seen faces pulled narrow by their sneers. Then proceedings had sped up again and his head had ached with the shouting, the scraping of chairs, the judge's gavel banging so hard and relentlessly, he'd feared his skull might crack open.

It had been so long ago and yet, in many ways, seemed as vivid as yesterday.

Samuel brought his attention back to the claustrophobic shiny white walls, allowing his long thin fingers to flick idly through the small paper squares of the perpetual desk calendar until he reached 17 May.

The date when his endless days here would finally cease was only a heartbeat away.

Four days. Just four more insufferable, featureless days, and he'd be back in the normal world again. Things would be very different out there, he knew that.

Samuel didn't like people much, didn't understand them. When he spent time around others, he found himself putting on an act so he might appear more normal. When it suited him, he showed sympathy and sadness at the misfortune of others. It was how he'd survived his time in prison.

He'd always known you couldn't trust people. They smiled

to your face and dissed you behind your back. Even the people closest to you were out to get you.

In his teenage years, after the death of his father, he'd been bad much of the time just to relieve the boredom of school and the endless hours alone at home while his mother worked two jobs to make ends meet.

There was only one person Samuel wanted to get closer to now. He wanted to get close enough to share the air she breathed. Once, in prison, he'd had a dream where he ate her up. Ate her all up so she was trapped inside him and could never, ever leave.

Just a few more long days to go but now freedom was close. He couldn't afford to mess things up. He had to get out of here and get back home to finish what he'd started.

This time he wouldn't mess it up.

This time, he would do it *just right*.

EIGHT

JOSIE

I'd only been at work for about an hour after dropping Ivy off at school and I'd already almost wrecked the joint. I scanned the mess on the kitchen worktops. The open packets, tubs, empty cartons; there was barely an inch of space still available. The whirring industrial ovens filled the space with their comforting hum and the tendons in my neck softened a little. The main thing was, we were on track to meet our baking targets for the day.

I bent forward and peered through the glass at the rapidly melting discs of biscuit dough that would frazzle in the space of a few seconds if left in there too long. Sheena was out front serving customers and I had one of the new part-timers shadowing her. I had little help and a mountain of work to get through.

My phone rang and I answered the call without looking at the screen.

'Josie speaking.'

'Ms Bennett? This is Detective Inspector Helena Price from Nottinghamshire Police. Is this a convenient time for a quick chat?'

Police? My heartbeat jumped up into my throat.

'I have a couple of minutes, if that'll do,' I said, trapping the phone between my shoulder and cheek and turning both ovens down by ten degrees to buy a little more time. Then, no doubt making no sense at all, I added, 'I'm in the middle of baking a mammoth batch of biscuits.'

She paused before speaking again. 'It's just a courtesy call. I wanted to let you know, in the interests of keeping you fully informed, that Samuel Barlow is due to be released in line with the conditions of his sentence at the end of the week.'

The past I'd worked so hard to push away reared up like a tsunami wave and took my breath. I don't know what I expected her to say, but it wasn't that. Foolish, maybe, but I'd expected someone from the parole board to call me back, or the prison.

'Ms Bennett?'

'This week?' My skin turned clammy, like something dead had just swept against me. I leaned back against the worktop and took hold of the phone in my hand again. He had five more years to serve. 'That can't be right. He's... he's not due out yet.'

She cleared her throat. 'He's been granted early parole, and his release date is fixed as Friday, seventeenth May.'

So the gossip Fiona had heard had been true.

'I'm supposed to be informed about any parole hearing,' I said. 'He's already applied three times and I've received a letter each time, confirming it.'

'Have you recently moved house? Sometimes people forget to keep the parole board informed.'

'Oh God,' I said faintly. When we moved here I worked through a list of who to inform and the board was not one of them. 'But... what was different this time? How come they're letting him out?'

She sighed. 'Sorry, we're not party to their decision-making process in individual cases. It would usually be based on his behaviour in prison, any accomplishments, that sort of thing.'

For more than half my life, I've dreaded hearing those words. Last month had marked the twenty-sixth anniversary of Jimmy's death and here the parole board were, patting Barlow on the back for being a good boy in prison and studying hard, or whatever his 'accomplishments' are.

'I... I don't know what to say. It's a shock.' Then, 'Where will he live? Will he be coming back to Mansfield, to his mother's?'

'I'm so sorry, I'm afraid I can't divulge any personal details,' Price said.

When Barlow was arrested for Jimmy's murder and awaiting trial, word got out Maggie had lied to police to try and save him. The locals took their frustrations out on the house when she was arrested, too. They smashed windows at her property, broke fences and daubed 'child killer' on her front door.

Maggie was tried and convicted of perverting the course of justice, and when she'd served four months of her eight-month sentence, she came back to the area and was regularly verbally abused in the street.

Then one day, a to-let sign went up outside the small, shabby ex-council house. She'd done a moonlight flit, moved out of the area for what seemed like for good. I heard a distant aunt had died and left her a modest sum of money, enough for Maggie to start again somewhere else. But about a decade ago, a neighbour who still lived on the street contacted me and told me the tenants had moved out and Maggie had quietly returned to the house. By then, people had left the area or passed away and the fury had long died down. Jimmy's death was just a distant memory in a town that had moved on.

I'd seen her twice since she returned to the area. Once outside the doctor's surgery years ago, and once at the super-market. Both times I'd been shocked at how she'd aged in both body and face. It was as if her lies had rotted her from the inside out. She'd tried to talk to me on both occasions, but each time I'd walked the other way. I couldn't face looking into her cold eyes, exact replicas of her son's.

'Is there... anything else you want to ask?' DI Price said and I realised there had been a long space of silence from my end.

'No, but thanks... for letting me know, I mean.'

She didn't reply for a few moments, as if I'd thrown her off guard. Maybe she'd been expecting me to panic or get upset but, in the end, I just felt numb.

'Right. Well, any questions or problems, you can contact me at our Arnold headquarters. I'll text you the number for my direct line. Just leave a message and I'll get back to you right away.'

The back of my neck prickled. 'What do you mean, "problems"?'

'Just that some people find an offender's release harder to deal with than others,' she said carefully. 'Especially when it's someone whose crime irreparably changed the course of the victim's family, as happened in your case. It can take some time to sink in, so if there's anything you're worried about or...'

Her words faded out as I flashed back to a six-foot tall Samuel Barlow, aged nineteen. He'd been spotty and skinny, leaning against the fence smoking a cigarette. Coolly watching me and Jimmy playing in the back garden. I was thirteen when he murdered my brother, a little boy of just eight years of age. Jimmy would've been thirty-four now, if he'd have been allowed to live his life. We'd have been best friends. He'd have been an amazing uncle to Ivy.

Something occurred to me. 'Samuel's not allowed to contact me, right?'

'There's nothing legally in place,' she said slowly. 'But it wouldn't be advisable to contact you from his point of view, and that will have been explained to him.'

Her words dropped to the floor, limp and toothless.

Explained to him. This wasn't a regular guy we were talking about who played by the rules...

Unease began its agonising slow simmer in the pit of my stomach. I'd never thought to plan for his early release; I'd lulled myself into a false sense of security by the fact he'd been refused parole so many times.

I wasn't a defenceless eight-year-old boy he could terrify, lock away and leave to die, like he'd done to Jimmy. But my daughter, the light of my life, was currently the same age that Jimmy was when he died. I had to protect her at all costs.

NINE

After DI Price's phone call, I stood for a moment and stared at the blank white wall in front of me. As sometimes happened, Jimmy's face appeared there, shimmering softly like a faded tapestry from long ago. Those cheeky dimples when he smiled, those soulful brown eyes... the exact same eyes Ivy had now.

I rubbed at my face. I'd loved him so much. I avoided the past and its terrible memories but I still thought about Jimmy every day because my daughter had so many of his mannerisms too. Tipping her head to one side when she felt puzzled, that cute way she'd flap her hands around when she got excited. Stroking her chin absent-mindedly when she was thinking.

Ivy. The sense of unease in my stomach grew. I'd known for a long, long time this day was coming. I'd thought I had the time to outrun it.

Terry and I had moved away from the area in which I'd grown up and we'd always intended to move even further in time. Then came the divorce, Mum's health worsened and I felt trapped between not wanting to see her and carrying out my daughterly duty despite her hatred of me. Then I opened the café, and it just seemed more sensible to stay put for a while. While Samuel was inside, the past stayed there with him.

I hadn't anticipated him getting an early release, and I hadn't considered how I might feel about my daughter's safety if it happened.

It made sense he'd come back here and stay with Maggie, at least for a short while.

'Josie! What's happening?' Sheena rushed into the kitchen and I snapped out of my daydreaming. A thin wisp of black smoke curled from one of the ovens. She pressed feverishly at the buttons.

'Sorry... I just...' I ran over and turned both ovens off. I opened the first door and thick, acrid smoke puttered out, filling the kitchen in an instant. We both coughed and Sheena rushed to the outer door, throwing it open to let the fresh air circulate. 'I just took my eye off the ovens for a moment and—'

I was standing right there in front of the ovens. What was I thinking?

Sheena grabbed the oven gloves and slid out a tray of incinerated biscuits. 'Nothing we can do for these, I'm afraid.' She looked at me and grinned. 'That must have been some daydream you were having.'

'I wasn't daydreaming. I was—'

'Hey, no worries. Tell you what, you sit down and tell me how to make the biscuit dough. It's time I learned and it's quiet in the café.'

I felt a swell of heat in my chest. 'Thanks for helping but I can take it from here.'

She placed a metal baking tray with its charred contents down on the oven top and peered at me. 'You don't look too good, Josie,' she said. 'Why don't you—'

'Honestly, Sheena, I'm fine!' I said tersely. She didn't say a word, just shoved her hands into her apron pocket and looked at her feet and I instantly felt bad. 'Sorry, I didn't mean to snap.' I swallowed. 'Leave me to sort out this mess; it's not the end of the world. And you've got customers to see to.'

I opened the other oven and took out two trays of what was essentially black ash. When I looked up, Sheena hadn't moved.

'Are you going to tell me what's wrong, so I can help?'

'Nothing's wrong. I've got a lot on my mind and some biscuits burned. End of story.' I really needed her to go away now. Nobody who worked here knew about what happened to Jimmy and that's the way I wanted it to stay. The young students were all from other parts of the country and were based in Nottinghamshire purely for their studies at the two universities. Sheena was in her late-twenties and had moved here when she met her partner, who'd lived abroad but had recently taken a job in the East Midlands. But Sheena too was originally from down south.

Sheena pulled out a couple of stools from the tall counter I usually did my admin on when the rest of the worktop space was covered in batter or dough. 'Why don't I make us both a coffee? You look hassled, Josie. You've been working so hard on the Brew contract, it's time to take a breath.'

I felt heat channel into my face, betraying the nonchalant attitude I was trying so hard to pull off. I pulled my hair – desperate for a colour and cut – up into a bun and secured it with a scrunchie from my wrist.

'OK. A quick coffee then, but I can't sit for long. There's far too much to do.'

I climbed up on to the other stool, reasoning that a few minutes getting my head straight would probably make me more productive anyway. Sheena walked over to the other side of the kitchen, pulling two mugs out of a cupboard, and spooning instant coffee in. She didn't usually cook because she was a waitress and took care of admin. I watched the easy way she moved around the unfamiliar space. Opening and closing cupboards and drawers until she found what she was looking for. I'd never had that sort of confidence. I did everything with a sense that something would probably go wrong.

She filled the cups from the boiling water tap. The hissing and spluttering of the steam added to the chaos in my head.

Unhurried, Sheena added milk to both drinks and brought them over. She went back to the double saloon doors and looked out into the café.

'Everyone's OK, there are only a handful of customers now,' she said, placing a coffee cup in front of me. 'You've done so well with this place. If we can keep on top of the Brew contract it could go from strength to strength.'

'Thanks. That's what I'm hoping.' I took a sip of my drink. The heat and caffeine were an instant hit. 'This is good.'

She nodded slowly, watching me. 'I just worry you're stretching yourself too thin, Josie,' she said gently.

I put down my mug. 'Sitting here isn't helping me get ahead though. So I'll just go and—'

'Josie, wait.' She pushed her hand in her pocket and pulled out a red and white packet that was very familiar to me. 'I found these on the floor. Right where Ivy was baking yesterday.'

'What?' I felt the colour drain from my face as I reached for the packet of sertraline. 'I... I don't know how that happened. They were in the bottom of my handbag last time I looked.'

'They must have dropped out. It's easily done when you're rushing around.'

'Ivy knows not to touch medicine. She wouldn't have taken one if she'd found them.' I knew I sounded defensive, but I had to say it.

'Course. She's a sensible girl,' Sheena said easily. 'There was something else, too. I wasn't going to say anything but...'

'No, go on,' I said, dreading it. 'Please.'

'When I got in this morning the window was open.' She pointed to the small window next to the door I remembered opening for a bit of air yesterday. Small, but probably just big enough that someone could squeeze through and enter the premises if they were so inclined. 'Again, it's easily done. I just wanted to let you know.'

My face burned. 'I probably do need to slow down a bit.' I walked over to the other side of the kitchen, my heart hammering. I had to get a grip. Forgetting to close a window could have been disastrous. Kids could have climbed through for fun and smashed up the equipment I was still paying for. Even worse, they could have taken cash. I'd got into the dubious habit of leaving takings in here two or three days before banking it, to save time.

'Well, I know you've got lots to do.' Sheena stood up. 'I'll go and see if the customers are OK.'

'Yes,' I said stiffly. 'Thanks... for telling me this stuff. I need to sort myself out.'

She sighed. 'The last thing I want to do is upset you. Believe it or not, I want to help out, not add to your stress levels.'

'I know,' I said. 'Thanks, Sheena.'

When she'd gone, I looked around me at the functional white shelving, the stainless-steel ovens I'd taken out a loan for when the café started doing so well.

I had a mountain of work to get through and, after DI Price's call, a new avalanche of worry to try and hold back. And, on top of it all, I was making mistakes here at work.

I had to get a grip. I refused to let Samuel Barlow ruin my life all over again.

TEN

MAGGIE

1985

Maggie Barlow finished mopping the kitchen floor and grimaced as she arched her twinging lower back. It was a nice day, so she decided to leave the back door slightly ajar to aid with the drying. When she reached to pull it open, she caught sight of the scruffy back yard and looked away. Each terraced house in their rundown row had the same dreary scrap of outdoor space.

It wasn't the life she'd wanted or expected. Reg had promised her the earth when he'd proposed to her. 'I'll give you the moon and stars if you'll let me,' he'd whispered, his breath sweet and clean then. His lean handsome face had just the right amount of stubble and had hovered just inches from her own.

Fool she was, she'd believed the words that slid so easily from his tongue every time he opened his mouth. As they'd both learned, time had a way of changing things and not always for the better.

Maggie sighed now and tiptoed gingerly across the wet

floor. No sooner had she reached the hallway than she heard a light tapping on the door.

'You there, Maggie?' a shrill voice called out. 'It's me, Pauline.'

Maggie turned to see her friend, Pauline Bennett, on the step, her adorable six-month-old son, Jimmy, balanced on one hip. Pauline's husband was a senior manager at one of the big hosiery mills in Forest Town and they lived in one of the detached houses with big gardens on the outskirts of Mansfield.

'I've just dropped our Josie off at school and thought I'd drop by for a cuppa,' she said.

Pauline's eyes swept critically around the clean but shabby kitchen and Maggie's heart sank. Pauline and her husband had money to spare. Maggie had never been invited to their house but, on the local grapevine, she'd heard about their new kitchen extension with its cherry wood cupboards and even a separate utility space for the washing machine and a dryer. She only had to glance at Pauline's face to know how awful her own house must look in comparison.

Still, five-year-old Josie was always round here. She seemed to feel more at home here than in her big, grand house. It hadn't escaped Maggie's notice that Pauline's interest in her daughter had waned since she'd had the baby, Jimmy. She only had eyes for him now. Still, Josie and Samuel played nicely together despite the age difference. He didn't really get on with boys his own age. Maggie loved having her around.

She pasted a smile on her face. 'Come through, Pauline.' Maggie beckoned her in, trying not to notice the dried mud on her boots that scattered over the clean floor with each step. 'I'll put the kettle on.'

She led Pauline through to the living room where eleven-year-old Samuel sat with his head down and completely absorbed with sorting each Lego brick into a strict colour code.

All the reds together, the blues and the yellows, each section set neatly apart.

'Where's Josie?' he said without looking up.

'She's at school, where you should be,' Pauline said firmly.

'He's feeling a bit under the weather, aren't you, Sammy?' Maggie said, tearing her eyes away from the baby's bonny face and plump little arms and legs. 'It's just a headache though, he's got nothing catching.'

'Doesn't look a thing wrong with him to me,' Pauline said.

Samuel looked up then and saw baby Jimmy. He stood, leaving his Lego unattended and sidled over to Pauline.

'He's nice and soft,' Samuel murmured, pressing his finger-tips into the smooth, plump skin of the infant's dimpled hand.

'Sammy loves babies,' Maggie said softly. 'He would've loved a brother or a sister.'

Pauline swung baby Jimmy on to the other hip away from Samuel's touch. When he attempted to move closer, she sat down on the threadbare sofa and bounced her tiny son on her knee, her elbows extended either side of him forming an effective barrier. She said, 'Have you been feeling a bit low again, Maggie? You seemed... I don't know, sort of sad the last couple of times I've called.'

'I'm fine!' Maggie gave a tight smile, suddenly desperate to get away from Pauline's scrutiny. 'Oh, I just remembered. I knitted baby Jimmy a new cardigan in the prettiest cornflower blue!' She dashed out of the room and ran upstairs.

When she felt it was safe to breathe again without bursting into tears, Maggie sat on the edge of the bed and collected herself. She should have never confided in Pauline last month that the doctor had prescribed medication to help with her diag-nosed depression and anxiety.

But it was true. Maggie felt the black cloud hovering again. It was seeing the baby, so perfect and wholesome. Why was she still fixating about having another child? As Reg had said time and time again, it wasn't the right time for them to have another baby.

'We're on our uppers, love, and you can't handle Samuel when he goes off on one as it is. Admit it.' Maggie knew he had a point, but she'd felt such a hatred for him voicing the truth so dispassionately that she found herself unable to respond.

After all this time, her mother had been proven right. In Reg, she'd backed a loser and now there was nothing to be done about it. Her father was dead from kidney disease, her mother had shunned her since she'd fallen pregnant with Samuel out of wedlock and now, she felt well and truly trapped.

As Maggie rooted around in the bottom of the wardrobe, she heard another knock on the back door. 'Get that, can you, Pauline?' she called down, pulling the crumpled paper bag out that contained her latest hand knitted garment for baby Jimmy.

She heard Pauline greet someone in the kitchen and the sound of laughter. It sounded like Janet, a new neighbour Pauline had only met once before. Maggie felt a smidgeon of annoyance at the extra footfall. She'd need to mop the kitchen floor again at this rate.

She stood up, grimacing at her protesting knees but then froze when a screech threaded its way upstairs. It sounded like a small creature in pain and Maggie's blood instantly ran cold. She dashed to the bedroom door and called out: 'What's happened?'

The sound of running footsteps across the kitchen and then Pauline's distressed voice screamed out at the bottom of the stairs: 'Maggie? Come quick!'

In what felt like one motion, she half-ran half-slid down the brown and orange patterned stairs' carpet.

'Samuel! What have you done?' Pauline's distressed voice changed into a shriek of anger as Maggie dashed into the cramped living room. 'Oh, you bad boy! You bad, bad boy!'

ELEVEN

JOSIE

2019

We entered the huge foyer of the Showcase cinema and queued at the food counter. Ivy chose a small bucket of popcorn, and we shared a diet soda. After getting our tickets checked on my phone, we made our way to Screen One. It was pleasantly busy but not rammed and so people were spaced out well.

We slipped off our jackets and sat through several trailers and I thought how much I'd missed the all-enveloping focus the cinema lent to a movie. I glanced down at Ivy, her arm linked through mine, face rapt and glued to the screen, and vowed to do this more often.

Five minutes before the film was due to start, I realised I needed the bathroom. Ivy didn't need to go, she said. 'Sit here and don't move,' I whispered back. 'I'll only be a few minutes.'

She nodded distractedly as she stared rapt at the flashing Disney animation on the screen, her small hand dipping in and out of the brightly striped popcorn carton. I slipped out into the artificial bright light of the corridor and headed for the well-signposted loos. Just before I turned left into the ladies, a short figure in a caramel-coloured mac moved out from behind a film poster and darted around the corner.

It was an older woman with dyed dark hair and grey roots who'd looked in a hurry to get away. I hadn't seen her face, but something about her reminded me of Maggie Barlow. I felt a new knotted sensation in my stomach, but I was desperate for the loo so I rushed inside the bathroom.

'It's not Maggie Barlow,' I muttered under my breath. 'It's not her.' I hadn't seen her for years. I'd become paranoid. This cinema was miles away from where she lived, and anyway, how could she possibly know we were here?

When I came back out of the bathroom, I looked around, relieved. No sign of anyone. Still, I felt nervous that I'd left Ivy on her own. Flustered, I rushed back into the darkened screen room. The trailers had finished and there was a message on the screen about turning off your phone.

I scurried up the steps to row five and stopped dead. Ivy wasn't there.

I checked the row number. Five. Seats three and four. Right here. This is where I'd left her. I looked around wildly.

The people on the row behind where we were sitting threw me daggers when I didn't sit down as the opening credits started to roll. I caught the eye of a woman sitting on the row behind us. I leaned forward and hissed, 'My little girl was here... did you see her go out?'

The woman shook her head and looked at her partner, who continued to stare straight ahead.

I turned around in a circle, peering through the darkness at the seats in other rows. Other people were starting to look visibly annoyed because I hadn't sat down yet.

'Ivy!' I called as I turned. 'Has anyone seen my little girl, she's eight, I left her sitting right here.'

'Sssh!' someone hissed impatiently a few rows back, but

then a few concerned others stood up and began to scout around.

The film started. I stared at the actor and frowned... then the screen froze, and the lights came on. Shouts of indignation and profanities rang out as people started bickering among themselves. A couple of uniformed staff came in and someone pointed as they headed up the stairs towards me.

I stared down at our seats and there was nothing... not even Ivy's empty popcorn carton. I remembered taking off my denim jacket when we first sat down... it too had gone.

And that, of course, was when I realised.

I was in the wrong screening.

'I'm so sorry. I'm an idiot, I don't know how I managed to get it wrong,' I babbled as the cinema usher led me through to next door and Screen Two.

'Don't worry, love,' the middle-aged woman said as we walked. 'You're not the first and I'm certain you won't be the last.'

My cheeks felt red hot and I felt sick. 'My little girl will be panicking. I said I'd only be a few minutes at the bathroom, and I've been gone at least ten.'

'We're here now. Can you remember where you were sitting?'

I nodded and rushed forward ahead of her, looking for Ivy's small silhouette. The room flashed bright and dark from the colourful images on screen and I saw her sitting there, tiny, her little face turned towards the screen. Then another flash illuminated the darkness and I felt an explosion of joy and relief. I ran towards her, waving my arm, but she was looking away now. Looking at a woman sitting next to her.

'Ivy!' I yelled. The woman next to her was Maggie Barlow. The dark hair, the light-coloured coat. It *was* her I'd seen outside the bathroom. 'Get away from her!'

People stood up, shouting for me to pipe down but I didn't care. I took the steps two at a time and lunged forward. The woman stood up and took several steps back as Ivy got out of her seat and wrapped her arms around me. 'I thought you'd gone, Mummy. I...' Her voice muffled as she buried her face in my side.

I turned with fury and pressed my face close to... a woman I didn't recognise.

'I saw you go out and she started to look a bit worried,' she said meekly. 'I sat next to her and said you'd be back in no time but even I was beginning to wonder.'

It was not Maggie Barlow. It was just a kind lady who'd spotted Ivy's discomfort and done a good turn.

'Thank you so much,' I said. 'Sorry to shout, I was confused. I went in the wrong screening. It was kind of you.'

'Sit down and shut up!' a man yelled from the back.

'OK now?' the usher whispered, one eye on the complaining man.

I nodded and guided Ivy back into her seat before sitting down myself. 'Thank you,' I mouthed over the aisle to the woman who'd settled again. 'Sorry!'

She raised a hand and smiled. Ivy slipped her little hand into mine and, for what felt like the first time in ages, I took a breath.

TWELVE

MAGGIE

Like any mother would do, Maggie had observed the changes in her son over the years and she'd been able to tell that he'd become bitter and twisted inside. On the last visit Maggie had made before Samuel's release, she'd left the facility with her skin crawling, an army of invisible creepy-crawlies marching up and down her entire body.

At first she'd wondered if it was nerves she'd detected. Re-entering the outside world after so long would be a challenge for anyone.

'Don't worry about people gossiping about you because you won't recognise anyone on the street. Everyone has died or moved on,' she'd said, hoping to reassure him.

'Oh, I'm not worried at all about that,' he'd said easily. 'I realise you've found yourself in the fortunate position you can forget I ever existed. Perhaps you've even been able to forget how you helped ruin my life by testifying in court.'

'I had no choice, Sammy. You can't refuse to give evidence, you know that. I suffered too, don't forget. Served time for lying for you.'

'Except you didn't lie, did you? You told the truth: that I'm an innocent man. You'd do well to remember that.'

'I meant that's what other people said, what the police said, at the time. That I'd lied.'

He had tied her up in knots, the way his father used to do.

'I don't care about other people. I don't care what you think, either. I used to care about Josie, but she abandoned me, too. For twenty-five long years, never visited once.'

Maggie had felt shocked at the extent of his denial. 'Jimmy was her brother, Sammy. You can't blame her for—'

'There you go again. Sounding like I was guilty. I was innocent. That's what I'll be telling anyone who asks.'

It was a waste of time even talking to him about it. He'd grown opinionated and arrogant inside the prison. He'd even started talking differently, in a strange, awkward manner. Choosing his words carefully and using convoluted language.

And now, he was upstairs in bed. In his old bedroom. His jacket slung over the banister, his discarded shoes tripping her up at the bottom of the stairs.

In other ways it was as if nothing had changed.

She'd never dare admit it to anyone, but she'd secretly hoped he would be getting his own place to live. She felt sure she'd heard they sometimes put people up in hostels or bedsits when they were first released. Maggie wasn't looking forward to having this critical stranger at home. Her beloved son had evaporated, and a cynical bully had taken his place.

Maggie had no friends and no support and, now, Sammy was home and it felt like he was ready to take over her life. It was hard to put into words, but she just had a feeling, a mother's intuition that he had something planned. Something bad.

There had been many times in her life when Sammy had been in trouble. When she'd known beyond doubt he'd been purposely cruel or hurt others. Times when she'd felt at a complete loss about what to do as a mother. She'd always come to the same conclusion, no matter how bad he'd been: she would stand by him, as she'd always done.

Now, Sammy was all grown up and a free man again, and Maggie had an awful creeping dread that those times were back with a vengeance.

THIRTEEN

1985

After hearing all the shrieking and racing downstairs, Maggie stood in the doorway and took in the chaotic scene before her. The living room reverberated with noise. Pauline screeching with fury and the new neighbour, Janet, nursing a screaming baby Jimmy in her arms.

Pauline had Samuel's arm in a pincer grip and was pulling at him roughly.

Maggie rushed over, grabbing him and snapping at Pauline, 'Stop that, leave him be!' She hugged Samuel into her. 'What happened?'

'Ask that son of yours!' Pauline's face was puce. She took her baby from the other woman, shushing and rocking him. 'He's a devil child. Everyone around here says so.'

Both women glared at Maggie as her eyes rested on the baby's damp, red face. A livid purple welt ran from his temple, across his cheek to his upper lip. In a couple of places, it had driven deep enough to break the skin and blood oozed out. She watched as the entire mark darkened further with each second that passed.

'Samuel, did you hurt the baby?' Maggie pushed him gently back from her so she could see his eyes, but the boy buried his face deeper into her side.

'Of course he hurt him!' Pauline seethed. 'That much is obvious.'

'You saw exactly what happened then?' Maggie challenged her.

Pauline hesitated. 'No... but he obviously attacked him when I answered the door to Janet. I ran back in when I heard the baby screaming and Samuel sprang away from him. Why would he do that if he's innocent?'

'Did you hurt the baby, Samuel?' Maggie asked again. Samuel stayed silent but shook his head vehemently against her arm.

'Liar!' Pauline spat out the words, her fury renewed by the boy's blatant denial. 'He's used something hard and sharp. A weapon! That mark is literally millimetres from Jimmy's eye.' Her voice wobbled. 'He might have blinded him!' Pauline stepped forward, her eyes narrowing. 'I'll search him. He must have something in his pocket, something sharp enough to leave such a mess.'

Samuel shrank further into Maggie's side. 'Don't you dare touch him. You've admitted you didn't see him do anything.' Maggie's voice sounded dangerously calm. 'Neither of you saw what happened. The baby's nails look quite long, perhaps he scratched himself.' Maggie looked from one woman to the other and Janet looked away. But Pauline's eyes burned into Maggie's.

'He's six months old, for Christ's sake! He hasn't the strength to make such a deep, long mark on his own face. You know that as well as I do. Samuel is dangerous, he shouldn't be around other children.'

'I think you should leave now,' Maggie said coldly. 'Both of you.'

To her relief, Pauline marched towards the kitchen, holding the whimpering baby boy close to her chest. Janet followed close behind. 'Wait here,' Maggie whispered to Samuel before walking into the kitchen.

When they reached the back door, Janet stepped out silently, but Pauline stopped and turned. 'Mark my words, that lad needs help before he blinds the next child, or worse. It's not natural, attacking a helpless baby like that. You should do something before—'

'Goodbye, Pauline.' Maggie stepped forward. 'Don't bother coming over here again.'

'You've got a cheek! I wouldn't set a foot inside this dump again even if you—'

Pauline's furious retort faded into nothing as Maggie slammed the door shut. She stood for a moment and looked down at her trembling hands. Seeing baby Jimmy in that state had been so upsetting. After a couple of deep breaths, she headed back into the tiny hallway.

Padding softly in her stocking feet, she waited outside the living room, watching through the crack in the door. Samuel stood in the centre of the room and carved the air with a piece of blue Lego, grimacing as he pulled it in slow-motion across what could be an imaginary face. When Maggie pushed open the door, he slipped the piece into his pocket.

She stared silently at him until, after a few seconds, his face crumbled. 'I hate that woman, Mummy. She tells lies. It wasn't my fault baby Jimmy scratched himself.' When Maggie didn't answer, he ran over and threw his arms around her, hugging her tight. 'I love my mummy more than the whole world.'

'And I love my Sammy more than the whole universe,' Maggie said faintly. She pushed away worries about who Pauline might tell and what might come of what had happened here today. There was no proof, that was the main thing. Samuel had been simply acting out a role just now when she'd secretly watched him. He'd just been pretending. Like all kids did.

Later, as her troubled son slept peacefully in his bed, Maggie retrieved the piece of Lego from his trouser pocket and examined it under her powerful sewing light. The sharp edge and corner of the piece was speckled in what looked like dried rust. Maggie washed it clean in the bathroom sink. She could see wasn't rust at all. It was blood. Baby Jimmy's blood. She took the plastic brick downstairs and out to the dustbin.

Later, while Reg was still in the Station Hotel and blissfully unaware of what had happened, Maggie poured herself a small whisky. She turned off the lights in the living room and stared out into the black night, trying to battle the rising sense of panic inside while she waited for her husband to return.

The day after the incident with Samuel and baby Jimmy, Reg had returned home from work steaming with rage at the end of his shift.

'I got told in front of all the men at the factory to go directly to Mr Bennett's office.' Reg winced, referring to Pauline's manager husband. 'When I got there, he told me what that—' he glared over at Samuel, who was keeping firmly behind his mother '—what that little savage did to the baby.'

'He did nothing wrong,' Maggie said, ushering Samuel further back, out of his father's reach. 'It all got out of hand.'

'I'll say it did,' Reg said from between gritted teeth. Maggie took in his knotted features, the rising colour in his face. 'You've got to face it; he hurt that baby, Maggie. He's done other stuff too over the years and he needs to see someone.'

'I didn't! I didn't do it!' Samuel screeched from behind her.

'If Samuel says he didn't do it then I believe him,' Maggie said shortly. She stood her ground between her husband and their son. This was the measure of the man. One who could not be trusted to control his temper in front of his own child.

'Mr Bennett says he's got a purple welt across his chops like someone slashed him in the face.' Reg's expression darkened.

Maggie lifted her chin defiantly. 'They've no proof. None at all. Pauline Bennett didn't see Samuel touch a single hair on that child's head.'

Samuel stepped out from his mother's side. 'I hate you,' he told his father quietly, his face pale, his eyes dark. 'I really hope you die soon.'

Reg seemed to suddenly wither before the two of them. His shoulders sagged, his chest sank inward. He turned and walked away. That night, without a word to his wife, he moved into the spare room.

FOURTEEN

JOSIE

2019

The morning of Friday, 17 May, I opened my eyes and stared at the ceiling. Today was the day I'd dreaded for so many years. The day Samuel Barlow became a free man again, thanks to a screwed-up justice system. Jimmy stayed dead and *he* got the chance to start a new life. How could that be fair?

Since DI Price's phone call on Monday informing me his parole application had been approved, my sleep had suffered. I'd struggled to get more than an hour or two's sleep at all without waking up. It seemed to take ages for me to drop off again each time and I was probably currently existing on three to four hours' quality sleep each night at the most.

'Train me up to make the biscuit dough,' Sheena asked for the umpteenth time yesterday when she cleared a customer table and caught me running between the ovens and the industrial mixer. 'I can oversee the Brew contract and take that pressure off you for a while.'

'It's fine, I can manage, I—'

Sheena dumped the dirty crockery on the side and folded

her arms. She waited until I stopped what I was doing and looked at her. 'Don't you ever get tired of trying to be Superwoman?'

I threw my hands up in the air and said, 'You know, you're right. Thank you, we can start today.'

Sheena was a quick learner and had really helped increase output in between serving in the café. She came over to my house after work a couple of times to go through the contract paperwork and now the new part-timers were trained up, she had more time to help me in the back.

I kept forgetting stuff at home and at work. Nothing serious. Ivy found a jar of coffee in the fridge, which we had a giggle about, and Sheena spotted a couple of minor mistakes in the invoices I'd prepared for Brew. I checked the security of the windows and doors scrupulously before I left the café each day and I left all medication at home, instead of tossing it carelessly in my bag and taking it at work.

But it felt like the right time to visit the doctor. I made sure she knew I was trying to help myself. Doctors liked that.

'Is there any reason for this increased anxiety?' She looked at me over the top of her glasses.

'Just the general pressures of life, I think. Running a business, coping as a single parent,' I said. 'I've started a yoga class and I'm in the process of cutting down my working hours. I just need a bit more help to feel calmer for a while, until I start feeling the benefits. Then I think I'll be fine.'

She wrote me a prescription for some stronger medication and something to help me sleep.

I'd told Fiona about Samuel Barlow's release. 'It's bad news for us all. A monster like him back on the streets,' she'd said, shaking her head. 'I was hoping it was just idle gossip but obviously not.'

It wasn't gossip, it was real. And even though I would like

nothing more than to take Ivy and hide away somewhere nobody could find us, I knew life had to go on.

For the first few days following Barlow's release, I'd been like a cat on hot bricks. Scanning the faces in the street, insisting to Fiona I'd keep Ivy at home every night.

I couldn't imagine how bad I'd be if the doctor hadn't given me the extra medication. Somehow, I'd imagined my life would change when he became a free man again, but there had been no contact, no strange happenings. If DI Price had not contacted me, I wouldn't have known Barlow was out at all.

'Ivy? Time to go, sweetie,' I called upstairs on Tuesday morning when it was time to leave to drop her at Fiona's house.

'I wish I could come to the café with you today, Mummy.' Ivy pursed her lips and folded her arms. 'And I wish you could stay at home like Darcy's mum does.'

'I know. It's tough for me too.' I swept the fringe out of her eyes. 'But it will get better, I promise. When things settle down, I won't have to be at work as much. OK?'

'Can I have a sleepover with Darcy tonight?' she asked, as if she could sense my nervousness. Since Barlow's release, I'd felt too nervous to let her out of my sight once I picked her up at the end of the day.

'I don't know,' I said cagily. 'We'll have to see.'

When we got to Fiona's house, Ivy asked again. 'She's very welcome to stay here,' Fiona said, tipping her head and watching my face. 'She'll be perfectly fine, you know.'

My initial reaction was to refuse. I felt like I needed to know she was safe upstairs at night. So I could go and watch her breathing, touch her warm skin, if I woke up panicking. But Fiona took me upstairs and pointed to the new bunk beds in Darcy's room.

'Dave assembled these yesterday. Ivy even gets her own bed. I've planned the girls' favourite teas and Darcy insisted I got Ivy a pair of matching pyjamas.' My eyes settled on the matching folded nightwear featuring pink-heart appliqués. 'The girls get on so well, I don't even know I've got her, so please don't worry, Josie.'

Ivy could barely conceal her delight at the prospect of staying over, but my sense of threat swelled bigger with each minute that passed. 'Pleeasse, Mummy, can I stay over? Me and Darcy have got matching teddy bears!' The girls stood, each clutching a pink bear aloft with pleading looks on their faces.

I'd heard nothing from Barlow, nothing from Maggie. My paranoia had been embarrassing at the cinema... was it fair to spoil Ivy's fun and weigh her down with my worries?

I gave a weak smile and turned to Fiona. 'Why do I get the feeling I'm outnumbered here?'

She grinned. 'Best to admit when you're beaten.'

'Well... if you're sure...'

'Honestly, we love having Ivy stay here. It's no chore on my part, I can assure you.' She nudged me. 'And OK, I admit, me and Dave usually get an hour of peace and quiet after tea when the girls are together!'

Cecil, Fiona's mild-natured whippet, sauntered in and sniffed at Ivy's legs, making her squeal in delight. She'd always wanted a dog, but I'd had to explain many times it wouldn't be fair on the animal as we were away from the house too long every day.

'We're taking Cecil out for a walk later, Mummy!' Ivy beamed, stroking his silky fawn fur.

I felt my stomach twist. 'Where do you walk the dog?' I asked Fiona.

'It'll just be around the edge of the park today. At the weekends we sometimes go to the woods, but the girls can have a climb and a run around if we do the park.' She hesitated and laid a hand on my arm. 'You've no need to worry about her safety, Josie. I'll look after her like she's my own.'

'I know and I'm sure she'll love it,' I said, pushing away the sense of dread. 'It's fine. She knows to stay close to you and not move away.'

'I should think so, we tell them often enough.' She looked at me. 'I hope you know Ivy is well looked after here.'

'I do, yes. Thanks, Fiona.' I scratched the dog's ear. 'You're going to enjoy your walk, aren't you, Cecil?'

Fiona busied around, making juice for the children, untangling the hair of two dolls that had become locked together... all with an easy smile on her face. It mirrored the fact that everything I did came with the shadow of work and the scarcity of time, and now the added worry about Barlow's early release.

Fiona was an effortless mum, never seeming to worry about whether she was doing things right. She just ran with her instincts, which always seemed to be on point. Her kitchen was clean but lived in, her short nails were painted, a half-done crossword sat on the side. She'd got things in balance, ticking lots of boxes. When I looked at Fiona, I saw what life might be like if we could make a fresh start where I wasn't bogged down with worry.

'I can't stay long, sorry, Fiona,' I said regretfully. 'It's so good of you to have Ivy later. I'm not going to waste the evening. I'm heading straight to the café to prepare the baked goods for the morning and make another few rounds of biscuits.'

'Those never-ending biscuits.' Fiona lowered her chin and looked up at me with chastising eyes. 'Don't wear yourself out, Josie. You can only do so much.'

Ivy ran past us to the hallway.

'Ivy... say bye to Mummy before you go upstairs to Darcy, darling,' Fiona called to her and she came rushing back over.

She looked so adorable with her little plaits, wearing her new checked school dress I'd bought her from the spring uniform range. 'Darcy has a proper vet's shop and I've brought some of my poorly toy animals to be seen by the vet after school.' Ivy patted her small pink rucksack. 'Patchwork dog has a sore paw and one-eared rabbit has a poorly eye.'

'Goodness, I hope the vet can give them some medicine,' I said, my heart squeezing at her furrowed brow, as she immersed herself in the story. 'I'm sure they'll feel better soon.'

'Love you, Mummy.' Her small arms clasped around my middle, squeezing tight.

'Love you more, angel,' I whispered. I felt my eyes prickle and I looked down, kissed the top of her head. My heart squeezed in on itself that I wouldn't see her until tomorrow, but at least she was happy and safe here.

I watched her scamper upstairs before turning back to Fiona.

'I know it sounds silly, but will you just drop me a text later when she's in bed to let me know she's OK?'

'Of course I will, and it doesn't sound silly at all.'

I glanced at Ivy to make sure she wasn't listening to our conversation. 'It's just, with Samuel being out now and... I know it might seem paranoid, but—'

Fiona laid her hand on my arm. 'It doesn't sound paranoid, Josie. I'd be exactly the same.'

I blinked a few times before looking at Fiona. 'I'll get off then,' I said. 'Just ring if you need anything at all.'

Fiona gave me a sympathetic smile. 'Don't beat yourself up, eh?' she said softly. 'You're a great mum and you're trying to make a good life for the two of you.'

I nodded and left before I dissolved into a hot mess in front of my daughter.

FIFTEEN

Back at the café, I opened the oven door and pushed in another four supersized trays of biscuit dough. I screwed up my eyes against the blast of heat. My skin felt raw and scorched but I had so much to do, I couldn't afford the three-second wait for cooler air.

Since I'd woken up this morning, I had a headache I couldn't get rid of. While Barlow was still in prison it had been much easier to push away the past but the thought of him free on the streets again – well, it was now an impossibility.

As it was, I had a productive day, managing to get ahead for the first time in ages. *Keep busy. Keep busy.* I repeated the words over and over like a mantra in my head. Later, when the café had closed and the part-time staff had gone home, I called Fiona.

'Is Ivy OK?' I said lightly. 'Has everything been alright today... when you took Cecil out?'

'She's absolutely fine,' Fiona said brightly. In the background I could hear the radio, the girls laughing. A proper home. 'Ivy? Come and say hi to your mum!'

The laughter and shouts got louder. 'Hi, Mummy!' Ivy's

breathless voice. 'We were playing hide and seek but Cecil keeps finding us and giving our hiding place away!'

'Oh, he's such a spoilsport! Everything been OK at school today?'

'Yes, I got a sticker for finishing my numbers worksheet first and someone's lunchbox broke in the dinner hall and their sandwiches went all over the floor. I have to go now, Mummy, it's my turn to find Darcy. Love you, bye!'

'Bye... love you...'

'Me again!' Fiona replied. 'Love you too.'

'Ha! She sounds happy.'

'She is, Josie. You shouldn't worry on that score.'

'Thanks,' I said. 'For everything.'

'Don't be daft. We love having Ivy here.'

'I know, but thanks for understanding. For getting it.'

'Course,' Fiona said gently. 'But you can sleep well tonight, Josie. Ivy is perfectly fine and we're not going out again, so no need to fret.'

I thanked her again, feeling tearfully grateful I had such good people around me. After the call, I sat down and stared at my hands.

The silence filled my head like a siren. Samuel Barlow was out there, back with his mother in the same street after all this time. So many years since Jimmy had been alive.

What was he doing now, this very minute? Having tea with his mother?

I pictured myself inside their dark little house as a child. Ironically, I'd felt at home there. I'd felt safe and wanted.

Perhaps Samuel was filled with regret, reflecting on his terrible crime. I seriously doubted that.

I wondered, if the detective hadn't called to tell me about his release, would I have sensed anything different? A feeling of unease, a restlessness in my bones? The world was a different place now he was a free man and yet life had seemed to carry on as normal, on the outside at least.

Maybe it was only in my head that everything had changed.

The next morning, I woke early, about five-thirty. But I'd had a decent night. Probably the best one for a couple of weeks.

As I hadn't had Ivy in the house and Fiona had reassured me all was fine, I'd taken one of the new tablets my GP had prescribed. 'Something to help you relax a bit better at night,' she'd said.

It had done the job. I'd woken a couple of times, visited the bathroom in the early hours and lingered by Ivy's bedroom door, thinking how strange the house felt without her presence. But, generally, I felt more rested than I'd done in ages.

I made a cup of tea and took it back to bed while I checked the new, helpful baking spreadsheets Sheena had created for the Brew contract. At eight o'clock, I texted Fiona.

Morning! Hope everything OK. Give Ivy a kiss from me.

Two minutes later my phone rang.

'Morning, Mummy!' Ivy's bright, clear voice rang out. 'Darcy fell out of bed in the night and hurt her arm.'

'Oh dear! Is she OK?'

'Yes, she's got a bruise coming.'

I heard laughter and whispering and then Fiona's voice came on the line. 'Hi, it's me. She's fine. This pair of little scally-wags got in bed together after lights-out and Darcy half fell out. No harm done though.'

'Oh good! Thanks for letting her ring. Just nice to hear her voice.'

'That's what I thought. Nothing to worry about. She's still

in one piece... just,' she said in a mock stern voice. I heard the girls giggling close by.

I said, 'I'm going to try and get to school to pick her up later, but I'll text you to confirm, if that's OK.'

'No worries. If not, I'll bring her back here, so no rush.'

'Thanks again, Fiona,' I said. 'You're a lifesaver.'

It was a busy morning in the café with lots of footfall. We had a full roster of part-time staff for once and it had freed me up to get lots of baking done. With Sheena's help, we'd managed to do a good morning's work.

While Sheena sorted out yet another supplies delivery, I made us a well-deserved coffee. When she brought the delivery note through for me to sign, I frowned at the quantity of butter. 'This is half what we usually have,' I tutted.

'The delivery guy says it'll be back to normal next week,' she said. 'He's really good. He's going to try and source more later today, so it doesn't leave us short.'

She disappeared again with the signed delivery chit, and I covered my face with my hands. Everything seemed to be such hard work nowadays. Two steps forwards and one step back. The second I thought I was on top of the contract, another curveball came in.

By twelve-thirty, the regular lunch customers were starting to arrive for both eat-in and takeout. When I was in the middle of making up a takeout order of our popular Snickers sweet toasties, Sheena came through to the kitchen.

'Sorry to disturb you, Josie, but there's a customer out front who's got a complaint and is insisting on speaking to the manager.'

I cursed under my breath. This was all I needed. 'Not one of our regulars, I'm guessing?'

She shook her head. 'Some grumpy bloke who says he got

the wrong order. But I served him and he definitely asked for a latte and a piece of red velvet cake and that's exactly what I gave him. Now, he's saying he asked for something different.'

'Don't worry, I'll sort it out.' I washed my hands and dried them before heading out into the café.

'Over there, in the Puffa jacket.' She nodded to a man with his back to the main seating area. He had short grey hair and sat staring out of the window.

'I could do without this today,' I said, sighing. 'Thanks, Sheena. Leave it with me.'

I took a breath. I really didn't feel like a set-to over nothing. Things were going well for once. Thanks to my late night yesterday I was on track to get in front with the orders for the first time. I was trying hard to keep positive and if another piece of cake and a coffee was what it took to set this guy straight, then it was a price I was more than willing to pay.

As I approached him, the strangest thing happened. The back of my neck prickled for no reason. I walked around the side of the complaining customer's table. 'Hello, I'm the manager. Can I help you?'

The man looked up at me and smiled. Those icy eyes and wet red lips, the crossed yellow teeth... I could never forget that grin. My throat tightened and revulsion rose in my chest. 'Get out,' I whispered hoarsely. 'You can't come in here.'

'Hello, Josie. I didn't know you worked here.' Barlow glanced around but Sheena had gone back to the kitchen and the tables either side of his had been vacated. When he realised nobody was listening, his voice dropped quieter. 'But then I'm entitled to visit any café I wish in the area. I'm a free man now.'

I cleared my throat, spoke clearly and with, I hoped, some authority. 'I'm the manager and I'm asking you to *leave*.'

Barlow leaned back in the chair and folded his arms. Just an ordinary middle-aged man to most people, but I could see he'd been working out from the broadness of his chest and arms, even though his jacket was bulky. The veins in his neck stood proud and his hands were large and substantial and looked at odds with his long, slender fingers.

'I wasn't happy with the service, see. I asked for a piece of carrot cake and your ditsy waitress brought me red velvet. I don't like red velvet. What are you going to do about it?'

I felt my heartbeat move up into my throat. I could ring the police but DI Price had already said there were no legal blocks in place forbidding Barlow to contact me. He hadn't done anything wrong here at the café and there were other customers who'd vouch for him, I'm sure. On the surface he was just making a minor complaint and asking to speak to the manager. I took a breath. I spoke slowly and focused on keeping my voice from trembling.

'I don't want you here. I'll provide you with a takeaway coffee and cake and then you can leave.'

'Why don't you want me here? Aren't you a forgiving person, Josie? I'm disappointed.' One side of his mouth tilted up in a sort of half-smirk. It was the same expression he'd had all those years ago when he'd stood smoking, watching Jimmy and me for hours over the garden fence. I'd always felt he'd hated me spending time with anyone else, even my own brother. It was impossible to meet those cold eyes without wondering if they were the last thing my brother saw before he died. I looked away but I could still feel his eyes burning into me. 'It's a bit breezy out today,' he said. 'I'd prefer to sit in and eat. If that's alright.'

'It's not alright.' My voice became high and strained. Some of the other customers looked up from their conversations and I realised I was speaking louder than I ought to be.

'You're not the forgiving sort after all, Josie. I can see that now,' he said smoothly, placing a pale hand on the table. His nails were longer than a man would usually keep them. 'Shame, that.' He stared down at the table for a few seconds as if he'd gone to another place. Then he looked up. 'Still. I'm out of prison now and that's what matters, isn't it? I've got a fresh start to look forward to.'

A fresh start Jimmy would never have.

'I want you out of my café.'

His smile widened, his cold eyes twinkling. Ivy's face came into my mind and my head filled with thunder. Rage shook my entire body. It felt like it shook the café, threatening to fracture my whole world. Then, as suddenly as it came, the thunder receded. When I looked around me, I saw alarmed faces, felt the weight of the thick silence hanging in the air around us.

I locked eyes with Barlow. The trace of a smirk remained but he was faking nonchalance. His eyes darted round the café, his fists clenched. I couldn't seem to get my breath.

'Are you OK, Josie?' Sheena rushed forward, looking accusingly at the ordinary-looking middle-aged man, who she'd assumed was just a troublesome customer.

A couple of customers stood up, the bell sounding as they left the café.

'I'm OK. This customer is just leaving.' I looked at him. Sheena, sensing my discomfort, folded her arms and stared him down.

Barlow stood up and gave me a disingenuous smile. 'Shame we couldn't have a civilised chat,' he said, pushing his chair out of the way. 'Maybe next time.'

'There won't be a next time,' I said, as I turned on my heel and walked away.

SIXTEEN

I couldn't get Barlow's piercing blue eyes and long, pale fingers out of my head. The way he'd sat there looking like an ordinary man to the other, unsuspecting customers when I knew he was the worst kind of monster.

I'd made an excuse to Sheena about feeling unwell and left for Fiona's house. It wasn't a lie. I felt dreadful. In the car, my hands shook on the steering wheel and I drove slower than usual because I didn't trust my reactions.

But I had to speak to Fiona. I had to warn her about Barlow.

I made a call on the way on hands-free and, to my relief, DI Helena Price answered right away.

'It's Josie Bennett,' I said, trying to keep my voice calm when really all I wanted to do was scream.

'Oh hi, Josie,' she said and then asked a little more cautiously, 'is everything OK?'

'No, I'm afraid not. Samuel Barlow just came to my café. He asked to speak to the manager, which is me, and I went out there and that's when I realised it was him.'

'Right, let me just make some notes,' she said and I could

hear the concern in her voice. Paper rustled and then she was back. 'OK, so what happened, exactly?'

'My waitress came to get me from the kitchen as a customer was complaining and demanding to see the manager.'

'And so you came out to speak to him?'

'Yes. I had no clue it was Barlow. I went over to his table and saw it was him.'

'And what did he say?'

'He said he was unhappy with the service he'd had.'

'He had a genuine complaint?'

'No, the waitress was certain he'd been given the correct order. He complained so he could get to speak to me. I immediately asked him to leave.'

'Right. Good. Did he threaten you at all?'

'No, but I *felt* very threatened. It was such a shock, seeing him out of the blue like that. Thanks to your phone call, I knew he'd been released last Friday, but I never dreamed he'd come to the café.'

'Is that what he said, that he'd come to find you?'

'No. He feigned surprise, said he didn't realise I worked there but... well, that's clearly rubbish. He knew I was there. He had to.'

'And did he leave when you asked him to?'

'Eventually, yes, but that's not the point, is it? He shouldn't have come anywhere near me.'

'Of course. I totally understand.'

'So, what are you going to do about it? Can he be cautioned?'

Price sighed. 'On paper he's done nothing wrong. He claimed not to realise you worked there, he didn't threaten you, and he left when asked.'

'That's hardly the point!' I pulled out of a junction too early and earned myself a prolonged beep from an oncoming car. I put my hand up and mouthed 'sorry'. 'It's obvious he did it to unnerve me.'

She hesitated. 'I'll give his probation officer a call and explain what happened. He'll be in trouble if he's found to be trying to make contact during his probation period.'

'He needs telling in no uncertain terms not to come anywhere near me or my daughter!' I cried out.

'Did he mention your daughter?'

'No, but... he can't be allowed to just do as he pleases. Can't I get a court order to keep him away?'

'I know how frustrating this must be for you and I'm sorry you had to face that today,' Price said. 'Sadly, our hands are tied unless Barlow threatens you or makes a real nuisance of himself. It's understandable you feel he tracked you down, but let's hope it was a genuine mistake on his part.'

'He's already made a nuisance of himself,' I snapped. 'I want someone to tell him to keep away from us.'

'I understand entirely,' Price said. 'As I said, I'll speak to his probation officer, explain you don't consider it a mistake.'

I gave a bitter laugh. 'You don't know him at all. Samuel Barlow doesn't make mistakes like that. He's cold and calm and calculating and he's no fool.'

'Leave it with me,' Price said, her tone a little cooler. 'I'll make his probation officer aware of the incident today.'

I ended the call and felt like punching my hand through the windscreen to relieve my frustration. How could they be so gullible? Barlow had only been out for a matter of days and he already had them hoodwinked.

When I got to Fiona's, I knew Ivy and Darcy would still be at school. 'This is a surprise,' she said brightly when she opened the door. Then her expression darkened. 'Is everything OK, Josie?'

'No... something's happened,' I stammered. 'At the café.'

'Oh no! Come through. I'm just feeding the babies, but it won't take long.'

Fiona was looking after her regular charges, eight-month-old twins. They both sat in highchairs at the kitchen table when I followed her through. One had bouncy golden curls, the other one straight dark hair that stuck up in random tufts. Both smiled and jigged when I came in and I wiggled my fingers to greet them.

I sat at the table and watched as she spooned macaroni cheese alternatively into the babies' mouths. She looked at me. 'What's happened?'

'You know Samuel Barlow was released last Friday?' She nodded and frowned. 'Well, today, he came into the café.'

'What?' The empty spoon froze in mid-air and the curly-haired toddler banged his highchair tray with the heel of his hand to signal his disapproval. Josie loaded up the spoon again. 'But... surely he's not allowed to contact you?'

'That's what I also thought but the detective I called seemed to think Barlow had covered himself because he pretended he didn't know it was my café.' My throat felt rigid with upset. 'He knows just how to play the system. Always did.'

Three years before he killed Jimmy, when Barlow just turned sixteen, his school had threatened to exclude him for pushing another boy off a rock-climbing face and breaking his collarbone. But they'd had to retract their threat because there had been no witnesses around when it had happened and the victim – obviously terrified – had voluntarily withdrawn his allegation against Barlow shortly afterwards.

'The detective said she'll speak to his probation officer.'

Fiona shook her head, scraping the bowl and offering the last two spoons up to the children. 'You must be out of your mind, Josie. You really shouldn't have to put up with that.'

'That's why I've come over here,' I said. I was struggling to find the best way to say how I felt. 'All I can think about is protecting Ivy from even having to lay eyes on him. I won't be able to let her stay over again until I know he's been told to stay away. I hope you understand.'

After today, I knew I'd never sleep a wink unless Ivy was safe at home in the next room. I needed to be able to check she was safe anytime I liked.

'I understand completely,' Fiona said, waving a hand to dismiss my concern, as she took the empty dish over to the sink. 'I couldn't bear to be away from Darcy at night, so please don't worry. I'll get the twins cleaned up and then I'll make us a cup of coffee.'

It sounded like she would never put up with so many sleep-overs for Darcy, although I'm sure she didn't mean it like that. Still, her words jangled my guilty bells, as if they weren't ringing loudly enough.

My mind soon returned to Barlow. Underneath his jacket I'd sensed his sinewed forearms and wide shoulders. That same wolfish smile I remembered from years earlier. Terrifyingly, he was the kind of man most people wouldn't notice in a café. There were no standout features, no air of threat, no prowling demeanour. He had looked, on the face of it, like a completely ordinary man.

But I knew different. Twenty-five years inside had done nothing to disperse the darkness I'd sensed writhing just under the surface of his skin. I knew the callousness, the wickedness that lurked behind his amiable appearance and his falsely apologetic attitude.

He was a predator who was now a free man again and my only driving desire was in keeping him away from my precious girl.

SEVENTEEN

After the twins' grandma had collected them, I went with Fiona to school to pick the girls up.

'Please don't mention anything about what happened with Barlow today to the other mums,' I said. 'It'll probably get out at some point, but I don't want people asking me questions about the past.'

'I wouldn't dream of it,' Fiona said. 'It's a horrible position to be in and I'll do anything I can to support you. I hope you know that.'

'I do,' I said gratefully. 'Thank you.'

Ivy wasn't impressed when she learned she wasn't going to Darcy's house to play after school.

She punched her small hands on to her hips. 'We're supposed to be taking Cecil out for a walk again.'

'Sorry, but there's been a change of plans,' I said wearily.

'Why though?' she pressed, as I said goodbye to the others and we made our way to the school gates. 'You said I could this morning.'

'I know, I'm sorry,' I said, feeling close to tears. 'I love you so much. I just need you at home with me.'

She looked at me then, concerned. Silently, she reached for my hand and pressed her head to my arm.

Later, I got Ivy settled into bed after her bath and read her a story. Since we'd left school, she'd seemed a little quiet. I tried to focus on improving her mood. By the time she'd snuggled down in bed, she seemed much happier.

Instead of looking at productions spreadsheets or zoning out with a boxset, I set Adele's new album playing at low volume on Spotify. The room filled with her soulful, mellow voice, and I allowed my head to sink back into the seat cushion. For the first time that day, I felt the knots in my shoulders finally begin to soften a little.

I'd just begun to drift off when a tap at the window, followed by a sharp rap on the front door, broke through my relaxed state. I sat bolt upright. There was only one person who knocked like that, and I didn't feel up to seeing him.

I realised with a jolt I hadn't given a second thought to telling Terry about Samuel Barlow's release, least of all his appearance at the café today. Maybe he'd found out somehow. He'd been so unreliable with Ivy in recent weeks, he'd been the furthest person from my mind.

I walked quickly into the small hallway. My handbag, shoes and coat were still discarded by the door where I'd dumped them, exhausted, when we got back home from school. I pushed them aside with my foot and peered through the spyhole, even though I knew exactly who to expect.

My heart sank when I saw Terry's eyes staring blankly forward, his mouth set in a tight line the way it did when he was looking for trouble. As I unlatched the Yale lock, I felt the tension returning to my neck and shoulders. I didn't expect, nor want, unannounced visitors at eight o'clock at night.

'Terry?' I opened the door just wide enough that I could see him clearly. 'It's late. What is it?'

'Can I come in? I need a quick word if that's alright.' His face looked thin and worried. He clearly had something on his mind.

I sighed inwardly. I hadn't got the inclination or the energy to start a doorstep argument. The last time Terry saw Ivy was three weeks ago. The court had given me full custody after our acrimonious split two years ago, but I'd readily agreed for him to have a weekly visit to be arranged between us by mutual agreement. I'd lost my dad young and I wanted Ivy to have a good relationship with her father more than anything. But we'd agreed back then, no turning up to the house out of the blue. Terry had been guilty of it before – especially when he was heavily drinking – but not for a long time.

'I'm tired, Terry. I've got a lot on at work and—'

He looked furtively over his shoulder, but the street was quiet. 'Can I come in?' he said again. 'What I've got to say won't take long.'

Behind him, the light was fading. The way it caught his face, the angle of it as he waited for me to invite him inside... I was reminded of the night we met. Christmas Eve, twelve years ago. I'd been out for a drink after work with a few girlfriends and they'd gone on to a club. I'd been tired and eager to get home. A cab came around the corner and a tall guy with longish wavy hair and a square jaw hailed it at the same time I did. Warmed and emboldened by our festive drinking, we ended up sharing the taxi and arranging to meet up for a drink the day after Boxing Day.

I stood my ground. 'I'm shattered, Terry. We agreed you'd call before coming round.'

His confident stance deflated. 'Josie, please. I really need to talk to you. About Ivy and... well, some other stuff.'

I looked at him, this man I had once loved, who'd had the

ability to flip my stomach just by walking into the room. A man who'd regularly looked at me like he felt lucky to have me, who I couldn't wait to be alone with so we could pull off our clothes and melt together, skin-to-skin. Now, all those things seemed like a fiction I'd imagined. The thrill of settling down, the contentment of marriage only eighteen months later and the fullness of our hearts when we found out I was pregnant with Ivy only a year after we got married... that had all been very real. It had. For a long time, we were so, so happy.

The gulf between us didn't open in an instant. The cracks began to appear, and we both ignored them. The solid ground we'd built our life on slowly crumbled with us barely noticing until we were free-falling down. Now, here we stood like two strangers, both still silently blaming each other. We knew each other's faults only too well and we'd forgotten the things that forged us together all those years ago. Upstairs, our perfect eight-year-old daughter, who still needed us both in her life.

I opened the door wider and stepped back. 'Half an hour tops, and then I really have stuff I need to do.'

Terry closed the door behind him and came inside, his head swivelling this way and that, taking it all in. This wasn't the family home we used to live in together. I'd wanted to move away to another part of the country for obvious reasons. But we bought our first house quickly with a ninety per cent mortgage. It had been just five miles away from my childhood home.

I'm going to be trapped here forever, Jimmy, I'd whispered to my late brother. *I'll never get away.*

I followed Terry into the living room. 'Did you want a drink?' I said, the implication of my tone being that I'd rather him not.

'Thanks. I'll have a coffee.'

I left him sitting on the sofa, knowing he'd be scanning the room, looking for clues that a man had been here. He seemed to think I shouldn't be allowed to date because of the effect it might have on Ivy. It was OK for him to date women, of course. Dating was the last thing on my mind, but I wasn't about to share that with him.

Our marriage had disintegrated for several reasons. Terry had really hated his job as regional development manager of a chain of popular budget hotels and, in a moment of madness after being turned down for a pay rise, he'd resigned.

Things were predictably grim on the financial front, but Terry quickly got work through a hospitality agency and landed a job working at an upmarket bistro in the city he dubbed French Pete's. He quickly rose through the ranks to become assistant manager.

I had a nosedive health-wise after losing our baby and the doctor signed me off work and prescribed some medication. Things weren't good between us. Terry began to wilt under work stress and trying to cope with coming home to my depression and mood swings at the end of his very long days.

Two days before Christmas, he told me he was leaving home.

On Christmas Day, after five-year old Ivy had opened her presents and we'd had breakfast together for the last time as a family, Terry moved out of the family home. He went to live with his new girlfriend, Christa. A twenty-four-year-old waitress who worked at the same bistro. Her wealthy father had rented her a penthouse apartment by the river. Terry told me she worked the job just for fun, for something to do.

I couldn't afford the mortgage on my own, so we put the house up for sale immediately. We had to reduce it before we got a buyer, but fortunately it sold just as the mortgage went into default.

We stayed in a tiny rented bedsit with a pull-down double bed. I made an adventure of it with Ivy, told her it was our secret hideaway.

We were there for nine months until I saw an advertisement

for this place; a rented semi-detached property with a small garden in Hucknall, nearly ten miles from Mansfield. I registered Ivy at the local primary school.

The kettle boiled and clicked off. I looked out of the kitchen window and the square of fading light beyond and realised I hadn't pulled down the blind. I'd been feeling more nervous than usual after Barlow's visit and that led me to thinking I should tell Terry he was out, and about the incident at the café. But first, I'd let him say what he'd come here for.

I didn't bother making a drink for myself, but I took his through and put it on a low table in front of him. 'So,' I said, 'what's up?'

Terry looked at his coffee but didn't touch it. 'I'm just going to come out and say it, Josie. I'm in trouble. I mean, *real* trouble.'

'What?' My heart plummeted. 'What's happened?'

He covered his face with his hands and sat like that for a few moments, not speaking. He was unravelling in front of me. His relationship with Christa had lasted all of eight months before she'd ejected him from her fancy flat and declared she was bored of Nottingham and of Terry, and planned to move back to the vast family mansion in Buckinghamshire.

He looked up now, let his hands fall away from his face.

'I had a bad bet,' he said in a small voice.

'No.' I stood up. 'Not again!'

'Josie, please. Just listen.' His face was so pale, he looked like he might throw up at any second.

I sat down again and shoved my hands under my thighs. I hardly trusted myself not to go for him. This wasn't the first time we'd been here. I'd given him a thousand pounds about a year ago when someone was after him for a dodgy bet. He'd begged me, in tears. 'I promise I'll get myself sorted out for Ivy's sake.'

'You swore it wouldn't happen again,' I said from between gritted teeth.

'This is not the same as last time. These people, they're...
professionals.'

'Professionals at what?'

'They mean business, Josie. If you can't pay, they'll break
your legs. They'll—'

'What's happened to you, Terry?' This was a world I didn't
know about. Didn't *want* to know about. What if these thugs,
these 'professionals', were watching him right now and he'd led
them to our home? 'Why are you making such terrible choices
in your life?'

His eyes darkened. 'All very well for you to say. Got yourself a nice house now, your own business, right? Don't want
your ex-husband tarnishing your success.'

I pulled my hands from under my thighs and jabbed a finger
at him. 'Don't you dare say it like it all just dropped in my lap. I
had to scrape myself up off the floor after we ended up in a
grubby bedsit because of you, so you could go and live with your
fancy piece. I've worked for every single thing I have.'

'Here we go.' His crocodile tears were long dried, and his
features screwed up into a tight knot. 'You got a couple of grand
from the sale of a house I mostly paid for, so stop whining.'

It was true he'd paid the mortgage on our home together,
but we'd agreed I'd only work part-time in a local buffet restaurant chain so Ivy had a parent to take her to and pick her up
from nursery. That had been a joint decision I'd thought we
were both happy with.

I stood up. 'Yeah? Well, we *both* got a couple of grand as I
recall, so why not use that to bail yourself out of this pathetic
mess?'

The sneer slid from his face, and he jumped up out of his
seat, pressing his hands in the air. 'Josie, Josie, sit down. Please,
I'm sorry. I haven't come here to fight.'

'No. You came here for money.' I sat down. 'And I'm trying
to tell you I haven't got any.'

He made a disparaging noise of disbelief. 'I'd rather you just say no than lie through your teeth.'

'What money I had went on a deposit for this place and the rest is tied up in the business.' Not that it was any of his concern, but I wanted him gone now. We were no longer together, and his problems were certainly not my problems.

He reached over and grabbed my arm. 'Josie, you don't understand. These guys are—'

'I *do* understand, Terry,' I interrupted, shrugging him off. 'You've got yourself in another terrible mess and you're looking for me to sweep up after you again. Well, this time I can't do it.'

'You're heartless.' His top lip curled back. 'I'll make sure Ivy knows you threw me to the lions.'

'Well, that's up to you. Rest assured I won't be telling her that her father turned into a gambling addict who put himself and us at risk. Don't come here again, unless you're interested in being a decent father to our daughter.'

He turned on his heel and walked to the door.

'You're no great shakes as a mother yourself, Josie. Working all the time, palming her off on that childminder. You don't deserve her.'

'Right, OK,' I said lightly. 'Bye, Terry. Enjoy your evening.'

It was only when he'd gone that I realised I hadn't told him about Samuel Barlow's release or him turning up at the café today.

But I had so much on my plate right now, what was one more thing to worry about?

EIGHTEEN

SAMUEL

Samuel opened his eyes, but he did not move an inch. He stared up at the ceiling in this drab, faded room in his mother's house. The same space as he'd grown up in all those years ago.

When she'd come into a bit of money from a relative, his mother rented out this house and moved to Bradford, a town about twenty miles, and a forty-five-minute bus ride, from HMP Wakefield where he'd been incarcerated. She'd stuck the stigma of having a son in prison for years, but moving to Bradford made her visiting him easier and for years she tried to make a life there. But she'd never settled and had missed Nottinghamshire.

'I felt more of an outsider in Bradford than I did among all those people who turned against me,' Maggie had told him on one of her visits.

About ten years ago she'd decided not to renew her tenants' lease and had returned to the family home. Lots of the houses around here had been converted to multi-occupancy accommodation and bedsits, and nobody cared less who she was or what her son had done all that time ago.

His eyes scanned his small bedroom and he felt sure that his cell had been bigger and cleaner than this dump. The dull, dirty cream walls that looked as if they hadn't been refreshed in all the time he'd been gone. The thin, floral curtains that let in the first spots of light, an enemy of lie-ins. The same threadbare sticky carpet underneath his bare feet as when he'd got out of bed as a teenager.

But at least he was alone in here.

In prison, thanks to overcrowding issues, he'd had to share a cell for some of his sentence. The last time had been eighteen months stuck with another con. A guy who was younger and a bully and he had forced him to take the top bunk when Samuel's preference had always been the lower bed.

During that time, he'd woken much the same way as this morning. He'd opened his eyes and stared at the ceiling until he felt able to move. This ceiling, that ceiling... what did it matter in the scheme of things? He'd never be free. Sure, he was out of prison but being stuck here with his mother was just another kind of prison at the end of the day.

It was while serving his sentence that he'd become a reader. When he was younger, he'd rather have pulled out his own hair than read a book. That shortcoming had meant he'd never fully engaged with his schoolwork. But over time, while inside, he'd come to appreciate that the printed page offered a very real escape from the mind-numbing boredom prison ruthlessly imposed on a person.

Over the years, through his books, he'd visited different lands, worked different jobs, experienced a myriad of emotions by metaphorically walking in the shoes of others. Empathy, the prison librarian had called it. It hadn't necessarily made him a better person but it had given him an understanding of how deep waters could run in other people. He'd always taken others at face value but now he understood that there was often more to folks than meets the eye.

It was through developing his reading across lots of subjects and genres that Samuel had discovered self-development books.

Vince, one of the rare lags who was actually serving a longer sentence than he was, had helped out in the prison library.

You could put in a request for a particular book and Vince would do his best. Samuel had been waiting weeks for the new Jack Reacher thriller and Vince had promised him he was next in line.

'Sorry, mate,' Vince had said regretfully when he'd reached Samuel's cell empty-handed. 'The powers that be pulled the new Reacher release because of the "gratuitous violence", as they put it.'

Something had snapped in Samuel's head. He'd felt like throttling Vince but, instead, had turned inwards and begun banging his head on the landing wall. It had taken three officers to restrain him. An hour later when he'd returned from the medical wing, freshly medicated and sporting a very sore head, Vince had left a book on his bed.

Samuel had picked it up and lobbed it at the wall. When he'd woken a while later, he'd seen, with irritation, there were still two hours to go before teatime. The book had lain where it had fallen, its pages splayed, on the floor. Grudgingly Samuel had got off the bed and picked it up. It wouldn't hurt to read a couple of pages, he'd supposed. Better than lying here with only his thoughts for company.

Two hours later, the bell sounding mealtimes had rung and shunted Samuel out of his reading bubble. He'd stuck a piece of notepaper in his place and put the book down, feeling dazed. He'd been reading stories of people – some just like him – who had discovered that their upbringing had contributed in ways they'd never believed to the choices they'd made and the way they'd lived their lives. Samuel had always just accepted the way things were. Acknowledged that life was hard, that you had to take what you wanted, or someone would take it from *you*.

Samuel's life at home growing up had played in front of him like a movie. Living with his mother after his dad's death a week before he'd become a teenager. The way she'd never showed him right and wrong, but told him he was perfect. That he'd had the power to do anything he wanted, to whom he wanted.

That's when he'd realised that *she*, his mother, was to blame for all of it... for him being stuck in here for over half his life. The book had helped him get it all clear in his head and it was like a powerful lightbulb illuminating the darkest corners of his mind.

His cell door had swung open then and one of the senior officers stood there. 'What's up, Samuel, still feeling queasy? You're usually first down for grub.'

Samuel had grunted and stood up. It was true that food had once been front and centre in his life and, despite what people thought, the grub wasn't bad in here. 'Coming, boss. I've been reading.'

The officer grinned. 'Ahh, I see. Looks like the clink has found the scholar in you at last. You'll be going back to college when they let you out, eh?'

Samuel had frowned as he'd followed the officer out on to the landing, the noise of the other prisoners ringing in his ears after the peaceful reading session in his cell. 'Nah, I've got more important stuff to do when I get out of here. I've got some stuff that needs setting straight.'

Samuel had carried that thought with him throughout the rest of his sentence. He'd started taking better care of himself physically about five years ago. Working out at the gym, skipping pudding and drinking more water. He'd reaped the benefits within a few months, growing stronger in mind and body.

He was still filled with a raging desire to set stuff straight, that much was true. But more accurately, Samuel now knew he had several *people* to set straight.

People who would pay for ruining the man he might have been.

NINETEEN

JOSIE

The next day, I grabbed my handbag and keys and turned the sign to 'closed' on the café's glass door. It had been a crazy busy day for a Thursday but I'd got a lot done and I felt eternally grateful there had been no further appearance from Barlow.

The café usually closed at five o'clock. Now, at three forty-five, in a reflection of the drop-off in physical trade, it was empty. I'd sent Sheena home early so she and Warren could go for a drink in the sun to reward her hard work the last few days.

I walked back through the café into the kitchen and did a final check to make sure all the appliances were turned off before setting the alarm. I didn't want to make a silly mistake like I had done and leave a window open again and had a new routine where I looked back before finally leaving.

I headed straight for the car, parked out back as always, when a stunning trill of birdsong stopped me in my tracks. I looked up at the expanse of unbroken blue sky, felt the warmth of the sun on my face. It felt more like July than late May. It would take me just over five minutes to drive over to Fiona's or twenty minutes to walk. If I left the car and walked, I'd prob-ably have a cup of tea and catch-up with Fiona then Ivy and I could walk back together via a small park we used to visit before my work became so manic.

I took out my phone and texted Fiona.

On my way. Decided to walk over... see you in twenty mins!

I set off at a steady pace, enjoying the feel of the warm, gentle breeze against my face. There was a school nearby to the café and parents and children were walking home together. I never usually got to see people out at this time of day and the warmth of the sun had always dulled by the time I'd finished at the café, usually after six or seven.

It had taken seeing Barlow again to bring me to my senses and I felt guilty about that. It was as if I hadn't valued what I'd got before, but had become blinkered to anything but work. It wasn't something I'd carefully considered and subsequently decided upon. I'd simply slipped into the routine of side-lining my life and focusing almost entirely on the café. How did that happen to people? We ended up spending most of our time doing something that, in the grand scheme of things, wasn't important at all but shouted the loudest.

I walked by the small park we'd call at on the way back. It was bordered by a tall hedge, so I couldn't see the kids playing in there from the pavement, but I could hear them laughing and squealing. The hum of parents chattering and calling out for their little ones to be careful. It took me back to the time before I'd opened the café.

We'd lived in the grotty bedsit back then. Terry was living in splendour with his new girlfriend, and I'd become very creative with the slow cooker, making bean stew and rice pudding; anything that would fill us up and not hammer the piggy bank. We didn't have much at all, but we had each other. Ivy and her non-stop questions: 'What's that bird called?'; 'Why is that boy rubbing his knee?'; 'What are we having for tea?' By the time we'd get home, my ears would be ringing but I'd loved every minute of it.

Somehow, life had since worn me down almost without me noticing. I'd got stuck somewhere between making ends meet and building a business that would ultimately free us from the past. And, in the mix of all that, something as precious as walking in the sun with my daughter had become a distant memory.

I felt like the problem was mine and mine alone. Every mother I stood with at the school gates appeared to get their priorities straight. The inadequacy felt like a millstone around my neck each and every minute of the day.

I turned into Fiona's road and saw a woman leaving with the twins Fiona looked after regularly. I felt a warm glow that I was picking Ivy up at a normal time like a normal mum, leaving us hours before bedtime in which we could do something nice together.

My phone rang and I fished it out of my handbag. Terry's name flashed up on screen and I pushed it back in my pocket without answering. He'd leave a message if it was important. I wouldn't let anything spoil my early finish, least of all the latest fix he'd got himself in.

I knocked at the front door and Fiona smiled widely when she saw me. 'Oh, you made it! Ivy will be pleased. She's in the garden with Darcy. Fancy a cuppa?'

'Why not?' I said, enjoying the feeling of not having to rush off for once. 'I'll just pop to the bathroom.'

Fiona disappeared into the kitchen, calling over her shoulder: 'I'll put the kettle on and let Ivy know you're here.'

I opened the door to the downstairs cloakroom and my phone pinged with an incoming text from Terry. Then an answerphone notification. Maybe it *was* important. Or maybe it was another plea for cash I hadn't got. I put the phone back into my pocket. He'd leave a message if it was important.

I was washing my hands in the cloakroom when I heard shouting, unmistakeable noises of alarm. Feet ran by the cloakroom door and thundered upstairs. I dried my hands hastily and stepped out into the hallway.

Curiously, the second I stepped out, the house seemed to fall deathly quiet. I headed for the kitchen but then heard the same feet thumping frantically back down the stairs.

Fiona reached the bottom and froze when she saw me. Her face looked stretched, bleached out. She sagged against the wall.

'Fiona, what is it? What's wrong?' I rushed forward and grasped her arms in case she fainted. 'Come on, let's get you in here. Do you feel ill?'

I tried to guide her into the living room and the nearest chair but her body went rigid, as if some hidden force had pinned her to the spot. 'I can't... I need to check...'

She broke free of me and ran through the hallway into the kitchen. By the time I'd followed, she was already out of the door and in the back garden.

'Fiona?' I leaned out of the doorway and looked at the garden, expecting to see both girls. But there was just Darcy, looking frightened and pressing close to her mum. 'What's happening? Where's—'

'It's Ivy.' Fiona sounded breathless. 'She's gone.'

'What?' I stepped on to the small patio area outside the back door. 'Gone where?'

'They were both in the garden, playing,' Fiona said faintly, her fingers fluttering up to her throat. 'Darcy went upstairs to get the water gun, but couldn't find it. She spent a while looking—'

'I couldn't find it,' Darcy echoed, her eyes wide.

'When she came down, Ivy was gone. We've looked upstairs and in all the rooms,' Fiona said hopelessly.

I ran into the garden, peering into every corner. It didn't

take long. It was a small, rectangular plot with bushes but no big trees.

A lump of bile rose in my throat. 'Where's she gone?' I ran around to the side gate that led to the front of the house. 'How long? When did she go missing?'

'Not long... five minutes. We'll look for her. She can't be far. The garden is secure and...' Her voice faded out and I felt myself begin to sway slightly.

'The gate is unlocked!' I cried out.

'I always make sure I've latched the gate properly, I—' Fiona's voice floated into the ether and faded away as a whooshing sound filled my ears.

I pushed open the gate and ran down the side of the house, across the small patch of front lawn and out into the street. 'Ivy!' I yelled, looking wildly up and down the street. 'Ivy!'

Fiona bolted out of the front door and rushed past me, clutching Darcy's hand. She called out to an older couple kneeling on pads as they weeded their front garden. 'Have you seen a little girl, dark hair in a blue dress?'

The woman shielded her eyes with a floral-gloved hand and shook her head.

'Everything OK, Fiona?' another neighbour called and she ran up to the fence to talk to them.

I raced down the steep slope of the street, looking into gardens, speaking to anyone who was out. 'My little girl's gone missing from the garden. She's eight with dark hair in a bob. She was wearing a blue and white checked school dress.' All I got back was concerned faces, and shaking heads. I ran back up the incline, interrupting Fiona talking to yet another woman.

'She's nowhere to be found. We need to call the police,' I said breathlessly, taking out my phone. It started to ring again. Terry.

'Terry, I'm at Fiona's house. Ivy's gone missing.'

'What?' Out of the corner of my eye I saw more concerned people coming out of their front gates on to the pavement.

'Ivy's gone missing at the childminder's. Can you come over and help us to search?' Terry had picked Ivy up from Fiona's on a couple of occasions, so he knew where she lived.

'I'm on my way,' he said and the line went dead.

'It's only been a few minutes,' Fiona said from behind me. 'Five minutes tops. Like my neighbour says, she's got to be around here somewhere. Everyone is looking for her.'

Five minutes turned quickly into ten and ten minutes turned into an hour and before you knew it, half a day had slipped by and it was too late. I snapped to. 'No. We need to call the police right now, Fiona.'

Fiona pressed her hands in the air. 'Look, let's just try and be logical about this, Josie. Ivy can't have gone far; we need to thoroughly search the streets for her. The police will ask if we've done that.'

'It's him. I know it's him,' I said, battling a sickly feeling.

'Who?' Fiona gave me a worried look before it clicked. 'You mean... Samuel Barlow?'

'It's got to be him,' I muttered, the queasiness in my chest rising higher and higher. 'It's too much of a coincidence.'

'But he doesn't know Ivy comes here.' Fiona leaned forward, her voice softening. 'She'll just have wandered off and got lost. She'll turn up in a minute or two, you'll see.'

'He came to the café,' I said vacantly, my mind's eye filling with his wolfish grin, the way he lied so easily, protesting his innocence in choosing to visit my place of work. If he knew how to find me there, I felt sure he could probably find out who looked after Ivy when I was working.

The floor seemed to rush towards me. I managed to stagger forwards a few steps, away from Fiona, before I bent forward and vomited at the side of the road.

'Christ!' I heard Terry's voice and running feet and a few

seconds later he was standing next to me, holding my lank hair away from my face as I heaved again. 'Here.' He handed me a grubby handkerchief. 'I've got some water in the car.'

He moved away and I straightened up. I ignored the hanky and wiped my mouth with the back of my hand. 'I'm OK.'

'What the hell's happened here?' He turned to Fiona. 'Where's Ivy?'

She explained quickly. 'She was there and then she wasn't. She's only been gone about ten minutes.'

'Have you called the police?'

Fiona stammered. 'Not yet, we... we're going to do a thorough search out here first. The police will ask if we've—'

'Stuff that,' Terry muttered and pulled out his phone and tapped at the screen. 'Yeah, police please.' He paused. Then, 'Yes, I want to report a missing child. My eight-year-old daughter. Her name is Ivy Gleed.'

When I heard him say our daughter's name, the taste of vomit filled my mouth again and I took another sip of the plastic-tasting water before replacing the lid.

Terry's expression was grim when he ended the call. 'They said they'll send someone straight out,' he said. 'Let's get searching for her and any luck we'll have her back here before they arrive.'

It felt like I had a lump the size of an onion in my throat. I couldn't speak. My breathing was shallow and ragged. But the worst thing was the feeling coursing through me.

The feeling that we were already too late.

Within minutes, the neighbours Fiona had spoken to had spread the word and there were people walking up and down the street on their phones, walking in and out of gardens. Others wandered down the side of Fiona's house through the open gate.

My feet felt rooted to the floor as I watched Terry work his way methodically down the street, knocking at one door, speaking briefly to the owner before moving on to the next. People milled around the small front gardens of the neighbouring houses. They peered behind bushes, raked through borders as though Ivy might be crouched down behind one of the leafy plants. Fiona's front door was wide open and neighbours had gathered outside their houses in small, gossipy groups.

'It's going to be OK.' Fiona drew closer, but I felt myself shrink from her outstretched hand. Her face was deathly pale with a little spot of pink heat on each cheek. 'We'll find her, Josie. I know it. She can't possibly have gone far.'

I stared at her, my eyes glassy and unfocused.

'I'd checked on her just before you arrived.' She grabbed my hands and held them. 'It's only been ten or fifteen minutes. We'll find her, you'll see.'

Ten or fifteen long, long minutes.

My precious girl could be anywhere.

TWENTY

Fiona and Terry ushered me back into the house. The hallway and kitchen were full of people and I hadn't a clue who any of them were.

'That's the missing girl's mother,' I heard someone whisper as I walked past.

'These are all good folks who've come to help the search,' Fiona said, noticing my bewildered expression.

I felt a strong hand on my shoulder. 'You're doing great,' Terry said. 'I'm right here, Josie.' When he'd come to the house asking for money, he'd seemed so weak and hopeless. But at this precise moment, he felt like the strong, dependable man I'd met and fallen in love with twelve years ago. I felt comforted by his presence.

I stopped walking to face him. 'Had any of the neighbours you spoke to seen her? Any sightings of Ivy?'

His pale face sagged. 'No. But I only did this street; we need to do a wider search.' He hesitated, and I noticed how dark the shadows under his eyes were. 'Josie, why the hell didn't you tell me Samuel Barlow had been released?'

I stared at him. I didn't know what to say.

'I've been ringing and texting you,' he said and I remembered ignoring his calls and pushing my phone back in my pocket when I'd first arrived at Fiona's house. 'Someone at the pub told me. Can you imagine how I felt?'

'I'd only just found out myself,' I said. 'I knew you had your own problems.'

That wasn't strictly true; I'd taken the call from DI Price informing me about Barlow's parole over a week ago now. But the last time I saw Terry, he was in no fit state to think rationally.

He shook his head, incredulous. 'No problem is bigger than our daughter being in danger.'

I pulled him to a slightly quieter corner of the kitchen. 'You told me those people who are after you for money are dangerous, Terry. If there's the slightest chance one of them took Ivy, we need to tell the police.'

'No way! They might not think twice before giving me a good kicking, but they're small fry compared to the kind of people who'd abduct a kid.' I felt even more colour blanch from my face. 'If that's what's happened, of course,' he added quickly.

'Barlow's taken her, I know he has,' I said feverishly. 'We have to do something, we can't just sit here and wait until—'

'Don't jump to conclusions, Josie. We know nothing for certain, yet. I'm praying Ivy has just wandered off somewhere.'

'When has she ever wandered off?' I snapped. I had to stop this fantasy. 'Ivy just doesn't do that sort of thing. You *know* she doesn't!'

I looked around, frustrated at the inaction. There were lots of people in here. A large older woman in a floral apron making coffees and teas, cheerily asked who wanted sugar and milk. 'Terry, we've got do something. I can't stand just waiting around in here.'

'Excuse me, everyone?' The chatter died away and people looked at Terry in surprise. 'We need a few minutes privacy in here please, to talk to Fiona.'

I walked over to the open kitchen door, looked out on to the small rear garden where, less than thirty minutes ago, my daughter had been happily playing in the sun.

Fiona came and stood next to me, but she stayed quiet.

There was a five-foot boundary fence all the way around the garden. In the middle of the patchy lawn was a little plastic table with a toy tea set arranged on top. Around the table, on the floor sat a teddy bear, a doll, and a blue hippo. I knew instinctively this was Ivy's doing. She'd done the same numerous times before in our garden at home. Tea parties for her toys were her favourite thing to do outside. I swallowed down a cry that rushed up from my throat. Hopelessly, I scanned every inch of the fence. No gaps or missing panels. There was a single side gate that led down the side of the house to the front garden that was now full of people.

Fear was a hangman's noose pulling tighter and tighter around my neck.

'Where did she go?' I said faintly, as people continued to reluctantly leave the room.

Fiona shook her head. 'One moment she was there and the next she'd gone. No exaggeration, Josie, that's exactly what happened.'

'Did you see... a man?'

'A man?' Fiona frowned. 'There was no man in this garden. I know you're bound to worry about Barlow but—'

'He's tall. Well built but quite ordinary looking. People don't seem to notice him and that makes him more dangerous.' I heard my voice rising and Terry touched my arm.

'Did you see anyone at all?' he asked Fiona.

'No! Don't you think I'd have said by now?' Her cheeks

were ruddy, her eyes darting around the room. She clearly felt attacked, but these were questions that had to be asked.

Terry frowned, looking round. 'All these people shouldn't be in the house.'

'They're all on our side, Terry,' Fiona said. 'Everyone here wants to help find Ivy.'

Terry led me to the modern industrial-style wooden table and pulled out a steel chair. I sat down, stared at the reclaimed wood and all its scars.

Out of the door I could see half of the little plastic table. I couldn't get Samuel Barlow's face out of my head; I could picture him there, looming over Ivy, who'd be unaware of his presence as she played with the toys.

I gripped the edge of the table until my knuckles shone white. 'It's him,' I whispered. 'Why won't anyone believe me? I know he's got her.'

Terry came to my side again. 'You're in shock,' he said. 'Sit down and I'll get you a glass of water.'

I felt dazed. Fiona said something, Terry answered her. The door opened. A person came in and went back out again. I was aware of it all, but I couldn't seem to process anything. I couldn't think of anything but the terrifying possibility that Samuel Barlow had taken my daughter.

A glass appeared on the table in front of me. As I stared at the water inside sloshing and finally settling, a bolt of hope shot through me.

There *was* someone who could help, who would believe me. Someone who'd told me to call if I had any problems. I upended my handbag on the table and plucked out my phone.

'What are you doing, Josie?' Terry said quietly. 'It's best to wait until the police get here now. Don't involve even more people.'

'Her name's DI Helena Price,' I said. 'She knows all about

Barlow. She was the one who rang to tell me he was being released. She also told me to call her if I needed her help.'

Then, as Terry and Fiona exchanged an exasperated look, I opened the text Price had sent giving me her direct number. I summoned up all the hope and courage I could manage and pressed call.

TWENTY-ONE

MAGGIE

Maggie had been surprised when Samuel got up early that morning and announced he was going out walking.

'I'm thinking of going to Sherwood Pines a bit later,' he said, with no further explanation.

Maggie had never been herself but knew it to be a vast park, once part of Sherwood Forest, that was full of walking and cycling trails. He would need to take a forty-minute bus ride before he even got there.

'Really?' She'd never known him to walk for enjoyment in his whole life. As a child, he'd had no interest whatsoever in nature or animals. 'What's brought this on?'

He'd looked up from shovelling his cereal into his mouth, his hooded eyes seeming darker than ever this morning. 'Maybe you'd want a bit of fresh air too, if you'd been banged up for twenty-five years.'

She clammed up then. She recognised the danger signs with her son's volatile moods and didn't want to provoke him. Let him go. At least she'd get some peace for a while.

While he was out, Maggie decided she'd try and improve his mood by baking Samuel's favourite sweet treat: lemon curd tarts. She weighed out the flour and butter, placed them in a bowl and started mixing it with her fingers. Baking had always relaxed her and it was something she and Josie had done together when she'd spent time at the house. Maggie knew she ran a dessert café now and she hoped she'd partly been responsible for nurturing her obvious creative talent.

Maggie had continued baking, even when Samuel was in prison, when she had nobody to feed. Often, the birds in her tiny garden were the only ones to benefit. Somehow the mixing and kneading and rolling unlocked a part of her mind that allowed her to think and freed her from the worries and regrets that pressed down from the moment she woke, extinguishing any chance of peace or joy.

She'd stood at this very counter, all those years ago, baking biscuits and cakes with a young Josie, trying to heal her broken heart with the magic of it. Seeing the child smiling and forgetting her troubles for a short time had been a balm to Maggie's soul.

She rubbed gently with her fingertips now, blending the butter and flour together. Lots of people didn't realise a light touch was far more effective and made for a lighter pastry. It was one of Maggie's little secrets. Just one of them. When folks looked at her, they just saw a washed-up old woman. It would stop them in their tracks if she spoke about the stuff she knew.

When Samuel went to prison, her neighbours, decent people she'd lived alongside for twenty-odd years, became terrorists overnight. Windows smashed in the dead of night, all manner of disgusting deposits through the letterbox and, on one occasion, even eggs thrown at her on the street. Maggie was shunned but hadn't got the funds to move away. Then years later her financial position had improved thanks to a small inheritance. Social services had helped her relocate to a different area of the country: Bradford. A town close to Samuel's prison. But ten years ago, she'd returned to this town, a place that had changed immeasurably in the time she'd been away but that she'd always thought of as home. People had moved on and those people who were still around didn't really care who she was any more. She was sixty-seven now and invisible. Nobody looked at her, nobody spoke to her. Not because they knew who she was but because that's the way people lived now. Everyone kept themselves to themselves, so taken up with their own lives, they barely looked around them.

Maggie had lived quietly, waiting for the day Samuel came home. Now that day was here and, far from feeling happy and grateful, as she'd imagined, her worries bore down even more heavily.

Maggie looked down at the bowl, the butter and flour now transformed into perfect breadcrumbs. She added a little cool water and mixed it in with a knife. Then repeated the action before binding it together to make a ball.

She smiled to herself as she wrapped the pastry in clingfilm to rest in the fridge. Funny how something could start off as one thing and end up as something else entirely. She'd loved Samuel so much from the day he was born. The strength of her feeling scared her. After her own childhood, raised by a mother who hadn't cared if Maggie had lived or died, it was terrifying to keep yourself from making the same mistakes. She'd never had the kind of money to buy her son mountains of toys or take him on holiday and spoil him silly. Instead, Maggie had smothered Samuel in love and indulgence. Maggie vowed to always have her boy's back. To support him in anything he wanted to do and, above all, to put him first. Always first. No questions asked.

He had begun life as a sweet, sensitive child. But she often asked herself the question: had the streak of cruelty been in him even then? Or had Maggie somehow fostered a sense of entitlement in Samuel... a right to hurt others?

Perhaps she would never know.

TWENTY-TWO

Helena had been working all morning on an investment fraud case that had cost a major UK bank several million pounds. An employee had figured out what had, until now, seemed to be a foolproof way to siphon off investments of very wealthy retired customers. That is, until the eagle eye of a banking intern, fresh out of university, had noticed a tiny discrepancy and decided to follow it up, inadvertently revealing a thread of deceit that had spanned nearly a decade.

They had a team of crack forensic accountants working alongside them on the case, which was a lot less exciting than it sounded. The forensic finance team were painstakingly trawling through the financial software and interrogating every single figure.

Brewster was enthusiastic about this one, having had a small timeshare investment go pear-shaped a few years earlier, but try as she might to summon up the necessary drive to power her through it, the case turned Helena cold. She'd never been a numbers person. She much preferred people and, although she'd never dare voice her opinions even to Brewster, she'd joined the police to make a difference to the lives of ordinary folk, not investment-hoarding fat cats.

Her direct line rang, jolting her out of the banking boredom. She picked up on the second ring.

'DI Helena Price speaking.' The line was quiet and, for a moment, Helena thought someone had called and then put the phone down. 'Hello?'

Then a small voice said, 'Hi, this is... this is Josie Bennett again.'

The detective hesitated, recalling the details. Then, 'Oh yes, hello, Josie. Is everything OK?'

'She's gone missing. My daughter is missing.' Her voice grew louder, higher. It sounded like she was out of breath, gasping to get the words out. 'She's only eight and... well, I think he took her. Samuel Barlow. It's too much of a coincidence. He gets out of prison and—'

'Slow down, Josie. You said your eight-year-old daughter has gone missing, is that right?'

'Yes. They've called the police and they're sending someone out, but they won't know the background like you. They all think I'm crazy, so I'm ringing to ask if you can help me because he's got Ivy. I know it's him.'

Helena reached for a pen and notepad.

'When did this happen?'

'About thirty minutes ago. I'm at the childminder's house on Papplewick Lane. Ivy was in the garden and—' Josie sounded out of breath '—Fiona – that's the childminder – she checked on Ivy and then the next minute when she looked, she'd gone.' Her voice broke. 'It's him. It must be him.'

'One second, Josie.' Helena covered up the mouthpiece of the phone and gestured to Brewster, who left his spreadsheet and came over immediately. 'Missing child, Papplewick Lane at Hucknall. Uniform en route, apparently. Can you get an update?'

'On it, boss.' Brewster moved quickly back to his desk and picked up the phone.

'Josie? Sorry about that, my colleague is just confirming details on exactly what's happening.' Helena's voice remained calm. 'Have you any evidence that Samuel Barlow is involved in Ivy's disappearance?'

'Yes. Well... not exactly, but he must be! Eight-year-old girls don't disappear from fenced gardens unless someone takes them, do they? I know he's got her. I *just know*. He wants to get me back for giving evidence at his trial and for what happened at the café the other day. You've got to do something. Please!' Her voice grew higher and higher.

'Try to calm down. Did Barlow come back to the café after that first time?'

Josie began wailing and then a man's voice came on the line. 'Hello? Who is this?'

'I'm Detective Inspector Helena Price, Nottinghamshire Police. Josie Bennett just called me. What's happening there? Who am I speaking with?'

'I'm Terry Gleed, Josie's ex-husband. Ivy, our daughter, has gone missing from the childminder's garden. Josie's in a state, as you can imagine. She panicked and insisted on ringing you, but the police are on their way and everyone is out looking for her.'

'My colleague is gathering details directly from the control room as we speak,' Helena said. 'Josie seems adamant that Samuel Barlow is involved. Can you tell me anything more about that?'

Terry sighed. 'Josie's convinced it's him, but I've spoken to most of the close neighbours already and nobody saw a man hanging around.' Helena heard Josie shout angrily at what he'd just said, but Terry continued. 'Fiona, the childminder, thinks Ivy has just wandered off, but she's a good girl. She's never done anything like this before.'

'Samuel Barlow was released from prison less than a week ago,' Helena thought out loud.

'Yes, I've only just found that out. But this house is full of neighbours, people who know the area well, and nobody saw anything. I think someone would have noticed a man hanging around.'

Helena tapped her pen on the desk. 'OK, I'll look into things our end, just in case there are any leads. And I'll keep in touch with uniform and their findings. Tell Josie I'll be in touch.'

'Thank you,' Terry said, sounding relieved.

When Helena came off the phone, Brewster appeared, referring to his notebook. 'So, about thirty minutes ago, a Terry Gleed reported his eight-year-old daughter missing from the childminder's back garden. He said they thought the kid had probably wandered off but he thought he should report it just in case. Two uniforms were dispatched and now those officers have just arrived and have put a call in for extra bodies to facilitate a search and door-to-door information gathering.'

'Any mention from uniform of Samuel Barlow being involved?'

Brewster pulled the sides of his mouth down. 'No. His name wasn't mentioned in the update but they've only just got there.'

Helena re-read her scribbled notes from Josie's phone call. 'Hopefully the child has just gone walkabout and we soon get word she's safe. Josie Bennett is convinced Barlow has taken Ivy and I totally get her logic; Barlow is released from Her Majesty's pleasure and suddenly her daughter is missing.'

Brewster frowned, the freckles on his forehead converging into one sandy-coloured shadow. 'That's certainly some coincidence.'

'Agreed. I've got Barlow's discharge documents here. I'll take some details from them. In the meantime, can you start a dialogue with uniform so we've got as close a live commentary on what's happening over there with the search as we can manage? We need to check out Barlow's whereabouts at the very least. I don't like the fact he's already contacted Josie Bennett at the café. I left that information with his probation officer, but I haven't heard back yet. Something's not adding up.'

Brewster stood up. 'If I remember rightly, boss, Barlow gave his mother's address as his first port of call upon release.'

Helena nodded. 'Can you try and get verbal confirmation of that from the probation service? Make sure he didn't change his mind and go elsewhere. Once we've got that, we'll pay a visit to the Barlow house.'

TWENTY-THREE

JOSIE

'You can't keep me here in the house, I need to be out there looking for her!' My eyes burned with fury and dread as Fiona and Terry stood in front of me, imploring me to sit down. But there was no way I was sitting down with a cup of tea and my feet up while my daughter was out there somewhere with the monster who killed Jimmy.

Terry stepped forward and touched my arm gently. I felt tears welling up behind my eyes. I looked down at my hands and saw they were trembling. Every single joint in my body ached.

Fiona said, 'Maybe she saw a puppy, or a balloon or something... she could have run out of the gate to have a look and—'

'The gate should have been locked... that was your legal responsibility as a registered childminder!' I yelled and Fiona took a step back. 'And if that's what happened, then why hasn't someone brought her back here?'

Someone knocked at the kitchen door. When Terry opened it, I saw frenzied activity out in the hallway. The front door was wide open and a larger group of people had gathered there.

'Have they found her?' I stood up, ready to fall to my knees and thank God that Ivy had been found safe and well.

'The coppers are here,' someone called through. 'Two of them.'

Terry turned to Fiona. 'For God's sake, Fiona, you need to get rid of all these people! It's an open house and they're trampling all over the garden. This could potentially be a crime scene.'

Two female, uniformed officers came into the kitchen. 'I'm PC Zahawi,' said the tall one, 'and this is my colleague, PC Baker.'

Fiona introduced us and Baker took out a notebook and sat at the breakfast bar at Fiona's invitation.

'Ms Bennett,' Zahawi said, 'I know this is an incredibly stressful and distressing time for you, but it is very important we get the facts right from the very beginning.'

I stood up, my fingers grabbing at my hair. 'We can't just sit in here chatting when she's out there and—'

Zahawi held up her hands. 'I totally understand your distress, but the sooner we get through our questions, the quicker we can look for Ivy. More officers are on their way to begin organising a formal search and door-to-door inquiry. Please, Ms Bennett, let's get this done. Is that OK? May I call you Josie?'

I nodded and sat down again, feeling utterly spent. All this red tape to battle and, meanwhile, Samuel Barlow had time to get my daughter further and further away from the police.

'This is all a waste of time.' I felt beaten but it had to be said. 'I know exactly who has taken Ivy. His name is Samuel Barlow and he got out of prison last Friday. DI Helena Price knows all about him.'

'We can certainly speak with DI Price,' Baker said calmly, 'but we still need to cover this stage of the inquiry. Let's start at the beginning of the day. You took Ivy to school first thing, I presume?'

'That's right,' I said. 'I closed the café early today too and walked over here. I wanted to pick her up from Fiona's early and call at the park with the weather being so good.'

Fiona looked at me pityingly and my mouth filled with the sharp, bitter taste of reflux.

Baker looked up from her notepad. 'Was that usual? For Ivy to come here straight from school, I mean?'

Fiona answered. 'Yes, most days. It helps Josie out, and my daughter, Darcy, loves having Ivy here.'

Zahawi spoke to Terry. 'And you are, sir...'

'I'm Terry Gleed, Ivy's dad and Josie's ex-husband,' Terry said. 'I only just heard that Barlow got out of prison from someone at the pub.' He glanced at me. 'I'd been trying to contact Josie and when she finally picked up, she said Ivy had gone missing. So I came straight over.'

'Right,' Zahawi said, looking at me. 'Josie, when was the last time you saw Ivy?'

'This morning,' I said wretchedly.

Zahawi nodded and turned to Fiona. 'We've established Josie was working all day. So can you tell us exactly what happened this afternoon?'

'My regular twins had been collected, so I'd just got Ivy, plus my own daughter, Darcy,' she said. 'Most parents just need my help a couple of days a week.'

It felt like a knife twisting in between my ribs when I heard those words. Other parents, *decent* parents, didn't palm their kids off on a childminder every day of the week, but me? Well, I just kept on going. Forging ahead, baking endless biscuits for the Brew contract, and leaving the care of my precious daughter to someone else.

'I picked her up yesterday and I'd left work early today, too,' I said uselessly.

Zahawi nodded and Fiona told her how the girls had been playing in the garden just before I got there. 'Darcy went upstairs to find her water gun and, when she came back down, Ivy had gone. She ran back inside to find her and when she realised she had vanished, she panicked and shouted for me.'

'And you'd already arrived at the house by this time, Josie?'

I nodded miserably. 'I was in the downstairs cloakroom. I heard shouting and people running up the stairs and I came straight out.'

Baker spoke next. 'And this—' she checked her notes '—this Samuel Barlow you mentioned. Do you know this person?'

I told her quickly about the call from DI Price. 'He got a thirty-year prison sentence for the murder of my brother twenty-six years ago. He wasn't due out for another five years, so it was a shock. He came to my café yesterday, pretended he didn't know I worked there. I told DI Price all that too.'

'I see,' Baker said and the two officers exchanged a glance.

'How long is this going to take?' My body felt racked with physical pain at my inability to do something useful towards finding Ivy.

One of Fiona's neighbours came thundering down the hall-way, tapping on the kitchen door before rushing through breath-lessly. It was the woman in the floral apron who'd been making drinks for everyone.

'A big van has just pulled up outside. It's full of coppers.' She looked from one police officer to the other. 'One of them is at the door now, wanting to speak with you.'

'Excuse me a moment.' Zahawi stood and calmly left the room.

I looked wildly at Baker. 'What's happening?'

'It will be the additional officers we mentioned,' she said, her voice measured and calm. 'They're here to begin the search.'

'I want to help look for her too.' I glanced at the kitchen clock and felt panic rising in my chest again. It was four-thirty.

There would only be a few more hours of daylight and then it would get really dark. Josie hated the dark. I always left a night light on in the hallway outside her room at night or she wouldn't go to sleep. I stood up. 'I need to get home.'

'Best to stay here, Josie,' Terry said, squeezing my hand. 'You need to be with people, not at home on your own.'

'I totally understand your concerns,' Baker said, 'but, as Terry says, you really are best staying here for now, so you're able to get a full overview of what's happening. We'll make sure you have all information as it comes in.'

'There's nobody at home,' I stammered. 'What if... what if someone finds Ivy in the street? She'd give them her home address.'

'They're posting an officer outside your house for that very reason,' Baker said gently. 'We're following a tried-and-tested procedure that you can have faith in. Rest assured we've covered all eventualities.'

I was shocked rather than reassured. Shocked at them thinking of that. Shocked that they were already so organised behind the scenes because this was a very serious situation. The sort of nightmare you might see unfolding on the news.

An eight-year-old child had gone missing. Only this time, it was *my* child. *My Ivy.*

TWENTY-FOUR

When PC Zahawi came back into the kitchen, I stood up. 'What's happening?'

'I've just spoken to the senior officer and he's organising a full search of the area as we speak. He's going to come and speak with you as soon as things are underway. They're also looking into Samuel Barlow's whereabouts back at HQ.'

Thank God they were finally listening.

'We've already looked everywhere,' Fiona said helplessly. 'All our neighbours have been out there since a few minutes after we realised she'd gone. These are people who know the area like the back of their hand, know every hidden pocket of land, every garden shed, every—'

'Things can easily be missed when a search is not carried out in a methodical way—' Zahawi gave her a tight smile '—plus, the door-to-door inquiries are about to begin. Maybe an elderly person has taken her inside and is unaware of the consequences happening right now. We have to consider all possibilities.'

It made sense that this could feasibly happen, didn't it? Ivy was a gregarious girl and if she had wandered out of the garden – which admittedly would be unusual but wasn't an impossible scenario – she could have easily got talking to another child who had innocently asked her inside. I'd drummed safety into my daughter just like every other mother, but if a child became distracted, they often wouldn't think of the panic they might inadvertently cause.

'We just have a few more questions to get through,' Baker said tentatively. 'Then we'll be off to help out on the street team.'

I suppressed a weary sigh. I just wanted it all to end. I'd trade anything to take Ivy home, bathe her, feed her, snuggle up together and thank my lucky stars she was safe.

'We've covered Ivy's movements today,' Zahawi said, shifting in her seat. 'There are just some details we have to confirm about your immediate family. I understand you're a single parent?'

'That's right, yes.'

Terry looked at his hands.

Zahawi trained her cool eyes on us both. 'Was there any problem between the two of you regarding the custody of Ivy?'

'No, no. Not at all,' Terry said too quickly.

'On occasion,' I said, feeling irritated. Terry hadn't been the most reliable father.

'It sounds like there might have been problems,' Baker said carefully. 'Please be honest. This all helps us build up a picture of your home life.'

'There are no problems,' Terry said shortly.

'Nothing big,' I said.

'What small things are there?' Baker pressed.

'Oh, you know, the usual. Terry sometimes arranges to pick her up and then doesn't turn up.'

Terry frowned. 'Be fair. That hasn't happened for ages.'

'Well, last month you promised to take her to the zoo and then showed up too late to go.'

'I took her to the park instead,' he said tightly. 'We had a great time.'

'Maybe so, but that stuff is a big deal to kids, Terry. They remember what's been promised. Ivy does, anyway.'

His eyes threw daggers but that was typical of him. Terry didn't like to face facts; he preferred to soften his own mistakes. Ivy had been drawing pictures all week, had told her teacher and classmates about her visit to Twycross Zoo where a baby hippo had just been born. On the day, she'd got up and come into my bed fizzing with excitement. We'd talked about baby animals – specifically hippos – for at least an hour until it got to eight o'clock. She'd had breakfast, got dressed and sat by the front window with her little backpack packed, waiting.

We saw his arranged pick-up time of nine o'clock come and go. Then ten. Terry's phone was turned off, but I left numerous voice and text messages. There was no response.

Ivy wouldn't move until it got to eleven o'clock and then, wordlessly, she put her backpack in the cupboard under the stairs and curled up under her blanket on the sofa. Her devastated little face filled my mind's eye now.

'We did have a bit of an argument the other night because Terry asked me to lend him some money and I told him I hadn't got any.' I felt my cheeks heat up as Terry's mouth dropped open, but I couldn't stop now. 'He needed the money to pay a gambling debt. He said he was in trouble, that the people coming after him were really nasty.'

The police officers looked at each other before turning to Terry, alarmed.

'People are after you for money?' Zahawi repeated.

'I didn't say that. I said I'd had a bad bet and—'

'You said they were the kind of people who'd think nothing of breaking your legs if you didn't pay, Terry. You need to tell the truth, for Ivy's sake!'

'Good grief,' Fiona muttered, shaking her head at me,

clearly wondering why I'd never mentioned it before.

'I – I didn't think, with the shock of Ivy going missing,' Terry stammered. 'It's only just occurred to me the two things could be linked.'

'Certainly this is something we need to be aware of,' Baker said gravely.

Someone tapped on the kitchen door and pushed it open. A tall, uniformed man stood broad and square in the doorway and nodded to the two officers.

Zahawi stood and opened the door wider. There were several other officers standing behind him, filling the hallway.

'Josie, this is Police Sergeant David Conway. He's co-ordinating a full search of the area, and a door-to-door inquiry.'

Conway stepped forward. 'Hello, Ms Bennett. I wanted to just say, we're determined to throw everything at this situation today. We'll be as thorough as possible and do our very best for you.'

'Thank you, but...' I faltered, 'I want to be out there.'

'Can we be part of this search?' Terry added. 'I can't just sit here not doing anything. I want to be out there if she's found.'

'We'll certainly keep you in full contact with all areas of the investigation.' I got the distinct feeling we were being side-lined in the nicest possible way. I battled with the urge to rush out there, to insist on being part of it all.

When the kitchen had cleared of police officers, Fiona made me a drink. She became quiet, even her movements light and unobtrusive in her effort to keep me calm. I knew on one level she was a good friend who'd suffered like everyone else in my life through my quest to keep on top of working. But I couldn't get over her sloppiness in not keeping an eagle eye on my daughter.

I took the tea and heard her leave the kitchen, leaving me to stare out at the small garden where my daughter had been playing happily about half an hour ago.

My whole body sagged into the seat cushions of the small, tartan sofa where Fiona and I had sat on numerous occasions putting the world to rights over a cuppa when I picked up Ivy at the end of the day. I felt bone tired, every inch of me aching and heavy in a way even long working hours hadn't succeeded in getting to me.

The kitchen door opened, and Fiona walked quickly across the room, holding out her hand.

'Come with me, Josie,' she said. 'I need you to see something.'

I didn't move. 'What is it? I'm so tired, I—'

'It's worth the effort,' she said, wiggling her fingers impatiently for me to take her hand. 'You'll feel better for it, I promise you.'

I sighed and hoisted myself up out of the seat as if I were eighty years old. Fiona led me down the hallway, which I noted, with relief, was now empty of neighbours and police officers. She opened the front door and stepped down on to the path. 'Look,' she said.

Fiona's house was about halfway up a gently sloping hill. From my vantage point of the slightly raised doorstep, I could see all the way down the hill to the left and all the way up when I looked to the right. The street was alive with police officers. Several uniformed officers stood chatting to neighbours in open doorways and Fiona's neighbours and members of the community, led by uniformed officers, were searching front gardens and following residents down the side of houses to look in back gardens.

'Everyone is focused on helping to find Ivy,' Fiona said softly. 'We'll find her. I know we will.'

I don't know what tore my eyes away from the activity on the street, but a slight movement caught my attention on the other side of a low hedge just a couple of houses up from Fiona's. A tall man, wearing a thin parka with the hood pulled up, stared over at me. I narrowed my eyes, trying to see beyond the shadows caused by his hood. I staggered back a step and held on to the door jamb when my legs began to shake. I heard myself call out to Fiona.

The man turned to look behind him. He looked as if he was about to take off running. A group of people came into view. They hovered in my line of vision. Some began to walk down front paths to speak to the householders. For a few seconds, I couldn't see the man any more. Then I saw the back of his parka moving away.

'Hey!' I shouted out, my legs springing forward. Then I was running down the path, opening the gate and dashing over to the hedge. 'That man... someone stop him!'

Some of the people stopped walking and stared at me.

'What's wrong, Josie?' Fiona called out and ran up behind me.

I stopped running when I got to the hedge. The people had dissipated now and we were the only two standing there. 'I saw Samuel Barlow!' I said breathlessly. 'He was right here. He had a parka coat on and his hood pulled up.'

Fiona looked around. 'I can't see anyone like that here.'

'He was right here,' I said again. 'He stood staring at me and then some people came and he... he looked around and started moving away.' My eyes darted everywhere at once. I walked a few steps forwards and backwards, craned my neck over hedges and fences to see into gardens.

'Maybe it looked like him, Josie, but I can see right up and down the street from here. There's no one around with that description. Stop for a moment and look yourself.'

I did what she said. I stopped and I looked up, down, across the street. There was nobody around that fitted my description.

The tall man who'd been staring at me, who'd looked so much like Samuel Barlow, had gone.

TWENTY-FIVE

MAGGIE

Maggie placed the last of the cooled tarts into the cake tin and looked up at a noise in the yard. Wiping her hands on her apron, she went over to the window and made a small noise of surprise.

It was Samuel back home from Sherwood Pines forest. He'd only been gone around three hours and two of those would have been spent on the bus.

Maggie watched as he lumbered across the cracked concrete in a big coat with a hood, his eyes darting wildly from left to right. He'd chosen to come around the back instead of using the key she'd given him for the front door. He always used to do that back when he was a teenager... when he didn't want to be seen.

He opened the back door and shut it quickly, leaning against it as though he had to catch his breath.

'You're back early!' Maggie said. 'I thought you'd be gone all day.' She glanced down at his trainers. They looked clean enough, no traces of dust from the dry earth. But he did look dishevelled. He looked hot and bothered, and he had a long scratch on the top of his right hand. 'Did you go walking, in the end?'

'What?' He squinted at her as though he'd only just realised she was there.

'Did you go to the forest? You're back much earlier than I thought.'

'Stop keeping tabs on me. You're as bad as the screws, watching my every move.' He scowled at her. 'I'm going upstairs. Don't disturb me.'

She said, 'I baked your favourites: lemon curd tarts. I can bring one up with a cuppa, if you like?'

'Watch my lips,' he snapped. 'Don't. Disturb. Me. Got it?'

'Fine.' Maggie's mouth set in a tight line. This was not how she'd imagined it would be. This was like having Reg back again after all those years. When he'd had a skinful down at the Station Hotel, he'd had a foul temper. She could certainly do without that.

Samuel stomped out of the kitchen but turned back when he reached the doorway. 'If anybody asks, I've been at home all day.'

'Who's going to ask that?' Her heart tipped slightly in her chest.

'Probably nobody. But just in case, to get things straight, I've been home all day.'

'Right you are,' she said and went back to wiping down the worktop.

When he'd gone upstairs, she walked over to the sink and stared out at the moody sky. Slivers of blue were visible among the buffeting grey clouds. Maggie didn't want much from life now. But she'd got used to having peace and routine, and she liked to watch her favourite programmes on television without being disturbed.

She didn't want this trouble, uncertainty, and a constant

sense of peril that Samuel had brought back into her life. She'd had years of it, and she didn't want to go there again.

A rhythmic banging started upstairs in Samuel's bedroom.

Thump, thump, thump... on the floor like an unleashed thud of rage.

Maggie could feel her quiet, orderly life starting to slip very slightly. She didn't know why her son had instructed her to lie, should some unnamed person ask where he'd been today. She'd tried lying to the police once before and she had ended up in a women's prison for four months. Living on her nerves and losing almost two stone in weight.

Now she came to think about it, Samuel had always been up to no good one way or another for the whole of his life. That would probably never change. But something else was different about him, something she couldn't quite put her finger on.

All she knew was that, despite his inclination to attract trouble wherever he went, they used to be close as mother and son. Now, it was as if a ravine lay between them.

A couple of days ago, he'd been out somewhere late afternoon and returned with a large canvas holdall full of something heavy. He'd taken it upstairs and told her to stay out of his bedroom.

'I don't want it dusted, hoovered, or anything else you can think of that doesn't need doing, just so you can nose about in there.'

'What about when your bed needs changing?'

'Never mind that, either. I'll be putting a lock on there soon, anyway,' he'd added.

The first time he'd gone out again, Maggie had put her head around the door and stifled a screech at what she'd seen. It wasn't right, what he'd done. This was still her house and he should have at least asked her if she minded. It was clear to Maggie he wasn't in his right mind... whatever that might be these days.

It disturbed her in a way she couldn't articulate, but she'd said nothing on his return.

She'd also noticed he'd been pointedly reading a book. He carried it with him around the house, with its loose pages and dog-eared cover. He'd sit near her and study it, following the print with his index finger, mouthing the words silently to himself. He'd never been much of a reader. Every so often, he'd look up and give her such a filthy look, it made her blood run cold.

Maggie had tried many times to sit with and read to him as a child from the Ladybird books she'd loved as a child. *The Three Billy Goats Gruff* and *The Magic Porridge Pot* had been two favourites. But Samuel had never had the patience to sit. He'd push her away and run off.

Maggie didn't mind admitting, she was worried. For herself as well as other people. She couldn't quite say why she was worried, just a sense that something inside Samuel's head was whirring out of control. Like a television that gives a strange flicker now and then but suddenly goes haywire and blows up. Anyway, if she could put her fears into words, who could she tell? She had nobody. No friends. There was no one around here that she even recognised any more. The only local she occasionally passed the time of day with was the woman who worked behind the counter at the corner shop.

Ironically, the person she felt closest to and saw most regularly was Josie Bennett. She knew so much about them, she almost felt part of her and little Ivy's life. But she could hardly approach her. Maggie had been watching her secretly for years now and that's where the false familiarity came from.

If only Josie could find it in her heart to hear her out, even for a short time. Maggie knew it was a lot to ask because, to Josie, she was a stranger now. A woman who Josie had made clear she hoped not to set eyes on again, never mind have a conversation with.

Thump, thump, thump. The troubling thud continued through Samuel's bedroom floor, and Maggie suddenly felt overcome by a panicked desperation.

Without stopping to think it through, she took a kitchen knife from the block in the kitchen and slid it into her knitting bag. Silly, really. She'd never have the strength or the will to use it but, somehow, it gave her a little reassurance.

How she wished she'd paid someone to put a lock on her own bedroom door before Samuel had come home.

Too late for all that now, she thought. Far, far too late.

TWENTY-SIX

Helena and Brewster headed out to the police car.

'Probation have confirmed Barlow is living with his mother,' Brewster said as they walked. 'They're obviously interested in why we want to know but I said you'll be in touch if necessary. I didn't want to involve them in Ivy Bennett's disappearance until we know more.'

'I spoke to his probation officer the morning after he'd visited Josie Bennett at her café,' Helena said when they were inside the car. 'She said she'd speak to him about it and asked me to keep her informed of any more incidents. I'll give her a call after we've spoken to Samuel. See what he's got to say.'

'Never a good sign when a little girl goes missing within days of a child killer being released in a neighbouring town,' Brewster said grimly. 'On top of that, though he claimed it wasn't planned, Barlow has already contacted Josie Bennett. I get the feeling it's one coincidence too many.'

'We'll soon find out.' Helena fastened her seatbelt. When she'd first seen the picture of little Jimmy Bennett all those years ago, her heart had gone out to Josie Bennett. An early chat with Barlow seemed sensible under the circumstances. She watched as Brewster fiddled with the satnav. 'We're heading for Ravens-dale in Mansfield, right?'

'That's right, boss. An area that was once named as one of the most deprived areas in the UK. The Barlows live on Sherwood Hall Road.'

'The Bennetts used to live next door but one after they fell on hard times,' Helena murmured. What a strange set-up this was. Josie had fled from the area soon as she got the chance, and the Barlows had now both returned.

Their address was about a half-hour car journey from the Oxclose Lane police headquarters in Arnold. Brewster put on his Neil Diamond playlist in the background and in what seemed like no time at all they turned into the area known as Ravensdale.

The houses all seemed well-kept, most of them on the main roads probably being bought privately from the local council in previous years. Then Brewster turned into Sherwood Hall Road and the impression changed.

'Four, five... six to-let signs!' Helena exclaimed, counting the various letting agency boards.

Brewster pointed to a collapsing brown fabric sofa in a small front garden they were passing. 'Some nice comfy outdoor seating installed at that one,' he quipped. He slowed as they reached the end of the road, a cul-de-sac, and then stopped.

'This is it,' he said. 'Number eighty-seven.'

Helena got out of the car and surveyed the Barlows' house. It didn't appear as rundown as some of the other properties but the small patch of grass at the front was badly in need of a mow and there were long-established weeds sprouting between the cracked concrete of the short path. Some of the houses had removed their fences and gates so vehicles could be parked directly on the front but the Barlows' gate and hedge were still intact.

'Quite a way for Barlow to get to Josie's café from here, to say he just stumbled on it. We should ask if Barlow has a car,' Helena murmured.

'There's a really comprehensive bus service in this area,' Brewster pointed out. 'One of my nephews rented around here when he did a foundation degree at West Notts college. He could get virtually anywhere in the country with the odd change here and there.'

Helena looked up the street and saw a bus shelter with several people waiting. Just a few steps away from the Barlows' house. Maybe it wasn't such a difficult journey after all.

'Here we go,' Brewster said, pushing open the small peeling gate. One of the hinges was broken and the bottom of it scraped noisily over the grey concrete path. 'Get ready for the fireworks.'

Helena smiled. Ex-cons were notorious for claiming police harassment. She'd had to check with the super before they called on him.

'We'll play it nice and casual,' Helena said. 'If we suspect he's got anything at all to do with little Ivy Gleed's disappearance, we'll bring him in for a chat.'

In Helena's experience, it was virtually impossible for individuals to hide involuntary signs of guilt such as eye movement, sweating and twitches and, after twenty-five years inside, Samuel Barlow would be way out of practice.

It had been precisely six days since his release. If he'd somehow managed to find out who Ivy's childminder was, and whip the child out from under her nose, then he'd been a very busy boy indeed. But it wasn't an impossibility and that's why they were here.

Brewster knocked and they stepped back and waited. Helena saw the net curtain in the front window move slightly, but nobody came to the door.

'Try again, Brewster,' she said. 'There's definitely someone in there.'

A few moments later, they heard locks being slid back and

the sound of a door chain rattling. The door opened about six inches and a woman's voice said, 'Who is it?'

Helena squinted into the opening. It was bright outside and dim in the house, so she couldn't see very well. But this would almost certainly be Maggie Barlow, Samuel's mother.

'Mrs Barlow? I'm DS Kane Brewster and this is DI Helena Price from Nottinghamshire Police. We—'

'What's happened? Why are you here?' the woman barked and opened the door a little wider. Helena just about recognised her as a much older, thinner Maggie Barlow from the photographs in the case file. Her reddish-brown hair had grey roots an inch either side of her middle parting and her skin looked grey.

Helena stepped forward, getting a whiff of cigarette smoke from the other side of the door. 'We'd like a quick word with Samuel please.'

'What about?'

'We'll need to discuss that with him, I'm afraid.'

Helena heard a metallic rattle again as the woman removed the security chain. She opened the door wider but stood in the opening, her arms folded. She had on a shapeless terracotta nylon shift dress and stocking feet. Maggie Barlow was a diminutive, wiry woman with sharp features. Areas of exposed pale skin on her forearms were dotted with caramel-coloured sunspots.

'Would it be possible to have a word with Samuel, Mrs Barlow?' Brewster asked.

Maggie looked from one detective to the other, her eyes narrowing. 'He's sleeping. I wouldn't want to disturb him.'

Less than ten miles away, a full police search was underway to find little Ivy Gleed before nightfall. It occurred to Helena that Maggie Barlow might be trying to mislead them into thinking Samuel was upstairs when in fact he wasn't home at all. She'd lied before to the police under caution and had disrupted a murder investigation, Helena reminded herself. It would take nothing for the woman to lie again.

'May we come in for a moment please, Mrs Barlow?' Helena asked, an edge of firmness to her polite tone. She glanced at a neighbouring house. 'We wouldn't want to draw any unwanted attention by standing out here.'

Maggie shrugged. 'The neighbours around here are off their heads on weed half the time.' She leaned forward and made a point of taking a deep breath in through her nose. 'Can't you smell it? You lot would be better off sorting them out, than hounding my son.'

Helena and Brewster didn't respond, but looked at her expectantly.

'I suppose you'd better come in,' she said grudgingly.

Inside, the house was clean and tidy and smelled strongly of furniture polish and cigarettes. Maggie led them into the living room and indicated for them to sit down on the chocolate-brown leather sofa. Maggie herself took the armchair. She leaned forward and folded her arms. 'So, what's all this about then?'

Helena had read the background notes of the case in Samuel's file. Maggie was a woman who brought her son up from his early teens as a single parent. A woman who'd bided her time and eventually returned to the very house where locals turned against her when Samuel was sent to prison. According to records, she had visited him twice a month, almost without fail, throughout his entire sentence.

It seemed her loyalty to her son could not be shaken. Usually, an admirable quality in a mother, but, in Maggie's case, one that had prevented her from telling the truth and had succeeded in interfering with a very serious police investigation.

Helena was in no mood to partake in her old games.

'Mrs Barlow, please answer this question. Is Samuel upstairs?'

'I told you, didn't I? He's probably asleep and I—'

'Could you please go upstairs and ask him to come down? If he's asleep, you'll need to wake him and tell him we need a word.'

Maggie muttered something under her breath and left the room. When her footsteps sounded on the stairs, Brewster stood up and stood by the slightly open door, listening. Muffled voices filtered down. 'He's up there and he's definitely not asleep,' he whispered before returning to his seat.

From where Helena sat, she could see photographs lined up like dominoes across the mantlepiece. Each one of them featured Samuel at different ages. A school portrait at five, a blurry image of what looked like a fishing trip at around ten. Several pictures of Samuel and Maggie at the seaside and one of Samuel in a dinner suit and bow tie that must have been taken shortly before he'd gone to prison.

The final photograph caused the breath to catch in Helena's throat. Brewster stood up again. 'What is it?'

Helena pointed to the large, framed photograph at the end. 'Look at that.'

'Strewth!' Brewster's face darkened. 'How could she leave that on display, after what he did?'

Helena stared wordlessly at the image of Samuel with a young boy and a girl of around thirteen. The boy was Jimmy Bennett, Helena would recognise his face anywhere, and the girl... well, it was clear she was Jimmy's sister, a young Josie Bennett.

TWENTY-SEVEN

As they stared at the photographs, they heard voices and footfall on the stairs. Brewster sat back in his chair and Helena turned away from the fireplace.

Samuel Barlow entered the room first. He was very tall – Helena guessed about six foot two – with sallow, pale skin and red-rimmed eyes that seemed to exaggerate the icy blue of his pupils. The flesh on his face looked as if someone had pulled it tight from behind his ears, giving him a hollow, almost cadaverous appearance. Her eyes were drawn to his big hands, like flat plates with long, bony fingers. She suppressed an involuntary shiver.

Samuel walked into the middle of the room and then, bizarrely, stood very still staring out of the window. Maggie fussed around him, pulling up a hardbacked chair from its position against the wall and patting for him to sit.

Barlow wore faded denim jeans and a baggy grey T-shirt. Helena watched as he sat down on the chair and pressed his thin lips together in a tight line, as if he'd already decided to remain silent in the face of any questions they might ask.

'Mr Barlow, I'm DI Helena Price and this is my colleague,

DS Kane Brewster.' Samuel kept his eyes on the window and didn't acknowledge either of them. 'I'm afraid there has been a serious incident not far from here and we need to ask you a few questions.'

'You can't hound him like this, you know,' Maggie said. 'He's done his time and he's got every right to get on with his life now.'

'Mum. Leave it.' His voice was higher than Helena had expected. He spoke quietly as if the last thing he wanted to do was cause a problem. Barlow trained his cold, pale-blue eyes on Helena and she suppressed a shiver. 'I'd be glad to answer any questions, DI Price. I've nothing to hide.' She found his calmness unsettling.

'A child has gone missing today,' Brewster continued. 'Just a few miles from here. An eight-year-old girl has disappeared from the garden of her childminder.'

'And what's that got to do with Samuel?' Maggie said. 'It's nothing to do with him if that's what you're getting at.'

Helena watched Maggie Barlow. On the face of it she seemed to be defending her son, but Helena noticed her fingers constantly twisting against themselves and she kept shooting glances at her son as if she'd been told what to say.

'Mother. Shut it!' Samuel spoke to Maggie through his teeth, his sore eyes bulging as he stared. Maggie swallowed hard and looked down at the floor, seeming to shrink a couple of inches. Barlow flinched as though he just remembered his act with the detectives. He turned back to them, assuming his calm demeanour once again. 'I'm very sorry to hear about the missing child,' he said, holding Brewster's cool stare. 'Although, of course, I wouldn't know anything about it.'

'The local news will no doubt pick it up very soon,' Brewster said tightly. 'And it's already being talked about on social media channels.'

'Well, as you can imagine, I didn't get to open social media accounts where I've been living for the past couple of decades.' Unruffled, he looked first at Baxter and then at Helena before shifting in his chair. 'As my mother just said, I haven't left the house all day.'

It was interesting, Helena thought, that Maggie hadn't said that at all. She'd said it had nothing to do with him.

DS Brewster shuffled forward to the edge of his seat. His eyes had narrowed to slits and there was no trace of his usual amicable nature. Helena sensed Brewster had taken a real dislike to Samuel Barlow.

'I believe you know the child's mother well. Josie Bennett,' Helena said, never taking her eyes off Barlow. 'You knew her growing up and you visited her café just a few days ago.'

'Did you?' Maggie addressed her son and he ignored her completely.

'I chose a random café to stop at for a coffee and a piece of cake,' Samuel said. 'There's no law against that, is there? I hadn't got a clue Josie Bennett worked at the place.'

'How did you get there?' Helena said. 'To the café?'

'Bus.'

'That's some ride,' Brewster said. 'How long... forty-five minutes?'

'Around that,' Samuel muttered.

'So, you took a forty-five-minute bus ride to a random café in a town a good few miles from here?' Helena said. 'That sounds like a lot of effort, for a coffee and a piece of cake.'

Barlow pulled a face. 'Anywhere is better than staying around this dump,' he said gruffly. 'When you've been stuck in a cell, it's normal to want to get out and about. Besides, I never knew Josie Bennett that well and it's nearly three decades ago now.'

'She used to come over here all the time when you were both younger,' Maggie said faintly, earning herself a vicious glare from her son.

'Well, you certainly knew her brother, Jimmy,' Brewster said dangerously. 'You were the last person that lad saw before he died.'

Helena turned to look at her colleague. She'd never seen Brewster like this and she suspected it had something to do with the eight-year-old nephew he was so fond of, the son of his sister who lived in the North East. It was always tough when the job infringed on family in some way but, regardless of this, Brewster was fully aware they had to tread carefully. He was clearly baiting Samuel, who was taking great pains to appear calm. They both knew he was a volatile man. When cross-examined in court, Samuel had turned violent and had had to be suppressed by security guards before the case could continue.

Brewster caught her warning look and seemed to come to his senses. He gave her an almost imperceptible nod, as if to register he'd got himself under control.

'Josie Bennett is convinced she saw you close to the house where her daughter went missing, Samuel. She claims to have seen you watching her as the organised search began.' Helena noted his relaxed posture. No tapping or twitching. When he spoke, his voice was soft, oddly laconic.

'You know by now not to believe a word she says, I presume?' Samuel said carefully.

'What do you mean by that?' Helena got the distinct feeling he felt he had the upper hand.

'She always exaggerated as a child. She'd tell lies, blame other people. What you've got to understand is that she's a fantasist. Some of the stuff she claims only exists in her head. Isn't that right, Mother?'

Maggie looked down at her hands. 'It's so long ago now, hard to remember,' she said, non-committal.

'Where were you today between twelve and five o'clock, Mr Barlow?' Helena said. Although Ivy had not gone missing earlier in the afternoon, she wanted to track Samuel's movements during the second part of the day.

'I was here,' Samuel said. 'At home.'

'Did you see anyone else or accept visitors, while you were here, at home?'

'Just my mother.' The corners of his mouth turned up a touch. He lifted a long, bony index finger and scratched his chin. It was nothing, an absent movement, but the back of Helena's neck prickled.

Helena turned to Maggie. 'Can you verify Samuel was here all afternoon?'

Maggie rubbed her eyes and stared at the photographs on the mantlepiece.

'Mrs Barlow?'

'I did some baking,' she said vaguely. 'He was up in his room.'

'You see, Detective Inspector, I have nothing to hide,' Samuel said brusquely. 'I've done nothing wrong. I'm just trying to live my life, be a good citizen.'

'Then you won't mind if we take a look around, I presume?' Brewster said coolly.

A fleeting look of surprise crossed Samuel's face and he glanced at his mother. 'Sorry?'

'We'd like to take a quick look around the house. Just routine, satisfy ourselves nothing's amiss.'

'Have you got a warrant?'

'No. But we can certainly ring in and get one organised,' Brewster replied easily. 'We can sit here and wait until it's ready, if you'd prefer that.'

Helena knew Brewster was bluffing. They hadn't got enough to apply for a warrant yet. There were no witnesses who had seen Samuel around the childminder's house and even Josie Bennett couldn't swear one hundred per cent the man she'd seen close to the house was him. He'd admitted he had visited Josie's café, but was still insisting it had been a coincidence.

'That won't be necessary,' Samuel said at last. 'Be my guest.'

Brewster stood up. 'We'll start upstairs, if that's alright. Shouldn't take long.'

Neither Samuel nor Maggie replied. Helena followed Brewster out of the room and upstairs. The tiny landing at the top was dark, with a coffee-coloured Anaglypta wallpaper that looked like it had been in place for years, emphasising the lack of light.

The first bedroom, overlooking the road, was a reasonable size and, although furnished in an old-fashioned manner with its heavy mahogany wardrobe and velvet drapes, it was tidy and the bed had been made with white pillowcases and a quilt cover. White walls, floral prints and a pale-pink carpet completed the feminine look.

'I'll check out the second bedroom,' Brewster said and disappeared.

Helena noted the half-filled perfume bottles on the dresser, the utility bills and pill bottles on the bedside table. An ornate silver frame held a photograph of a much younger smiling Maggie with Samuel. He looked about sixteen and towered over his mother, staring sullenly at the camera. A pair of worn slippers sat neatly by the bed and a threadbare dressing gown hung on a hook on the side of the wardrobe. Maggie Barlow seemed to Helena to be a woman without many pleasures in her life.

'Boss?' She turned quickly to see Brewster back in the doorway. 'You need to see this.'

She followed him across the landing and into the other room. Samuel's bedroom. Her eyes widened when she stepped inside, and she brought a hand up to her nose at the eye-watering odour.

The room was almost completely devoid of furniture except for an unmade single bed, a wooden dining chair with an empty holdall on it by the window, and a large, filled black bin bag in the corner. There was no carpet, just unvarnished floorboards with bits of underlay still stuck on in patches, as if the previous floorcovering had been ripped up. But the most startling feature was that the wallpaper had been stripped from the walls and lay in tatters around the edges of the room like discarded wrappings.

'Now we know why he took so long to come down,' Helena remarked.

A large five-litre tin of paint and a brush in turps sat under the window. A paint tray and roller, still gleaming with wet paint, lay beside it. The wall behind the bed had been freshly painted but was dry. The wall under the small, closed window had been started recently, accounting for the strong smell.

It was the colour of the paint that Helena found disturbing. Pure matte black. Not just the walls but the woodwork and even a small section of the ceiling had been started. The matte finish swallowed up all the light around it. She could imagine how overpowering this small room would look when it was finished, certainly not a space most people would relish spending time in.

'Weird, right?' Brewster frowned. 'Wait until you see this.'

He walked over to the large bin bag in the corner and dragged it closer to the middle of the room. He tipped out the contents, clearly Samuel's possessions given to him on his release. Helena crouched down and saw all the expected items. A few self-development books, some letters, paperwork pertaining to Samuel's probation arrangements and regulation toiletries.

She looked at Brewster, puzzled as to why he wanted her to see this stuff. When he moved the paperwork aside, she saw his point exactly.

Underneath was a ten-by-eight framed photograph of Josie Bennett. Judging by her appearance, it was a recent picture.

There had been a child in the photograph. From the height and the small crown of dark hair Helena could still identify, it was clear it was a picture of Josie with her missing daughter, Ivy.

The skin on Helena's arms began to crawl as she stared at what once must have been a lovely image of a mother and her young daughter. But Ivy's face and body had been blacked out by what looked like indelible marker before the photograph had been framed. Ivy had been effectively excised from the image.

'I think we need to have a serious chat down the station with Mr Barlow,' Brewster said. And Helena, for once completely lost for words, nodded her agreement.

TWENTY-EIGHT

MAGGIE

1986

Although Maggie's neighbours would still chat over the fence, they'd stopped coming round to the house for a cuppa and a gossip since the incident with baby Jimmy a year ago. They avoided any conversation about the injury that had scarred baby Jimmy's face.

Days after it had happened, Samuel had sat out on the front step to watch the other boys playing football and they'd moved the goalposts and played further down the street.

Seating was discreetly rearranged in Samuel's classroom, so he was no longer sitting near to the other children. Maggie had marched down and confronted the teacher.

'We've had so many requests from parents concerned for the safety of their children, we had to do something,' she'd said. 'We can't ignore the majority. I'm sorry, Mrs Barlow.'

Over the past year, Reg had spent more and more time in the Station Hotel and now, he often didn't bother to come home for his tea. That suited Maggie just fine. The house was far more harmonious when it was just her and Samuel.

She didn't care one jot that Pauline had stopped coming round, but she did miss seeing baby Jimmy. A bonus was that Josie seemed to come around more often. That's when Maggie had realised there was a problem. Would any decent parent allow her child to come to the very house where her baby had supposedly been attacked? The Bennett house was a ten-minute walk away and although there weren't any busy roads, a child who had just turned seven oughtn't to be out wandering alone.

There was always trouble when Samuel played with other children. They'd constantly mither and moan he'd kicked them or snatched away a toy. There was none of that with Josie. She seemed to understand Samuel – even though she was young, she could manage him in her own discreet way – and he, in turn, displayed a gentleness with her. The more they saw of Josie, the more Maggie realised her mother seemed to have lost all interest in her and she didn't seem in the least concerned about the time she was spending at Maggie's house.

Maggie would often stand at the kitchen and watch them play a game of Twister on the rough patch of garden. Or sip her tea quietly and marvel how Samuel would focus for long periods on a game of Monopoly, patiently explaining the rules to Josie.

'That lad's soft on her,' Reg sneered one day, worse for wear after an extended session at the Station Hotel. 'He's got an unhealthy obsession. You'd better watch him.'

His drinking had taken a step up when he lost his job. He stopped drinking cider and spent a large chunk of his severance pay on neat whisky and gin. Far from trying to reason with him, Maggie stayed quiet, saying nothing about Reg's profligacy when they badly needed the money to tide them over.

Within three months he was rushed into hospital with a swollen liver and two months after that he was dead from alcohol poisoning.

The day of his funeral, when everyone had gone home and Samuel had gone to bed, Maggie sat and poured herself a small glass of sherry. She felt lighter and happier than she'd done for years. She hadn't realised how the impact of the animosity Reg showed their son had settled on her like a crushing weight.

Now, without Reg to battle, Maggie felt like she might have a chance to turn Sammy's behaviour around and, in time, people would realise he was maturing into a decent, law-abiding young man. Someone they wouldn't object to their sons and daughters spending time with.

She could but hope.

TWENTY-NINE

JOSIE

2019

Time was racing on. In a few hours it would be dusk and, after that, darkness. My baby girl was out there somewhere, all alone and afraid. And there was nothing... *nothing...* I could do about it.

Fiona stood wringing her hands, making endless cups of tea and doing her best to help but failing. Terry stood close to me, looking at his feet. Neither of them could help me. It felt like nobody could help at all.

The search and door-to-door exercise had been going for some time now and the police had uncovered no clues. Nothing. Nobody had seen Ivy leave the garden or walk down the street. Nobody had noticed anyone hanging around Fiona's house or skulking around outside. Officers had now checked every house and garden on the street and the labyrinth of streets running alongside Papplewick Lane and, although nobody dared voice the obvious, the cold fact was: Ivy had seemingly disappeared into thin air.

'Don't lose hope,' Fiona said gently. 'They could find her at any moment, Josie. In a couple of hours, she might be back with you, safe at home.'

Her words sounded hollow. I know she wasn't really buying into this happy ending. She was just desperate to believe Ivy would be found unharmed.

'I saw him,' I whispered. 'I saw a man out there, near the hedge. You didn't even see him.'

Terry listened but didn't speak.

'Could you have been mistaken?' Fiona said. Then she quickly added, 'I'm not doubting you. It's just that... I don't know, sometimes our brain can play tricks on us at stressful times.'

'I know who Samuel Barlow is, Fiona,' I said blankly. 'His face is branded in my brain and I'm certain that's who I saw out there.'

My worst fears were realised when the senior officer knocked and entered the house.

'We'd like to search this house,' he told Fiona, 'and also Ivy's home,' he said to me. Next, he addressed Terry. 'I understand your daughter hasn't been with you recently, sir, but we'd also like to search your flat. We do, of course, require all of your permissions to carry out these searches.'

'Fine by me,' Fiona said. 'Terry? Josie?'

'Can't see how it'll help bring Ivy home, but if it has to be done, then fine,' Terry said.

'Ivy's not at home,' I said hopelessly. 'We haven't been back home since we left for school this morning.'

'I realise how it must sound,' the officer said apologetically. 'Please understand, we're required to explore all angles. We don't expect to find Ivy in one of the properties but there could be other clues to her disappearance. It all boils down to the fact we can't afford to rule anything out. The search of this area will continue. We have a few daylight hours left but we'll also continue into the evening with door-to-door in adjacent streets and housing estates in the vicinity.'

'And what if she isn't found?' I said, my eyes prickling. 'What if she's been taken – possibly far away by now – in a car? I saw Samuel Barlow out there on the street. You should have taken him in for questioning by now.'

'Believe me, Ms Bennett, we are taking the connection very seriously. DI Price is dealing directly with that particular issue as a separate line of inquiry.'

Terry moved towards me. 'Josie, come and sit on the sofa. We can—'

'I don't want to sit on the sofa!' I yelled and he stepped back, holding up his hands.

'If you give me your keys, I'll go and pick your car up from the café and drive you home, Josie,' he offered. 'The police will need access to carry out the search.'

I pulled my keys from my handbag and handed them to him.

'I don't want anyone at the house, I don't...' I covered my face with my hands. 'I just want Ivy back. I need her back now.'

'And you'll get her back,' Fiona said, wrapping an arm around my shoulders. 'She'll soon be home safe, I just know it.'

I wriggled out of her embrace and turned away, heading for the sofa. We both knew she had no idea if I'd get my daughter back or not. Ivy was missing and nobody had a clue where she was.

I must have fallen asleep on Fiona's sofa. I woke with a start. 'What's happened?'

'You've just napped for twenty minutes or so,' Fiona said. She sat at the breakfast bar, staring at her phone. 'You need to rest.'

I looked wildly around me. 'Have they... have they found anything out?'

She shook her head, her face long and blank.

'There's nothing yet, we're waiting for them to start the searches. They want to do your house and this one first,' Terry said from the chair. He seemed exhausted, too.

'I want to go home now, Terry,' I said.

He looked relieved. 'Course. Your car's outside now. Ready when you are.'

'I'll let the senior officer know you've gone home,' Fiona said.

'I'll stay with you at the house while they carry out the search,' Terry added.

When Terry stopped the car outside my house, I laid my hand on his arm as he unbuckled his seatbelt. 'No need to come in,' I said. 'I really appreciate you bringing me back, but you need rest, too.'

'Sure?'

'I'm sure,' I said. 'It shouldn't take them long. There's nothing to find here, we know that.'

'OK but I'll leave my phone on all night. If you need anything at all, just call, OK?'

I nodded, wondering how the power between us had shifted so quickly and completely. Only last night he'd begged me for my help and now, I felt like I needed him.

The strangest thing was, all this seemed to be giving Terry something back of himself. Like he'd finally remembered the man he used to be.

THIRTY

Inside, the house looked dreary and dim without the lamps on. It was missing Ivy's upbeat spirit and therefore barely a home at all. No comfort, no character. No joy.

I went up to her bedroom, walking past discarded toys on the landing. I picked up a white fluffy seal and held it to my face. I'd bought it for Ivy from one of those little shops full of the tat kids love on a day trip to Scarborough last year with Fiona and Darcy. She'd got so many soft toys, but she'd really loved this one. I closed my eyes and pressed my face down. When I took it away, the fur was damp and marked with mascara.

In my bedroom, I put my phone on charge and took a sedative the doctor had prescribed me. I got into bed fully clothed and pulled the covers over my head, snuggling Ivy's soft seal to my chest.

I wanted to disappear, to fall away into oblivion. I needed my daughter back so badly, every inch of my body felt raw with searing pain. I felt the heavy blanket of sleep roll over me and this time, I didn't fight it.

· · ·

I woke up in a flat panic, cold sweat trickling down my back. I'd dreamed I was wired up to a heart monitor and I'd flatlined. Sitting bolt upright as the digital line petered out had shaken me out of it. Now, the horror of waking from a nightmare to find reality was a hundred times worse. My world was falling apart and there wasn't a thing I could do about it.

I turned on the lamp as dread pressed heavier on my chest when I looked at the window. I hadn't closed the curtains and I watched as rain hurled against the window. They'd soon be calling off the search, stopping the door-to-door inquiry and going home to their beds. Parking my missing daughter like just another case for the in-tray, to be revisited in the morning.

I sat up and grabbed my fully charged phone from the side. I'd been sleeping for nearly two hours and there were two messages: one from Fiona and one from Terry. Both just checking how I was and reiterating for me to call them if I needed anything at all. Radio silence from the police.

I cried out, a long wail of misery. But there was nobody here to hear me because I'd pushed everyone away. I walked back into Ivy's bedroom and moved towards the army of soft toys she kept on the windowsill.

She knew exactly which toy sat where and could immediately spot if I'd knocked one into another position when I'd cleaned her room. I looked down into the small, thin garden at the back. It had started to rain. Next door's cat dashed across their garden and activated the motion sensors, which lit up our garden, too.

When we'd moved here, I'd had such plans for it. 'Gardens don't have to be big to look fabulous,' I'd told Ivy. 'You and me, we'll dig and plant and make our very own secret garden full of the flowers we love.'

'Can we, Mummy? I want lots and lots of pink roses and some yellow buttercups on the grass. And daisies too, so I can make you a bracelet.'

We drew up some plans and even visited a couple of garden centres to research what we wanted. Then the café got busier and I landed the Brew contract and the secret garden tumbled off my to-do list so fast I never gave it another thought.

My head jerked around at movement over by the fence. A flash of reddish-brown hair, a person... a white hand grabbing at the wall of the small shed I kept the mower in and the barbeque we hadn't used yet this year.

I stood very still and kept watching but there was no further movement. Could it be press? I hadn't checked what was happening on social media, but the police had warned me local reporters would soon get to know about Ivy's disappearance. 'When they do, they'll be after more information and they're not fussy about how they get it,' the senior officer had said. 'I'd strongly advise you not to open the door to strangers asking questions.'

I went downstairs into the kitchen. I left the light off and walked over to the window. We had no outside lights at the back. It had still been fully light when I'd gone up to bed, so hadn't pulled down the blind. Now, the light was fading fast. The rain lashed harder than ever against the window and my heart squeezed when I imagined where Ivy might be now. Was she at least inside? Was she warm? Had she got shelter from the weather?

My eyes felt so sore with salty tears welling up yet again. The pain felt too much to bear. I stared into the empty night. Looking down towards the bottom of the small garden in search of any movement but it was hard to see much further than the patio because of the lack of light.

As I reached for the toggle to close the blind, out of nowhere, a ghostly face loomed up and pressed up against the window. I shrieked and staggered back. Skin so pale, a gaping mouth and those eyes... those cold, ice-blue eyes... and then knocking. Calling out.

'Josie! It's me, Maggie Barlow! Let me in. I have to speak to you… it's important!'

I backed away from the window. It must have been her in the garden when I was upstairs. How did she know where I lived?

'Josie! I can help you find her. I can help you find Ivy.'

I looked up and she fixed me with those eyes, exact replicas of her son's. I tried to compute how she was here, right now, in my back garden. How she knew Ivy was missing… had she seen her? Had Samuel told her he had my baby? I stepped back from the window, moved to the side and she watched me hungrily.

'Just five minutes of your time,' she called, her white hands splayed on the glass. 'I want to help you.'

I felt rooted to the spot. I didn't want to speak to Maggie; I didn't trust her. I didn't want her here, inside my home. She tapped on the glass, pressed her face forward and mouthed, 'Five minutes?'

I broke out of my inertia. All those years ago, I'd made a deal with myself that I'd never speak to Maggie Barlow again. But things had changed. If she could really help me find my daughter, I'd take it.

'One second,' I shouted and ran into the hallway, looking for my keys.

When Samuel was sentenced for murdering Jimmy and went to prison, and after Maggie had served time herself for lying to the police, she had tried to contact me for weeks. She'd followed me when I left the house, waited for me outside school. She'd even bribed other kids to give me notes, all saying the same thing: that she wanted to talk. That she hadn't lied and Samuel had been wrongly convicted.

It hadn't stopped until the headteacher had alerted the police and they'd warned her off. After that, she'd backed off and years later, she left the area and tenants moved into the house.

Everyone in the area knew that Maggie was a liar. She'd given Samuel an alibi that had sent the police investigation in a different direction for a while, meaning Jimmy wasn't found until it was too late. I'd refused all her attempts at communication back then.

But if she knew something about where Ivy was, then it was a dealbreaker. I couldn't afford to ignore her now. I had to hear what she wanted to say.

I finally found my keys, tossed on to the stairs instead of in the key tray. I rushed back into the kitchen, snapped on the light and ran over to the back door, my heart battering at my chest.

My fingers fumbled at the lock as Maggie rapped impatiently on the other side of the door. I wrenched it open, my heart thudding so hard I felt sick.

She staggered forward slightly, her foot on the step.

'Has Samuel taken Ivy?' I demanded.

She didn't answer but slipped past me, small in her flat shoes and black polyester trousers. Her tan-coloured mac was dark and damp with rain, her hair stuck flat to her head. Her skin, once smooth and creamy, now looked creased and grey and, when she spoke, there was an unmistakeable smoker's rasp to her words.

We sat at the table. She slipped off her wet mac and draped it over one of the chairs next to her. I thought how small and harmless she looked. She'd always been kind to me when I was a kid. When she'd lied for Samuel, it felt like an even bigger betrayal.

'Do you know where Ivy is?' I said. 'That's all I want to hear.'

'Not exactly,' she said and I felt myself deflate. 'I don't know where she is *yet*. But I can help you find her. I know I can.'

My eyes burned into hers. 'Samuel's taken her, hasn't he?'

'I can't say for sure. I'm not saying that, not yet.'

'Then why are you here, wasting my time?'

She sighed and laced her fingers together in front of her. 'We have history, you and me.'

'Your son murdered my brother. That's the only history that counts.'

'No, no. I don't mean that. *I* didn't do anything to Jimmy, Josie. You need to remember that.'

'You lied to the police, tried to get him off!' I took a breath and tried to calm myself. 'I haven't got time for debating who did what back then. My daughter is missing, Maggie. I'm waiting to hear from the police who want to search this house. I don't know what to do with myself. If you can't help me then I need you to leave.'

'I beg you, just listen. I *can* help you,' she said in an urgent, quiet voice. 'I can't tell you where she is at this precise moment, but... if you agree to us working together, we can get Ivy back. There are things you don't know. Things that have happened.'

'What things?' I froze, staring at her. 'You said you didn't know anything.'

'I need you to work with me, not against me. Samuel is cleverer than you think. I barely recognise him since his release and he won't talk to me but I've known he's been up to something. That place has changed him. Hardened him, but he's not well. You should see what he's done to his room at home. I'll level with you, Josie, the only way to get him to open up is for him to fully trust me again.'

'I won't play your sick games. If you know something, then you need to tell the police.'

'I've nothing to tell them yet, aren't you listening?' She sighed. 'Samuel came out of prison a closed book, even to me. But I want to help you, Josie. I don't want another child to suffer like Jimmy did.'

I couldn't even bear to think about where my daughter was, what might be happening to her... my heart felt crushed.

'The police came to the house earlier to speak to Samuel.

They searched the house and garden and they found nothing. They've taken him into the station for a chat, but they've got nothing on him. They can't help you, Josie. The only person who can help now is me.'

Something collapsed inside of me. The resolve to turn her away crumbled. 'If you can help me then I accept,' I said. 'But if you think I've forgiven you for—'

'There's a condition,' Maggie said quickly. 'You can't involve the police.'

'What?' I let out a hard, broken-hearted laugh. 'You must be crazy if you think I'm going to protect your crazy son. If you—'

'Listen to me. You *cannot* involve the police. I need your word on that or I can't help you. Ask yourself; what's more important? Getting Ivy back or putting your faith in the police who are more interested in slavishly following the rule book than doing what it takes to bring her home?'

Her words resonated clear and loud with the truth. The police wanted to help but their hands were tied with red tape. They had to tick each box before they could move on to the next stage. I thought about my call to DI Price when Samuel had turned up that day at the café. She'd assured me she'd speak to his probation officer when she should have dragged him in for questioning. Instead she'd taken the softly, softly approach and now Ivy was missing.

It choked me to think how right Maggie was. The woman I'd vowed never to speak to again in my life might be the only person who could truly help me. My heart felt lifeless, hanging uselessly in my chest.

'If I find out Samuel has taken her, there is no way I'll protect him,' I said. 'He's a monster, a danger to children everywhere. He should never have been let out.'

She looked at me steadily. 'This is not about Samuel, Josie,' she said. 'This is about Ivy. This is about finding her before...'

'Before what?'

She grasped my hand and pushed something into my curled fingers. 'Before it's too late.' I opened my clenched fingers and stared at the crumpled scrap of notepaper she'd pushed into my hand. On it, she'd scrawled a mobile number. 'Ask yourself this, Josie: what have you got to lose?'

THIRTY-ONE

Maggie wanted to talk about the past, about the time before Jimmy had died.

'I can't even think about the past,' I told her. 'My head is full of the now, and how I'm going to find my daughter.'

She promised to contact me when Samuel returned from the police station. 'I'll try and find out as much as I can and call you,' she said. 'He'll easily hoodwink the police, but I'll work to try and get his trust.'

If my trust in her was misplaced, I'd end up making everything worse... maybe even jeopardise finding Ivy. And I was painfully aware of every second, every minute, every hour ticking past and the devastating feeling that Ivy was falling further and further out of my grasp.

'I need to use the bathroom,' I said, desperate for some space to think.

I went upstairs and into Ivy's room. I stood by the door, the way I always did before going to sleep myself. The soft glow from her unicorn night light always illuminated her enough so I could see her small chest rising and falling.

Tonight, the room was dark, the bed cruelly empty. I walked over and switched on her night light and sat on her bed.

'I love you so much,' I whispered. 'Wherever you are, I'm with you, my darling.' I lay down and buried my face in her pillow, inhaling her smell before sitting up again, afraid my tears would dilute the scent of her.

Maggie's words echoed in my head. The stuff she'd said about finding Ivy before it was too late. How could I ever trust a thing that woman said? I'd be a fool to give her the time of day, and yet... what else had I got? Even though DI Price had reservations about Samuel, of her own admission, she had next to nothing to go on in terms of Ivy's disappearance. Nobody but me had seen a thing at Fiona's house. Nobody had spotted Samuel in the vicinity. Sure, customers had seen him at the café, but he'd sat quietly, never raising his voice. He'd pretended he didn't know I worked there and stuck to his story ever since.

The circumstances of Jimmy's disappearance had been similar. Samuel had known our family well. He'd been seen talking to Jimmy when he first left the house that day but he was our neighbour. Nobody had seen him leading Jimmy away; nobody suspected him.

And earlier today, I swore I'd seen him among the people out on the street who had come to help the police search for Ivy. In the moment, I had been so sure it was him. And yet, because of everyone doubting me, I could now feel myself wavering in my certainty. I'd started to question myself. It was true I hadn't seen his face clearly but... the build of the man, the way he'd stood so arrogantly staring back at me... everything in me at that moment had screamed: 'Samuel Barlow.'

Everyone was trying their best to bring Ivy back home. People I knew and trusted. The police, Terry and even Fiona. Yet what if the only person who I could really trust was Maggie Barlow? The one person I didn't want anywhere near me, who I could never forgive for trying to save Samuel's murdering skin all those years ago. Right now, she was the only one who believed what I believed: that her son was responsible for Ivy's disappearance.

I glanced again at the scrap of notepaper she'd pushed in my hand. Her voice, so pleading, so full of empathy...

I'm here to help, Josie. I can help you more than you know. You just have to trust me.

My phone stayed silent. No news, no updates. Now it was getting late, and I was about to endure my first night not knowing where my daughter was.

Could I really afford not to give Maggie Barlow a chance? If the worst happened to my daughter, and it turned out Maggie could have helped, I don't think I could live with myself. I stored her number in my phone and then sent her a text so she had mine, too.

THIRTY-TWO

Maggie sat in the chair by the window and I sat in one corner of the sofa, squashed up to the arm as if I could make myself smaller that way. I shifted about in the seat, sat more upright. I didn't want to show her my weakness.

'You always felt the odd one out in that family, didn't you?' she said softly. 'I used to sometimes hear how your mum used to speak to you in the garden. How she only really wanted Jimmy.'

I started to feel hot. She was trying to make trouble.

'Do you remember your parents when they were wealthy?'

If she thought I couldn't remember anything, she was mistaken. 'Yes. I know when I was very young, they lived in a big house. But they fell on hard times and, sadly, they had to come right down in the world and live near you.'

She smiled. 'They had everything in life in the early days. Me and your mum, we knew each other from school. We'd always got on and kept in touch. Then we both got married at similar times. I married Reg and she fell on her feet and wed your dad. She changed after that, became all la-di-da! Had money to burn, and yet... there was one thing she couldn't have.' Maggie turned and stared at me. 'She couldn't get pregnant.'

'Well, she obviously did in the end because they had me, and then they had Jimmy.'

Maggie continued as if I hadn't spoken. 'They tried and tried but she couldn't have a baby. So, do you know what they did?'

I said nothing.

'Your mum got down off her high horse and begged me to help her. "You're my oldest friend," she said. "I trust you completely." They paid me and Reg to have a baby for them.'

Cold, clammy fingers were tracing their way up my spine. 'What?'

'Your mum and dad paid me and Reg to have a baby together and give her away. Just like that. Pop her out and hand her over like a wonderful gift. And she was beautiful, our baby. Big trusting eyes; not pale and blue like my own and like Samuel's, but brown like Reg's.'

Her voice sounded like it was coming down a tunnel. I could feel my breathing coming in shallow bursts, making me light-headed even though I was sitting down.

'That baby was you, Josie. It was all agreed, like a contract. Like a job. Your mum would fake a pregnancy and I would stay in the house for the last four months and that's what happened. It worked a treat.'

She stood and walked towards me. I fought to get the breath in. She looked blurry and too close to me.

'I'm not a stranger, my love.' She sat down next to me, stroked my hands with the tips of her fingers. 'I'm your biological mother.'

'You are a liar!' I screamed, standing up, my head spinning. 'I should never have listened. Never trusted you. I must be crazy, even giving you a chance. I want you to leave.'

'Josie, listen to me—' she stood up, raising her voice above mine '—that's why Samuel was so taken with you. He was both jealous and entranced by you. He heard me and Reg talking one day. He knew you were his sister.'

'I'm not interested in your lame excuses, your lies!' I had to bite down on my tongue to stop myself from screeching. Then something occurred to me. 'What about Jimmy? Were you paid to have him, too? You're a liar!'

'It was your dad who couldn't have kids. Your mum found out she was pregnant when she had a one-night stand. Someone who worked at the doctor's surgery leaked it.'

Mum sitting at her dressing table flashed into my mind. The final months Dad lay in bed dying, she went out, night after night. Red lipstick, blue eyeshadow, perfume so strong I could still taste it at the back of my throat the next day.

I knew her faults but... I didn't want to believe *this*. And I didn't have to believe it.

'You lied to the police. You led them off into a whole other line of inquiry by trying to save your murdering son's skin.' I jabbed my finger close to her face. 'You lied then and you're lying now.'

'This isn't a lie,' Maggie said, keeping her voice calm and level. 'This is the truth and if you want to find out what's happened to Ivy, then you're going to have to face up to it.'

'What do you mean, face up to it?' I stared at her. 'Do you know where Ivy is?'

'No. If I knew, I'd tell you. She's my granddaughter, after all.'

I had no reply to that. It was ludicrous. Impossible.

'I can't be certain that Samuel is involved but there's one thing I know beyond any doubt.' She looked at me earnestly. 'Samuel *is* your brother. He has always loved you in his own way and, if you want to find out what he knows, you're going to have to face the past instead of running from it. You're going to have to speak to Samuel yourself.'

THIRTY-THREE

SAMUEL

On the way to the station, Samuel sat quietly in the back of the police car, his hands folded in his lap, his eyes closed.

He knew the male detective, DS Brewster, would be watching him in the rear-view mirror, looking for any signs of panic. Samuel would ensure he didn't find any.

While he was inside, some of the other lags had called it his 'poker face', but Samuel preferred to think of it as his mask. He'd used it all his life to appear 'normal' at those times he needed to fade into the background. He'd also pop it on when he needed to cover any signs of guilt. Like now.

Still, he had to put everything in perspective. He might be on his way to the police station – he had a feeling he was their number one suspect – but they hadn't arrested him yet, and there was a reason for that. They had absolutely nothing to pin on him. What's more, both detectives knew it. The woman was assuming a cocky and confident stance and failing. Judging by the look on DS Brewster's face, he was watching and waiting to make a strike.

It was crystal clear to Samuel that they'd hauled him into the station in a thinly veiled attempt of intimidation. To trick him into blurting out some detail, some damning piece of information that they could then incriminate him with.

He opened his eyes to find, exactly as he'd suspected, Brewster's glare trained on his face. Samuel gave him a lazy smile. One of his 'I know what you're up to' smiles that had the power to drive cops and prison guards crazy.

He'd learned his craft well.

Samuel had never been one for schoolwork as a boy. Instead, his education had served a different kind of apprenticeship: how to read people and establish their weak spots. How to fool them, and gain their trust. His teachers and classmates had been unwitting guinea pigs and his school years had been very well spent because of it.

He'd already read the male cop like a book. He'd spotted Brewster's weakness shining like a beacon in the living room back at the house. All the time they were talking, Brewster had kept dragging his eyes away from the framed photograph of Jimmy his mother had on the mantlepiece.

It was entirely apparent to Samuel that DS Kane Brewster had not been blessed with a poker face or a mask. Every thought he had translated on to his pale flabby features. When the detective looked at Jimmy Bennett's photograph, the revulsion he'd felt for Samuel had burst through in the form of a vivid red flush that spread rapidly up from his neck to his cheeks.

Amusing, thought Samuel, meeting Brewster's eyes briefly before looking out of the window again. Amusing and interesting because he now had something to work with if things got too heated in the interview room.

Samuel's mind turned, as it inevitably did, to Josie. He'd seen the hatred and the fear flashing in her eyes when he'd turned up at the café. Usually, he liked that sort of reaction in people. It meant he'd got to them.

When she'd ordered him to leave, his natural inclination had been to sit tight and cause the maximum amount of trouble.

Then he'd seen her face, and he'd felt a real dread that she hated him.

All those years ago, he'd despised it that she'd loved Jimmy with all her heart. He was unprepared when he'd emerged from prison to find another clinging brat sapping all her affection. It had felt like he was losing her, and he couldn't bear that.

That's why he'd had to resort to drastic measures.

THIRTY-FOUR

JOSIE

When Maggie finally left, I'd barely had time to get my thoughts in order when the police arrived. A uniformed officer introduced himself when I opened the door.

'We'll be as quick and tidy as we can, Ms Bennett,' he said. 'The purpose of the search is to cover best practice, so we don't miss anything at all, and we're confident every area has been covered.'

In other words, they didn't think I'd got Ivy hidden away in the house somewhere. If only she was here.

'Are you searching Samuel Barlow's house, too?' I said, even though I knew they had.

He looked momentarily flustered and then recognition of the name flashed over his face. So, the foot soldiers *were* aware of Barlow's possible involvement.

Predictably, he said, 'Sorry, I'm not at liberty to discuss other aspects of the investigation.'

I stood aside. 'Come in, and do what you need to. Do you want me to show you which is Ivy's bedroom?'

'No need.' He hesitated. 'I should mention we will need to go in all rooms, including your own. Sorry.'

I waved his apology away. I just wanted them to do what they had to do and go.

'I'll stay in the kitchen if you need me for anything,' I said blankly.

'Can I just ask, do you have a loft space?' He looked sheepish.

'You'll only find Christmas decorations and boxes of old clothes up there but, yes, we do, and yes, there's a ladder.'

He thanked me and indicated to two other officers to come inside, who nodded respectfully as they passed me without making eye contact.

Is that how they got through the job, when they met desperately worried or grieving families? I could almost imagine the training content: *Distract yourself. Be polite but don't look at them. Avoid engaging in unnecessary communication.* How else could they go home, watch TV, maybe call for a drink at the pub when they had knowledge of an underbelly of life where people's children could just disappear without a trace?

I sat in the kitchen cradling a cup of tea. Heavy boots stomped above my head. The bathroom cupboard opened and snapped shut again. The boots moved on. They were in Ivy's bedroom now. Her room hadn't got a door on, so I could clearly hear sounds and identify what they were doing in there. When we moved here it was one of those dated opaque glass designs and I was terrified she'd pull it closed too hard one day and smash it, cutting herself. Fiona's husband, Dave, had taken it off and I'd never got round to replacing it.

I knew every inch of this house and yet I felt like a stranger, sitting here, waiting for it to become mine again. I looked around me, at the new Nespresso coffee machine I'd treated myself to when the café business took off and stabilised. I only really used it on a Sunday because I always seemed to be in too much of a rush during the week. The roman blind with its subtle sand and candy-coloured stripes that I agonised for hours over, insisting Sheena flick through the fabric swatches with me each time we got a spare minute at the café. I'd fretted: 'Is it too summery-looking for the colder months?'; 'Do you think it looks like deckchair fabric?'

What did it matter now, all that umming and ahing? Nothing mattered. Nothing but finding Ivy and bringing her home safely.

In the middle of my random thoughts, another one occurred to me. I picked up my phone and texted Sheena. It was gone eight o'clock at night and I'd only just remembered she'd need to know I wouldn't be at the café in the morning.

> *Ivy gone missing from childminder's. Can't talk now but can you put a note on café door saying closed until further notice?*

A few seconds later, Sheena's reply came through.

> *OMG!! Don't worry about café, I will open up in morning. Let me know if there's anything else I can do. Are you at home? Xx*

> *Thanks. Yes, at home. Police here, searching house.*

I honestly didn't care if the café went bust and the Brew contract failed. But I did employ people, and they all relied on their wage, so I had a responsibility to try and keep it ticking over.

For the next fifteen minutes, a scraping, bumping sound filled the house from upstairs; they were moving Ivy's bed. Sliding it away from the wall. They lifted it, dropped it back down, probably checked out the drawers underneath that were filled with clean bedding and towels. I heard the window open, and slam shut again. Next, the double wardrobe was pulled out and inspected. I imagined the officers peering behind it, on the lookout for a concealed door where I might be keeping my daughter prisoner.

I sighed, shook my head to dispel the crazy, unhelpful thoughts. It was procedure. Just standard procedure to the police officers up there. All in a day's work for them, while I sat down here waiting for them to wake up and focus all their resources on interrogating Samuel Barlow. Then, we might get somewhere.

I heard someone pull down the loft ladder. I turned on the radio to disguise what was happening. But the songs were too upbeat, too jolly, and I soon turned it off again.

I walked into the hallway and stood at the bottom of the stairs looking up. I nearly jumped out of my skin when the door-bell rang.

I opened it. 'Sheena!' Her eyes were shining with tears as she put her arms around me.

'I hope you don't mind me turning up but... oh, Josie, I'm so sorry.' I closed the door and we went into the kitchen. 'I was on the bus coming back from my mum's when you text and I got off at the next stop. It was only about a ten-minute walk here and I had to see you.' A hefty bang from upstairs startled her. 'Good grief, are they taking the place to bits?'

We sat down on the kitchen sofa. 'It's just routine, at least that's what they've told me. They're searching Fiona's house, Terry's flat and here. They have to rule it out.'

Sheena shook her head sadly. 'I can't stop thinking about making the waffles with her in the café just a few days ago.'

I covered my face with my hands. 'It's... it's just a night-mare. I can't begin to even describe it.'

I felt Sheena touch my arm. 'Listen, I know it sounds crazy, Josie, but... how well do you know your childminder? I mean... what the hell happened?'

'Fiona's a good friend, I've known her a few years now. She said Ivy went to play in the garden and she only looked away for a few seconds,' I said. 'But here's the thing: Ivy wouldn't just wander off like they're saying. She just doesn't do that sort of thing.'

Sheena nodded. 'She's such a good girl. I hope and pray it's true, that she just wandered off, maybe saw a dog or something. She loves dogs.'

I nodded sadly but we both knew it wasn't likely.

'You've had so much stress lately. The Brew contract, that creepy guy who came in the café causing trouble and now this.' She looked at me. 'Don't take this the wrong way, Josie, but... I know you're on tablets for anxiety. Are you going to be OK? Is Terry being supportive?'

I cursed myself again for being so lax as to drop the packet of sertraline on the floor at the café that Sheena then found. A simple Google search would show it was an anti-depressant also used for generalised anxiety in adults.

I nodded. 'Terry's being really good, actually,' I said. I didn't mention the dodgy people he'd involved himself with and I didn't refer to the medication. But it occurred to me I might need Sheena's help in other ways. She needed to know who Samuel Barlow was in case he came in the café again when I wasn't there.

'There's something I need to tell you. The guy who complained that day at the café?' She nodded. 'Well, I know him. His name is Samuel Barlow.'

She frowned. 'You know him? You didn't say.'

'There's a reason for that. This is going to sound mad and I can't explain it all now. But twenty-six years ago, my eight-year-old brother, Jimmy, was murdered.'

She gasped and her hand flew to her mouth. 'What? You never—'

'It's not something I like to talk about,' I said. 'The man who killed him was called Samuel Barlow. He's served twenty-five years of a thirty-year sentence and he's now out on parole.'

Sheena looked pale. 'And Ivy has gone missing? You don't think...'

'I do,' I said. 'The police know everything but it's important you keep an eye out at the café. If you see him, or even think you've seen him, please call me right away.'

'Course,' Sheena said faintly. She looked worried. 'I mean, is he still violent?'

I sighed. 'Look, I know nothing must be making sense to you and I'm sorry. I'm just not strong enough to go through it all now.'

Another hefty crash came from upstairs.

'Sorry, Sheena. I think you ought to go, they'll be down here soon,' I said.

'Course.' We hugged. 'Let me know if you need me to do anything. And I mean anything at all.'

'It's nearly dark out there, will you be OK getting the bus?' I said faintly and opened the front door.

'I'll be fine and Ivy is going to be OK, Josie. I feel sure of it.' Sheena stepped outside and turned to look at me again. 'Please do let me know if you find her.'

I nodded and closed the door as she walked down the path.

Back in the kitchen, I listened to heavy boots descending the stairs again. They searched the living room, the porch, the small cupboard under the stairs. I peered through the crack in the door and saw one of them lift the brightly coloured runner in the hall and look underneath it.

The senior officer approached me. 'OK if we look in the kitchen now, and the back garden? We've got torches.'

'Be my guest,' I said wearily.

I stood aside and a couple of officers came into the kitchen, opening each cupboard door and scouting through. I went into the living room and sat by the window looking out on to the road. This morning, I'd been chasing Ivy around the house chivvying her to get her reading folder ready for school. She'd sat here, in this chair, buttoning her cardigan and looking outside dreamily.

'Come on, Ivy,' I'd groaned. 'Get a move on, sweetie, or we're going to be late.'

If only I had that moment again, I'd throw down my car keys, ignore the clock and just hold her. Instead of asking where her school reading folder was, I'd tell her how much I loved her.

My phone buzzed with an incoming text. Fiona.

Everything OK? Have you heard anything?

Sheena's words came back to me. *How well do you know your childminder?*

I replied, *Police here, searching house.*

They've been here too. Keep me up to speed and I'll do same. Speak soon.

It was normal for Fiona to wonder if the police had been in touch. How could I even entertain the thought that she had anything to do with it? She didn't even know Samuel Barlow.

Fiona loved Ivy. She'd looked after her for years.

I hated the person I was becoming.

THIRTY-FIVE

NOTTINGHAMSHIRE POLICE

It was late when they arrived at Mansfield station. Samuel was left in the care of a uniformed officer to be duly processed. He'd been booked in by the desk clerk and then installed in one of the interview rooms with a glass of water. He was now waiting for the detectives to begin their interview.

'We'll give him a good five minutes,' Helena said, opening a bottle of sparkling water and taking a swig. 'Won't do any harm to let his nerves percolate a little.'

Brewster frowned, checking through the paperwork he wanted to take through to the interview. 'I'm not sure he suffers from nerves. Frankly, I'm not sure he's human at all.'

'I beg to differ, Brewster. So far as I'm concerned, he's not clever, mysterious or a monster at all. My attitude is that he's a pathetic man who's hopefully going to trip himself up in there.' She glanced at her colleague's fingers, tap-tap-tapping on the edge of the desk. 'I suggest you might do well to think the same.'

'You might be right, boss,' Brewster said dutifully. 'There's every possibility he'll trip himself up. If we ask the right questions, that is.'

Helena patted him on the back. 'All in a day's work for us, Brewster. Ready?'

He stood up, taking a moment to check yet again that he had the correct paperwork. Helena might be imagining it, but she detected a slight hesitation in Brewster she hadn't seen before. If she didn't know better, she might think Samuel Barlow had somehow gotten under Brewster's legendary rhinoceros skin.

They entered the stuffy interview room, one of two in the station without any means of ventilation. It would suit them perfectly. The last thing she wanted was Samuel getting comfortable. The furniture consisted of a scratched table, three hardbacked chairs and recording equipment. A threadbare artificial yucca plant stood forlornly in one corner, completing the depressing, claustrophobic effect. Totally fitting for their guest today, Helena thought wryly.

The uniformed officer left the room and when Brewster began to run robotically through proceedings for the benefit of the tape, Helena took the opportunity to study Samuel.

At first glance, he appeared an unremarkable man in so many ways. The sort of person you might walk past in the street without noticing at all. His baggy grey T-shirt and well-worn jeans seemed to aid his 'everyman' disguise. When she took a closer look, Helena's eyes were drawn to his bulging biceps and strong, thick neck. She'd seen other impressive physiques honed during time spent at Her Majesty's pleasure. The result of many hours in the prison gym.

Samuel noticed her watching him and gave her a thin smile, placing his hands on the table and steepling his long, thin fingers in prayer-position. Helena kept her face impassive and she did not falter as his ice-blue eyes burned into hers.

It occurred to her that everything about this man was cold: his eyes, each one curiously red-rimmed but framing a startling white sclera and a blue iris; his skin looked clammy and cool to the touch; and his voice contained not a scrap of warmth.

'We'll be recording this conversation and a written statement will be prepared for your approval in due course,' Brewster continued. 'Do you have any questions?'

'I do not,' Samuel said and, at that point, he switched his incisive stare from Helena, to Barlow's flushed face.

After spending just a couple of minutes in his presence, Helena had to admit to herself that Samuel no longer appeared like the ordinary man she'd anticipated. Close up, he seethed with a sort of calculated calmness. It seemed to ooze from his pores like infected pus from a boil. Revulsion traced its way down her spine and she gave an involuntary shiver.

It was time to break the spell.

'Mr Barlow, could you tell us where you were today between the hours of twelve until five?' Helena's voice rang out strong and clear in the sparse surroundings.

'Please, call me Samuel, DI Price. All my friends do,' he said pleasantly. 'Now, let me see. Between twelve and five, you said?' Helena did not respond. 'That's easy. I was at home. At home with my dear mother.'

'When was the last time you left the house?' Helena said.

Samuel looked up to the ceiling. 'It was early. I went out about eight, I think it was. I fancied a bit of a stroll to stretch my legs after breakfast.'

'You went where, exactly?' Brewster said.

'Oh, not far, DS Brewster. Just round and about, doing a little reminiscing.' He fixed his stare on Brewster. 'Come to think of it, I walked past the small park near us. I love to hear the children laughing and having fun there. Such a joy.'

Helena glanced at the pen in Brewster's hand, which he was currently screwing into the stack of paper in front of him with some force. 'That would be Maun Valley Park?' she confirmed.

'That's the one.' Barlow beamed. 'Lots of trees and greenery. Nature makes me glad to be alive. I'm so fortunate to have another chance at life.'

'Not everyone's as lucky,' Brewster muttered under his breath, clearly thinking about Jimmy Bennett. Helena cleared her throat, hoping her colleague would get the message to remain calm.

'What was that, DS Brewster?' Samuel smiled widely, showing his strong yellow teeth with pronounced incisors. 'As an officer of the law, surely you support the power of the criminal justice system to rehabilitate prisoners?'

Helena breathed a sigh of relief when Brewster failed to bite.

'As we mentioned earlier, an eight-year-old girl has gone missing from the garden of her childminder,' Helena said.

'Indeed.' Samuel shook his head. 'A terrible business.'

'The missing girl is the daughter of Josie Bennett,' Brewster added. 'Josie being the sister of Jimmy Bennett. Do you see the pattern?'

Samuel seemed happy to sit for a few moments in silence without the need to fill the space.

'You know Josie Bennett well, of course,' Brewster continued. 'You grew up together.'

'Well, not quite. I was six years older. She sort of looked up to me.'

'In court, Josie gave crucial evidence against you,' Brewster continued. 'Before she had the car accident that landed her in hospital for two days, she saw you talking to Jimmy, close to the warehouse where his body was found three days later.'

'Which was perfectly true,' Samuel said easily. 'I can't blame her for telling the truth, can I?'

'Really?' Helena said. 'Twenty-five years is a very long time. Some people might get to thinking about who's to blame for putting them there in the first place.'

Samuel laughed. 'Oh, I see where this is going. Your logic is that Josie gave evidence against me all those years ago, and now I'm out to exact revenge by abducting her daughter. Is that about the size of it?'

He thought he was clever, playing games, but Helena wasn't fazed. She'd been here before in the interview room. When people took this line, you just kept chipping away at them until you got through the veneer. She usually managed it in the end.

'You must admit, it's quite a coincidence,' Helena remarked. 'You, a convicted child killer, released on parole and, days later, the eight-year-old daughter of your victim's sister goes missing.'

'It must seem that way to a cynical person, DI Price,' Samuel agreed. 'But I can assure you I'm a man who learns from his mistakes.' Everything he said seemed to have a hidden meaning. 'The last time I looked, you couldn't arrest a man for a coincidence. I know I could insist on a solicitor for this chat, but I'm not going to do that. But I would like to know what actual evidence you have in order to suspect I had something to do with Ivy Gleed's disappearance. Or is it the case that you have precisely no evidence against me at all?'

Brewster reached down by his chair and placed the evidence bag on the table.

'Could you explain to us where you got this?'

Helena caught a momentary flicker, the slightest hesitation when Samuel set eyes on the framed photograph.

'I've never seen it before,' he said quickly.

'Now, we both know that's not true, Mr Barlow,' Brewster said easily, back in his element. 'This was found in a bin bag full of the sad little items you brought from prison.'

A flare of fury sparked in Samuel's eyes. Then he seemed to gather himself and the anger cleared from view. 'Oh yes, now I remember. It was a photograph my mother gave to me.'

'And she gave it to you, why?' Helena said. 'Where did she get it from?'

'She took the picture herself, I believe.' He leaned forward slightly as if he didn't want to miss their reaction to what he was about to say. 'All this time I've been inside, she's been stalking Josie. She knows everything about her... about her and the child, I might add.'

Brewster took down some notes.

'So, your mother gave you the photograph. But why did you block the child out of the picture?'

He looked affronted. 'I didn't. Mum did that, said it wasn't right for me to see the child.'

'How do you know Maggie had been following Josie and her daughter when you've been in prison?' Brewster said. 'Did your mother tell you?'

'She let it slip on one of her visits that she'd seen Josie and her daughter out. She admitted she'd followed them to a petting farm in the school holiday. I told her to get me a picture of the two of them or I'd write to Josie and tell her what Mum was up to.'

'And how would you have known the address to write to Josie?' Helena said.

Samuel smiled. 'Mum told me that, too.'

THIRTY-SIX

MAGGIE

She walked down the hallway and watched Samuel from the door of the living room. He'd only got back from the station ten minutes ago and now lay on the sofa, trainers still on, feet propped up.

The television blared, the curtains half-closed to cut out reflection on the screen. Empty bags of crisps and beer cans littered the floor around him from earlier in the day. The cup of tea she'd made him when he returned from the police station, boasting how they'd got nothing on him, sat untouched on the coaster she'd placed it on.

The stack of lifestyle magazines Maggie liked to keep fanned on the coffee table were in disarray. When she was in the right mood, she could leaf through them for hours, immersing herself in the pages. The dreary surroundings would fade out and she'd be sitting on the veranda of one of those modern white beach houses overlooking the ocean. She'd hear the screech of the gulls and smell the salty breeze. For a few minutes, she could live the dream.

She'd always had an excellent imagination. Her English teacher had taken her aside one day when she was around fourteen. 'Margaret, you have real potential. If you apply yourself a little more, you could be a teacher of English yourself.'

She'd never forgotten his words, but the instant they'd been out of his mouth, Maggie knew, as sole carer for her mum, it was an impossibility to sink more hours into her reading, or writing more stories filled with characters that made her classmates laugh or cry. She simply couldn't see a future for herself other than emptying bedpans and cooking.

When Sammy was growing up, her skill had played a part again. Maggie would dream about her son turning a corner, stopping his bullying of others, and constantly getting in trouble. She'd imagine how life might be when he was older, perhaps getting a good job and moving them both into a nicer place, a better area.

Maggie considered her own job was to get him through the tough times to allow the better days to come. She defended him and spoke up for him, even when she suspected he was in the wrong. That had been her plan and it had unequivocally failed.

'Mum?' Samuel bellowed without looking away from the football. 'Bring us another can.'

She slipped away from the door, back down the hall and walked back into the kitchen. Just in time to see her mobile phone flashing with an incoming call. She snatched it up, hopeful of talking to Josie but it was an Unknown Number. She answered.

'Mrs Barlow? This is DI Helena Price of Nottinghamshire Police. I know it's late, but I wondered if you'd be able to get to the station for a chat today? Or we could come to the house if that's easier? We have a few questions following on from your son's interview earlier.'

'I'll come to you,' she said. The last thing she wanted was Samuel listening at the door and chastising her for giving the wrong replies when the detectives had left.

Without telling Samuel where she was going, Maggie slipped on her shoes and her coat and headed for the bus stop.

Mansfield Police Station was only a fifteen-minute bus ride away from Maggie's house but it was nearly ten p.m. when she got off at Great Central Road and made the two-minute walk to the industrial estate where the station was located. The area was deserted at this time of night.

Maggie checked in at the desk in the fluorescent-lit reception area and, before she'd taken a seat, DI Price came out. 'Thank you for coming in, Mrs Barlow,' she said. 'We can go through now.'

Part of Maggie liked the detective, but a bigger part was cautious. Ultimately, they were looking to make an arrest in connection with little Ivy's disappearance. She'd do well to remember that.

Price led her through several security doors and down a long, echoing corridor.

Maggie cast an admiring glance at the younger woman's flattering black trouser suit and slim figure as she strode confidently ahead of her. She could have never imagined herself in that job as a younger woman. She guessed DI Price was in her mid- to late-thirties and by that time, Maggie was a widowed, single mother, trapped in a life she knew she'd never escape.

'Just in here.' Price opened a door and led her into a small but clean room. It had a small window that overlooked a small grassed area with the car park beyond. 'Can I get you a cup of tea, coffee... or water, Mrs Barlow?'

'I'm fine, thanks,' Maggie said, sitting down and unbuttoning her short beige mac. 'You can call me Maggie.'

'Thank you for coming in at such short notice, Maggie,' Price said. 'I'm sure you're a busy lady.'

'Not really. I've done the laundry and the ironing.'

'Do you have many hobbies? I'm sure you know lots of people in the area. You've lived there a long time.'

'It's mostly young renters now,' Maggie said. 'The people who do remember what happened to Jimmy Bennett keep their distance. I do alright; I like watching my soaps.'

Helena nodded. 'Well, as I said on the phone, this is an informal chat. I'll be recording it just so I don't have to interrupt our conversation to take notes. Are you OK with that?'

Maggie grunted her agreement. 'Isn't the other detective here? DS Brewster?'

'I thought it best to keep it just the two of us today. I'm sure we understand each other well enough to feel relaxed and open enough to talk honestly together.'

Maggie was uncomfortable with Price's polite approach. She couldn't imagine they'd been this hospitable with Samuel, although she wouldn't know because he'd refused to talk about it when he returned home.

DI Price was smart, cunning even. No doubt she would have already worked out the softly, softly approach would work better here, but Maggie was on her guard. She might not have had the benefit of Price's education, but she was no duck egg. People had under-estimated her for the whole of her life and Maggie was well-practised in using it to her advantage, playing the innocent, life-weary older woman.

Price pressed a button and started the recording.

She made the introductions for the tape. Then, 'As you're aware, Maggie, we interviewed your son earlier today regarding the disappearance of eight-year-old Ivy Gleed.'

'Yes,' Maggie said.

'He said one or two things that I just wanted to clarify with you. Firstly, he told us that you've been following Josie for years. Is that true?'

'No, it isn't,' Maggie said, keeping her face impassive.

'You don't follow Josie around and take pictures of her without consent?'

'I don't, no.'

Helena reached down and put a framed photograph on the table.

'Samuel told us you gave him this photograph. Is that correct?'

Maggie peered down at the photograph but didn't touch it. It was the one of Josie and Ivy at the petting park taken in the school holidays last summer. Maggie had stood well back to take the shot.

'I did give him this, yes.'

'Can I ask how you got this photo? Did you take it yourself?'

'I found it online,' Maggie said.

'Online where?' Price pressed her. 'Facebook? Instagram, perhaps?'

'I don't do any of that stuff. It was just from a website about things to do with kids during the school holidays.'

'I see,' Price said. 'And did you block Ivy out of the picture?'

'Yes,' Maggie said.

'Why did you do that?'

It had taken Maggie a surprisingly short time to feel backed into a corner. But she couldn't show any weakness now. She had to battle her way through and make a good job of it.

'It was Josie he was interested in. I didn't want Samuel seeing Ivy.'

'Why was he interested in Josie?'

Maggie hesitated before speaking. 'He's always had a soft spot for her, ever since they were kids. He was jealous of Jimmy when he came along.'

'And you didn't want him to see Ivy, why... because you were worried about her safety?'

'No. I wasn't worried; more that I didn't want him obsessing in there.'

'Obsessing about an eight-year-old child?'

'I didn't mean that!' Maggie snapped and silently cursed herself. She modified her tone. 'Samuel has always been strange about Josie having friends or being close to other people, even her own family. My visits to see him were already strained. I didn't want him dwelling on the fact Josie had a child.'

'Did you talk about Josie and Ivy on your visits to the prison?' Price said.

'He was interested in what Josie was up to. He'd ask if I'd heard anything about her.'

'And you'd tell him things?'

'Sometimes.'

Helena sighed. 'See, here's the thing, Maggie. You've said you didn't follow Josie around but she lived nearly ten miles away from you. She's got no links to Ravensdale any more, hasn't had for years. So how do you know so much about her?'

Maggie stared at the ticking digital timer on the recording equipment. DI Helena Price was getting the better of her.

'There's gossip in Ravensdale like anywhere else,' Maggie said.

Helena stared at her, waited for her to elaborate. But Maggie did not.

'What I can't understand is why both you and Samuel are still so interested in Josie Bennett,' Helena said, referring to her notes. 'Josie made a complaint against you harassing her many years ago, not long after her brother's death.'

'I just wanted to talk to her,' Maggie said.

'To say what?'

'I wanted to talk through everything, explain why I'd said what I did to the police.'

'Why you lied and interfered with the investigation, you mean?'

Maggie looked steadily at the detective. She was certainly in her stride now. The niceties and pleasant attitude were long gone.

'I wanted to talk to her. We'd been so close and then... it was all destroyed.'

'I see,' Helena said. 'Maggie, do you know anything about the disappearance of Ivy Gleed?'

'No, I do not,' Maggie said emphatically.

'Has Samuel intimated any detail about Ivy? Do you suspect he knows anything about what's happened?'

'No. If I knew where that little girl was, I'd be the first person to come forward.'

'Really?' Helena looked up from her notes. 'Even if that meant divulging information that could incriminate your son?'

'Yes.' Maggie met her eyes. 'And that's the truth.'

THIRTY-SEVEN

JOSIE

Magnolia Fields care home was in the middle of a housing estate about five miles away from the café. There were no fields around it and no magnolias for that matter, either.

Mum had been here for the past eight years since she'd been diagnosed with advanced dementia. Occasionally, she still had lucid moments when the fog would clear and she'd say something to remind me she'd loathed me before she became ill and loathed me the same afterwards.

'It makes you ill to go there,' Terry used to say. 'It takes you days to recover, sometimes. Why do you keep putting yourself through it?'

'It sounds stupid, but even after all this time, I keep thinking she'll change,' I'd admitted once. I didn't even know it until I heard myself say it out loud. 'Maybe she'll finally realise how she's hurt me and make amends. Say something that takes all the hurt away.'

Terry shook his head and looked away. 'We both know that won't happen and it kills me to see you keep going back for more.'

'I know, but she's my mum, Terry. Maybe one day I'll be strong enough to give it up,' I'd said.

Today, I'd come here for a different reason.

Visiting opened at ten a.m. and I got out of the car on the dot and stood for a moment in the sunshine, a warm breeze cooling my bare legs and my feet in sandals. I felt exhausted through lack of sleep. I couldn't bring myself to take a sedative in case there was any news during the night. Instead I got up in the early hours, made tea and sat on the sofa wrapped in a blanket. My daughter's face filled my mind's eye every minute of every hour.

'Where are you, Ivy? I miss you so much,' I whispered, my eyes filling with tears.

My chest felt tight, as if gripped by a metal band I just couldn't shift. I took out my phone and called DI Helena Price. She answered almost immediately.

'It's Josie Bennett,' I said, dispensing with the niceties. 'What's happening? Has there been any progress?'

'The search and doorstep inquiry is still ongoing and we've—'

'It's not working!' I cried out, causing a man who was heading into the care home to turn and stare for a moment. 'Nothing is working and you keep doing the same old things. Have you got someone watching Samuel Barlow? What if he's got Ivy imprisoned somewhere? That's what happened to my brother, you know. Jimmy was trapped in a refrigeration unit and—'

'Josie, please, try to calm down,' Price said calmly. 'Please believe we're doing everything in our power to—'

'That's just it! "Everything in your power" is stunted by paperwork and processes. Doesn't anyone there go on gut feeling any more? Why won't anyone listen to me?'

'Josie, I understand your frustration, of course I do. We are doing—'

'I don't want to hear it,' I snapped. 'I have to go.'

I felt like throwing the phone down hard and stamping on it until there was nothing left to destroy. What the hell was I going to do? Ivy was out there, somewhere, and the police were just so ineffectual. They should have forces everywhere in the country looking for her. At the very least they should have Samuel Barlow under twenty-four-hour surveillance. I felt the inevitability of them failing to find her creep over my skin like toxic waste.

I stood for a little while longer. Stared at the incongruous colour of the flower beds that bordered the gravel car park, prettying up a place where people came to live out their final years. Then I walked into the porch, signed the visitors' book, and buzzed reception stating my name and who I'd come to see.

The door clicked open, and I held my breath like I always did when I stepped inside. I hadn't been here for quite a while... too long. It always took more from me than I felt able to give and I felt sure today would be no exception.

I walked along the corridor with its glossy white walls and black tiled floor. I knew the smell would hit me, but I wanted to delay it as long as possible. It was the usual odour you found in these places: Dettol and bleach with something deeply unpleasant beneath it that I didn't care to identify.

I often thought, when I came here, that this whole place – and the people in it – were slowly decomposing. Forgotten by the outside world, each patient resided in their own little medicated bubble and, in Mum's case, trapped in the distant past.

'Hi, Josie!' Monica, a care assistant sing-songed as she passed me. I felt in awe of her upbeat mood. The people here were hardworking and underpaid.

'Hi, Monica. How's Mum been?'

I forced myself to sound normal. Soon, everyone here would

know about Ivy's disappearance, but I didn't want to discuss it with them today.

She pressed her lips together. 'She's been a bit anxious, I think. Seb's been looking after her, so I'll ask him to pop by for a chat before you leave today.' She began walking again then stopped. 'By the way, thanks for sending in the letter with the new visitor. It's nice she's got someone else coming to see her.'

'What?' I felt suddenly cold despite the stuffiness of the place.

'That new guy who visited. An old friend of the family, Seb said.'

'I don't know what you're talking about, Monica. I haven't sent a letter in.'

Her face changed. 'I've probably just got mixed up,' she said quickly, resuming her walk in the opposite direction. 'I'll tell Seb to pop in and see you.'

I stood there for a moment or two, deciding what to do. Should I go up to the office now and demand to know who'd been allowed in to see Mum?

I was convinced Monica had backtracked too quickly just now, worried she'd spoken out of turn. If Mum really had had a visitor who'd possibly faked a letter from me then the police needed to know about it because so far as I was concerned, there was only one man who'd be arrogant and dangerous enough to do that: Samuel Barlow.

I was nearly at Mum's room now. Very occasionally, she had lucid moments when she seemed to have awareness of reality again. Maybe, just maybe, she could tell me something about it.

I walked to the end of the corridor, my heels clipping the hard wooden floor. Mum's was the last door on Corridor A. She had a private room, and it was being funded from her savings, the proceeds from the sale of her house.

When I first brought her here, to Magnolia Fields, she'd fought me.

'I want to stay in my own home. I want to live there with Jimmy.'

'Jimmy's gone, Mum. There's just you and me now.'

'No! You're a liar!' She'd turn on me, her eyes blazing. 'Jimmy's not gone, he's back at the house. You're just jealous we have each other. We don't want you around. We've never wanted you around.'

Other times, she'd dissolve into tears, wailing, 'Where's my Jimmy, where's my boy? He got killed. The only one I ever loved got killed.'

It was the cruellest thing how her brain warped and flipped the truth as if its only aim was to cause her the sharpest pain.

In the early days, I'd try to wrap my arms around her. 'It's OK, Mum, I'm here. I'll always be here for you.' But nine times out of ten she'd push me roughly away.

One day, she looked at me coolly. 'Why couldn't it have been you that died? Why did it have to be Jimmy?'

Every time I came here, she said something akin to plunging a knife in to the hilt. The fact was, she hated me. Pure and simple. She'd hated me before the dementia and she hated me just the same now. But after Maggie's visit and revelation, I'd had no choice but to come again. I was holding Maggie's claims at a distance to protect myself. All that mattered was getting Ivy back. I didn't care who I was, or where I'd come from. Not right now. I had to limit what I let in and there was only one thing that really mattered. Finding my daughter.

Still, I'd felt compelled to come here today. There were questions I needed to ask whether I got answers to them or not. Some things just need saying, need putting out into the ether and making real. That's what my task was today.

When Mum first came to live at Magnolia Fields, I'd leave the place feeling wrung out. After I got home and put Ivy to bed, I'd open a bottle of wine before drinking most of it. I got to know the staff better and confided in them and they in turn fed back to the doctors, who adjusted her medication and that helped a little bit. But of course, the staff put her attitude down to the disease and I knew it was more than that.

Still, as the dementia advanced and took more of a hold, her ability to reason at all faded quickly and, mercifully, the fire in her belly cooled.

Sometimes now, she still cried for Jimmy, but other times – most times – she simply believed he was still alive and constantly begged me to take her home to him.

THIRTY-EIGHT

I reached the end of the corridor and took a breath before tapping on the door and pushing it open. 'Hello, Mum.' She sat by the window looking out on to the car park and didn't turn around.

I could see my car from here and I wondered if she'd watched me standing there on the phone call, if she'd seen the sadness that hung like a storm cloud over my head, so real it felt like a living thing.

I told myself every time I visited that it was the dementia, not Mum, who said the hurtful things. It was the dementia that blocked her powers of recognition. It was my way of trying to numb the cold fact that she despised me way before she became ill. I soon found out, after forcing myself to sit through her often abusive visits, it only reminded me more of how she'd shunned me as a child. It was as if all that was left of her now was the anger. Anything good had finally faded away.

I closed the door behind me and walked across the room, sitting on the other chair. 'Mum?' Despite everything, it was all I could do not to burst into tears, to empty out my frustration and fears about Ivy. For her to hold me close. Just this once.

She looked around hopefully. Her eyes fluttered over me, and I saw the possibility die on her face. 'I thought Jimmy was coming,' she said, frowning.

'I think he's coming later, Mum,' I said. I'd come a long way since the days of trying to reinforce the harsh truth by saying Jimmy had died. The staff at Magnolia Fields had encouraged me to play along rather than cause her distress over something she wouldn't even remember in a matter of minutes. 'I just thought I'd pop in for a quick visit before Jimmy gets here.'

She nodded and turned back to the window. I started chatting about this and that in our usual one-way conversation, running through what we'd been baking at the café. Usually, I'd tell her about Ivy's week at school. Even though she hadn't a clue who Ivy was. I'd never brought my daughter here. I didn't want Mum upsetting her. I could put up with it myself when I had to but when it came to Ivy, she was off limits. Mum didn't deserve her then and she doesn't deserve her now.

I said, 'I need to ask you about something. Something very important.'

On some level, she must have sensed something different about my voice because she turned to look at me in her seat.

It was silly, but I felt nervous. Even though I knew she probably wouldn't register what I was saying, just uttering the words out loud felt dangerous. But I had to do it. I had to say the words here, in front of her, so they existed.

'Am I your biological daughter?'

She flinched.

The words hung there in the air, and I waited. I waited for her to speak, but she remained silent although she carried on staring. 'Am I your daughter, or is Maggie Barlow my mum? Did you...' I faltered. 'Did you pretend you were pregnant and pay her and Reg to give me away?'

There was no further reaction. Just the stare. I looked back at her, harder than I'd ever done. Her angular face, her sharp features and grey eyes. Jimmy. I could see Jimmy in her, but I couldn't find a thing about her that reminded me of myself.

'You got pregnant with Jimmy when Dad was ill. I know there were men... is that how you had Jimmy, with another man?'

Some people closely resemble their parents, but lots don't. If you look hard enough, you can always find at least one feature you share, even with a stranger, that you can identify with. I didn't look like Maggie Barlow but I didn't look like Mum, either. Perhaps I looked more like my biological dad. I wondered, for the first time, if Maggie could show me some photographs of him.

I wasn't going to get anywhere, that much was obvious. But there was something else I needed to say.

'You've never done right by me, Mum. You've been cruel and cold for most of my life. You loved Jimmy with all your heart. He was your son; for the first time it's starting to make sense. Maybe Maggie Barlow is telling the truth, and you couldn't relate to me the same because I wasn't yours.'

'Jimmy,' she whispered softly, her eyes clouding.

'I didn't ask for you to pay her to have me. I did nothing wrong, being me. *You* were the one who did wrong.' I looked away from her. 'I wanted to say that. I want you to know you've failed me.'

I looked out of the window and noticed, for the first time, the channel of lily of the valley running alongside the hedge. I remembered at school we once learned that the flower signifies a 'return to happiness' according to Victorian myth. I'd always loved the plant with its sweet-scented, bell-shaped flowers. There used to be a carpet of them in the wood where Jimmy loved us to play hide and seek...

I pushed the memory away as Mum turned back around.

'Did you have another visitor this week? A man?'

'A man?'

'Yes, someone who came to see you who hasn't visited before. A family friend, they said.'

The strangest thing happened. She stood up and turned full circle, looking around the room. 'He's in here somewhere,' she whispered fearfully. 'He hides so they don't see him and, when they've gone, he crawls out to talk to me. He claws at my feet from the bottom of the bed.'

It was nonsense, but totally real to her. I could only imagine the terror of truly believing you were right and that everyone else was wrong but not being believed.

I reached for her hand and when I looked down at her bare fingers, my heart missed a beat. 'Your rings... where are they?'

She snatched her hand away. 'None of your business,' she snapped and then looked around the room again, her face panicked.

'You're safe here, Mum. Nobody is in the room and Seb is always around to check you're OK.'

'I don't trust him. Don't trust any man.' There was no talking to her when she was like this. I started talking about the café again, but she cut in. 'Don't you ever shut up? You've always been the same. Only interested in yourself. That's what he said. He told me everything.'

'Who?'

'The man!' She rolled her eyes. 'The man who's been to prison. He's out to get you.'

I couldn't breathe. I stood up when there was a tap on the door and Seb stuck his head round. 'Hi, Josie. Monica said you wanted a word?'

Mum turned to look at him and then went back to staring out of the window without acknowledging him. 'I'll come outside to talk,' I said.

We stood in the corridor outside Mum's door. 'Monica said she'd had a new visitor. A man.'

'That's right. An old family friend, he brought a letter in from you.'

My throat tightened and I struggled not to raise my voice. 'No, Seb. I did not write a letter giving permission for anyone else to visit.' His face paled. 'What was this person's name?'

'Hang on, I can check.' He pulled out a tablet from under his arm and tapped away. 'The office gave him clearance. As you know, we don't just let anyone in.'

'I can't understand why they didn't call me to check.' I was finding it increasingly difficult not to explode.

Seb pulled a regretful face. 'They don't call because everything has to be in writing these days, sadly. Here we go.' He flipped his phone round to show me a digitised version of a visitor form. 'A Mr S. Barlow.'

'What?'

'That was his name, the visitor. Mr Barlow. We asked Pauline if she wanted to see him, and she said yes.'

'Well, she would, wouldn't she? She's got dementia, for goodness' sake, she wouldn't have a clue who it was!' I pinched the top of my nose. 'And this person... he was in here unsupervised with Mum?'

'No, no. Strictly close family only in the rooms. She met with him in the communal lounge.' He hesitated. 'Look, I wasn't on duty that day but I'll investigate exactly what happened here.'

'I want to speak to the manager about this, Seb. I think we're going to have to get the police involved.'

'What? That's a bit overkill, isn't it?'

'He wrote a letter pretending to be me!' I cried out and then immediately lowered my voice again. 'That's illegal. I want to see him on the CCTV.' There were cameras everywhere, so we'd soon find out exactly who this person was.

'Sure. That's fine. If you go back in with your mum, I'll see if the manager is available.'

'She'd better be,' I mumbled under my breath.

Fifteen minutes later, I was summoned to Serita's office. She was a neat, pleasant-looking woman in her late thirties with short black hair, a discreet diamond nose stud and minimal make-up. She wore a navy shift dress and matching jacket with low black court shoes and tights.

'Hi, Josie, how are you?' she said in her trademark sunny manner. But it wasn't washing with me today.

'I'm not good at all, Serita. I want to know who this guy is you let in to see my mum without my permission.'

'Well, that's not strictly accurate, Josie,' she said pleasantly. 'He had a letter. Signed by you.'

I felt my nostrils flare. 'I've already told Seb. I didn't write a letter. It's obviously been faked.' I fixed my eyes on her. 'And her rings are missing, did you know that?'

She looked momentarily stricken before gathering herself. 'I... I'll check with the staff about that.'

'Can I see the CCTV?'

'Please, sit down a moment,' she said. 'Can I get you a tea... or coffee, perhaps?'

'No, thanks. I want to get this sorted before I involve the police.'

'Right. Well, I'll level with you... we have no CCTV footage of him.'

'What? This place is full of cameras!'

'True, but sadly it's malfunctioned. We're still waiting for an engineer to come out. She looked at the visitor book in front of her and passed it over. 'Here's his signature, S. Barlow, showing he visited six days ago on 18th May. Sadly, there are no CCTV records available from last week.'

I placed the book back on the desk. 'OK. So I need the staff who saw him to give a full description to the police. You should have checked with me personally, Serita. I'm not going to let this go.'

'The office did carry out all the necessary checks.' She sighed, pulling out more paperwork and passing it over. 'Here's the original permission slips you signed when Pauline first came to Magnolia Fields. These forms state that you are the only authorised visitor unless we receive written permission from yourself to the contrary.'

'That's right,' I said shortly. 'And I absolutely haven't given you that.'

'This is the letter Mr Barlow brought in.' I took the sheet from her. 'The office checked the signature, and it matches the original forms you completed.'

My eyes scanned the short, typed letter giving permission for a Mr S. Barlow to visit Pauline Bennett on 18th May. The letter ended: 'Kind regards, Josie Bennett'.

When my eyes reached the final line, I could do nothing but stare in disbelief because there was no doubt about it. That was my signature.

THIRTY-NINE

Friday morning, just after ten, Helena and Brewster stood outside and looked up at the block of flats where Terry Gleed lived. A tall structure, testament to the brutalist minimalist architecture of the fifties, it stood stark and incongruous against the brilliant blue sky.

There was a sandwich board with a handwritten chalked message outside the entrance door. 'Great. The lift's out of order and our man is on the fourteenth floor. Fancy tossing a coin, see which one of us gets the big climb?' Brewster said.

'Good try, Brewster, but we're a team if you hadn't noticed. That means we go up together.' Helena stood a little taller and threw back her shoulders. 'Come on. Onwards and upwards.'

Helena wrinkled her nose when they crossed the concrete floor of the foyer and reached the bottom of the stairs. The sharp smell of ammonia filled the air, the steps littered with wrappers and even a discarded pizza box.

As they climbed, Helena did her best to avoid looking at dark stains in the corners and a used condom on one of the steps. Halfway up, Brewster stopped abruptly. 'I need a rest right now, or you'll be calling me an ambulance.'

Helena raised an eyebrow. 'You've spent the last month bragging about how you're killing it at the gym. I'm starting to suspect you might be having me on, Brewster.'

Brewster assumed a hurt expression. 'Have a heart, boss. It's early days. It's one thing running on that treadmill in a nice air-conditioned gym with piped music and bottled water, another thing altogether hiking up fourteen floors in this godforsaken place.'

'I'd believe you, thousands wouldn't,' Helena said cynically, hoisting her bag further on her shoulder. 'Try to see it as extra thinking time. We can get things straight in our heads as we go. Distraction will help you get up there.'

'You'll tell me anything,' Brewster grumbled as he began to climb behind her.

'So, just to recap, Terry Gleed and Josie were married and they split up when Ivy was five or six, as I understand it.'

'Sounds about right. Josie got full custody of Ivy, but wanted her to have a full relationship with her father, so they came to an informal arrangement that he'd see her regularly by prior arrangement.' Brewster made a big deal of taking in a big gasp of air.

'But it sounds like Gleed has been unreliable,' Helena remarked, easily scaling the steps without noticeable effort. 'Recently, according to what Josie told us, he's managed to get himself involved in some undesirable company.'

'But according to officers at the scene yesterday, he was present at the childminder's house and fully supporting Josie after Ivy went missing. Perhaps he's redeemed himself.'

'I'm wondering if the reason he's being so present is because he feels guilty. A cynical person might think he has an idea who's taken Ivy... maybe a revenge act... from one of his enemies?' Brewster eventually managed, every few words punctuated with him gasping for air.

Helena stopped climbing and turned around. 'For goodness'

sake, Brewster, just take a few minutes to get your breath back, will you? Don't make me haul you over my shoulder and carry you the last couple of floors. You'd never live that one down at the station.'

Five minutes later, they stood outside a scratched, patchily painted front door with the number 1418 clumsily painted on by hand.

'Looks like someone's kicked seven bells out of this door,' Brewster said, eyeing several clear boot imprints and scuff marks along the bottom of the main panel. He rapped his knuckles hard on the wood and scuffling sounds emerged from the other side of the door. There was a spyhole and Helena presumed they were being checked out. After a few seconds, they heard the rattling of chains and bolts being pulled back before the door finally opened.

Terence Gleed was about six foot with wavy dark hair, the colour of which Helena thought mirrored his daughter's exactly. He was unshaven and on the skinny side, but looked impoverished rather than ill, like he hadn't eaten a hearty meal for some time.

Helena thought about Josie Bennett, her neat appearance even in the face of her desperate situation. Love often worked in mysterious ways but Terry and Josie were two people she couldn't imagine ever being together.

'Mr Gleed? I'm DS Kane Brewster and this is DI Helena Price from Nottinghamshire Police.'

Gleed didn't move from the doorway. 'What is it you want?'

'It might be best if we come inside,' Brewster said, glancing at the next door. 'We'll be discussing personal matters.'

Gleed stood for a moment longer as if considering his options. Then he stood aside. 'I suppose you'd better come through then.' He closed the door behind them and led them down a very short hallway into a large sparse room that featured a worn two-seater couch set in front of a television, a pull-down double bed, and a chaotic small kitchenette. There was a door on the far side that Helena assumed led to a bathroom.

'Sit down if you like, but it's a mess,' Gleed offered without apology. 'Didn't feel up to tidying round under the circumstances.'

The sofa was littered with discarded clothing and there were empty beer cans and half-finished cups of coffee on the floor. Helena wondered if he ever brought Ivy here and if Josie had seen the state of the place.

'Mr Gleed,' Helena began.

'Terry.'

'We wanted to discuss Ivy's disappearance, Terry.'

'Right,' he said, suddenly guarded. 'No news yet?'

'Sadly not, but the search and door-to-door inquiries have now resumed,' Helena said. 'And we're making other inquiries.'

Brewster took out a notebook and pen. 'We wondered if you had any thoughts on what might have happened to your daughter.'

'What? I don't know what's happened to Ivy. What do you mean?'

'Your daughter is missing, Terry,' Brewster said. 'I'm sure you've racked your brains to think of what might have happened to her.'

'Of course I have. I'm as devastated as her mother is.' He stared at the two detectives in obvious disbelief. 'Are you trying to say I've got something to do with it?'

Helena said, 'I'm afraid we are duty-bound to ask exactly where you were between twelve and five yesterday afternoon.'

His expression darkened. 'I went straight over to Fiona's house and I was there with Josie until I took her back home. Ask anyone there.'

'That's not what I asked, Terry,' Helena said. 'What were

your whereabouts before that, specifically between twelve and five o'clock?'

'Here. I rang Josie and she told me Ivy had gone missing.' Clearly agitated, Terry stood up and began pacing up and down the room. 'I used my last tenner on a cab.'

'We need you to keep calm, Terry,' Helena said. 'It's important you answer our questions, so sit down. Please.'

He sat down on the small sofa. 'I was here. I... I haven't been out much during the last week.'

'And why is that?'

He stood up again. 'Staying at home's a crime now, is it?'

'Looks like you might've had some visitors who didn't take kindly to you not coming to the door.'

'What?'

Brewster jerked his head behind him. 'Looks like someone's been using their size tens on your front door.'

'Kids,' he said quickly. 'Teenagers. They run riot in this place.'

'Thing is, Terry, Josie mentioned about your money worries,' Brewster said. 'There was some bet you had that had gone wrong. Can you tell us about that?'

'That's got nothing to do with Ivy going missing,' he said, belligerently.

'Under the circumstances, I beg to differ,' Helena said curtly. 'We need to investigate anything and everything that might be relevant.'

'So then, this bet?' Brewster pressed him.

'Just an unofficial bet in the pub like lots of people have,' Terry said casually. 'I made some foolish decisions, had too much sauce.' He mimed drinking from a pint. 'I got shafted and ended up owing them a couple of grand.'

'Them?' Brewster pushed.

'You know, the guys that run the book. Not the kind of people that provide you with a full ID, if you get my drift.'

'What pub was this?' Brewster barked.

Terry hesitated then sighed, as if he'd resigned himself he had to come clean. 'Hare and Hounds on Forest Lane.'

Helena knew that unregulated gambling was rife in the area and it often had a toxic effect on people's lives, gaining an iron grip on gambling addicts in an alarmingly short time. Often, shame and fear kept illegal activities invisible and shrouded in secrecy.

Brewster made a note of the pub and Helena knew he'd be following it up with a view to a possible premises licence suspension while an investigation took place. He'd once confided in Helena that his own late father had become involved in an illegal gambling den when he retired. 'People think it's just a laugh, but it can ruin families,' Brewster had said grimly. 'Dad bet away most of his pension pot without my mother even knowing.'

When the scam was exposed, he told Helena his father had turned to drink and eventually died from alcohol poisoning while Brewster was still in uniform.

Now it seemed Terry Gleed was experiencing gambling-related intimidation and possibly violence and he clearly didn't want to talk about it for fear of violent reprisals. Helena wondered if the seriousness of Terry's situation might extend to his daughter's safety.

Helena thought Terry looked genuinely dazed as Brewster outlined the lengths gambling gangs were prepared to go to in order to get their money. 'I'm sorry to say we have to consider the possibility that someone took her in order to put pressure on you to pay your debts.'

'Like I told Josie, these fellas are rough but they don't hurt kids. I can't bear to think that something I've done could have harmed her.' He covered his face with his hands.

'You'll understand that we have to follow procedure by the letter in cases like this, Terry,' Helena said. 'We'll need to take a little look around the flat, too, if that's OK with you. Just to tick the box.'

'This basically *is* the flat.' He swept his hand around the room they were in. 'Look where you want. I've nothing to hide.'

'Back to your gambling debt, Terry,' Brewster said. 'We'll need times, dates, full descriptions of these men. Any names or nicknames you used or overheard.'

Terry looked bewildered. 'I... I can't think straight. Not worrying about Ivy like I'm doing. My mind's a blur.'

'No rush. Have a think while DI Price has a little look around,' Brewster said carefully. 'Let's start with the pub, the Hare and Hounds. Now, remind me who the landlord is there.'

Reluctantly, Terry began to speak and Brewster nodded to Helena to make a start.

FORTY

Helena left Brewster and Terry talking and walked over to the kitchenette, her nose twitching unpleasantly as she got closer.

The worktop was littered with rancid bowls of half-eaten cereal and congealed takeaway food that had hardened on plates. She glanced over at Terry, who was still begrudgingly answering Brewster's questions before opening the fridge. It was completely empty except for a small tub of margarine and half a rotten cucumber. Hard times indeed and this was no place for a little girl. No place for anyone, really.

Helena had learned long ago that it was dangerous to make assumptions about whether people were innocent or guilty based on their circumstances. Saying that, it was obvious Terry was very scared of someone. Scared enough to shut himself up in this hole with nothing to eat.

That meant there was someone out there who was angry enough to want to punish him in any way they could. Some people were sick enough to do that in several ways – even abducting an innocent child.

When she turned away from the fridge, Helena's eye was caught by the splashback area between the bottom of the cupboards and the start of the worktop. Not even an inch of wall was visible because the entire space had been covered in child's paintings, secured on there with Blu Tack. On a few of the pictures, Helena could discern 'Ivy' printed in a childish scrawl.

Next, she walked over to the foldaway double bed that had been pulled down from the wall. The bed was unmade, and the sheets looked like they might get up and walk off by themselves any moment, unless someone gave them a good scrub. Beer cans littered the side of the bed but, again, lining the wall, at carpet level, were several propped-up images – school photographs of Ivy this time – standing proud in their photographic studio cardboard frames.

In the first one, Ivy was just a baby. She wore a fancy party dress and had been propped up in front of a fake Christmas tree backdrop. The others covered Ivy's progression through nursery, pre-school and probably, Helena guessed, one for each year in her infant classes. Tucked away in the corner, next to Ivy's photos, was a snap of the three of them. Terry, Josie and Ivy, looking happy and windswept on what looked like a trip to the east coast or similar.

It seemed to Helena, that even though Terry lived alone here with very little to his name, he still cared very much about his daughter and, judging by the display of photographs, he clearly wanted to remember the happy times when they were still a family.

'Jeez. This is starting to feel like an interrogation!' Helena turned at Terry's affronted tone as he glared at Brewster from under hooded lids making the dark shadows under his eyes even more pronounced.

'I'm sorry if that's the case, Terry,' Brewster said matter-of-factly. 'But as we've already explained, these are questions we simply have to ask.'

Helena opened the door close to the pull-down bed. She

found it curious Terry appeared so affronted by Brewster's questions. Most parents of missing kids couldn't do enough to help and that included giving full answers to the police's questions. Unless they had something to hide, of course.

She walked through the door and found herself in a tiny, grubby bathroom that was badly in need of a freshen-up. There was a toilet, sink and small shower. A damp hand towel hung over the shower rail and Helena spotted a sprinkling of mould across the bottom of the faded yellow shower curtain.

She opened a small mirrored wall cabinet. The doors had begun to de-silver and her reflection was marred by unsightly black spots. The cabinet was packed with toiletries. Several roll-on deodorants, half-empty bottles of aftershave and shaving lotion. Carefully, Helena pushed these items out of the way and found some packets of strong, prescribed co-codamol painkillers.

She replaced the items as she'd found them and made her way back to the main room.

'You're not working right now,' Brewster said. 'Is that right?'

'I do bits and bobs,' Terry said defensively. 'Agency work, mostly.'

'Which agency do you work for?' Brewster wrote something down.

'A few. I do a bit of building site labouring now and again.'

When Helena approached the sofa, she gave a nod to Brewster which indicated, in their shared silent repertoire, that she'd take over the questions. She sat down next to her colleague.

'You've got some lovely photographs of Ivy around the place, Terry. And lots of her artwork; I bet she loves that.'

'She's never seen the flat. I'd never bring her here,' Terry said miserably. I usually take her out someplace, maybe the cinema or tenpin bowling. But... well, I admit I've been a crap dad for a while. I've had no money, not much work and... I've been staying in a lot.'

Helena nodded. 'How do you and Josie get on?'

He sighed. 'OK, most of the time. She loses patience with me when I stay away. Understandable really, but she's as bad in her own way.'

'How do you mean?' Brewster said.

'That business of hers. She's obsessed with it. The child-minder has been looking after Ivy a lot lately because Josie's got too much on but she won't stop. She's got this crazy idea she'll make her fortune and life will be different. But she can't run away from her past forever.' He looked at the detectives. 'You know about... what happened to her brother when she was a kid, right?'

'Yes,' Helena said. 'I'm just coming to that. Josie seems convinced Samuel Barlow is the one who has taken Ivy. She thinks she saw him in the street outside Fiona's house and he visited her café on Wednesday, the day before Ivy went missing.'

Terry shrugged. 'Josie's always been obsessed with Barlow. She puts on a good show, but she's screwed up in ways nobody ever sees.'

'Can you give us an example?'

Terry swallowed, as if he realised he'd said too much. 'She's got a lot of guilt about her brother dying. When we were married, she used to go on and on about things being different if the accident hadn't happened. She blamed herself for giving Samuel Barlow the chance to harm Jimmy.' He looked at his hands. 'I used to try and make her see sense. I mean, she was just a kid herself. But she wouldn't listen. Even the therapist couldn't break through her mental blocks.'

'Which therapist is this?' Brewster said.

'Dunno. It was a couple of years ago now. Some shrink that tried to straighten her out and failed.' Terry studied his bitten fingernails. 'She's over-protective with Ivy cos of what happened back then. Doesn't even like me seeing her unsuper-vised although she'd never admit it.'

'When did you last see Ivy?' Helena asked, as Brewster scribbled down some notes.

He shuffled his feet and looked down at them. 'Couple of days ago when I went to the house. But she's told you that already.'

'Did you speak to Ivy?'

Terry shook his head miserably. 'It was late, she was already in bed, I just put my head around her bedroom door. It was gone eight o'clock, so I didn't stay long. I had a conversation with Josie.'

Brewster pursed his lips. 'A conversation about...'

'Borrowing some money to pay my debts among other things,' Terry said archly.

'What other things?' Helena asked.

He shrugged. 'Just a bit hard-up at the minute, you know?' His eyes flicked over Helena's suit and her black leather Radley handbag. 'You probably haven't got a clue what being hard-up feels like. You lot with your nice salaried jobs, pension for life and suchlike.'

'Oh yes, we've got a cushy number alright. Apart from when little girls go missing and we must deal with people who won't give us a straight answer, that is,' Brewster shot back in a flash.

Terry looked away.

'Your daughter's out there somewhere, Terry,' Helena said. 'At this precise moment, we don't have much to go on. We're asking a lot of questions because it isn't just about you any more, it's about the safety of your daughter.'

Terry started to chew the inside of his cheek, his eyes welling up. 'I'm sorry... I am. I want Ivy back no matter what the cost. I'm going to really think, when you've gone, of any other names I can remember.'

They stood up to leave.

'Thanks for your time,' Brewster said. 'We'll be in touch if there are any updates.'

Helena opened the door and stepped out on to the echoing, sparse landing. The stuff Terry had said about Josie was interesting. They hadn't known about the therapist.

One thing was for sure: there was something about this fractured family that didn't quite add up. Josie had been adamant Ivy's disappearance had something to do with Samuel Barlow and the murder of her brother, Jimmy. A tragedy rooted way back in the past. At the same time, she seemed to be blaming Terry for hanging around with the wrong sort of people.

Helena was intrigued by what he'd said about Josie blaming herself and seeing a therapist. She'd been in the job for long enough to tell if somebody was holding back information, and she'd bet her bottom dollar that Terry wasn't telling them the whole story.

FORTY-ONE

JOSIE

The house was quiet, just the occasional hum of a passing car outside. When my phone rang, I jumped up to sitting and snatched it up. 'Terry?'

'I'm outside,' he said. 'Can I come in? I could do with a chat.'

I was surprised to find I felt uplifted to have him here. I went downstairs and opened the door. He looked tired and haggard, like he'd had a similar night to me. 'Sorry,' he said. 'I know you probably want to be alone... but I thought you might forget to eat. I could make you a sandwich.'

He came inside and I closed the door. 'Thanks,' I said. 'For caring.'

'I don't want to add to your problems, Josie but—' his hair fell over his eyes, shadowing his face '—I wanted you to know the police have been to the flat.'

'I assumed they'd already searched it. What for? Have they got news?'

'No, no. They came to question me.'

'Surely they don't think you've got anything to do with it?'

'Well, they obviously do because they were there a while,

even looked around the place. They asked me loads of questions about the people who are after me for money and I've had to give them details of the illegal betting shop they run at the Hare and Hounds. They're probably going to close them down.'

'Sounds like they're more interested in the gambling den than they are finding Ivy.' My face burned. 'They have nothing to go on. They literally have no idea where she is.'

'Listen, I... I might've said more than I meant to. I mentioned the therapist you saw.'

'What? Why did you do that? It makes me sound like... I dunno, but you had no right to tell them.' I felt angry with him and embarrassed about the detectives knowing something so personal. It had no bearing on Ivy's disappearance. 'It makes me sound like a sappy woman who can't cope.'

'No, it makes you sound like an ordinary person who needed a bit of support after your brother got murdered,' Terry said bluntly. 'It would be weirder if you hadn't sought help, don't you think?'

I felt so hopeless, so infuriated. I hadn't started seeing the therapist until after we got married. I'd always felt I should have been strong enough to deal with what happened to Jimmy by then. So many years and time was a great healer, they said.

Without warning, the anger evaporated and a crippling sadness enveloped me. I laid my cheek against Terry's shoulder and began to cry. 'We're never going to get her back.'

He wrapped his arms around me and just held me. 'It's going to be OK, Josie. We must keep believing that. We'll do whatever it takes to find her.'

He felt warm and strong. I wanted to blurt out about Maggie being here, about her offer to help me, but her words echoed in my ears. *Don't tell another soul or the deal is off.* So I said nothing.

'I've been to see Mum this morning,' I said.

'I can't believe you've done that.' His arms dropped away

from me. 'In the middle of all this, I mean. You could do without more stress.'

'I know. It's just...' I could hardly tell him I wanted to ask her about Maggie being my biological mother. 'I just felt I needed to go and now I'm glad I did.'

'Yeah?' He raised his eyebrows in question.

'Barlow's been to visit her. Faked a letter from me.'

'That's... mad. Are you sure?'

'Yep. He signed in and everything. But the CCTV cameras are broken so there's no evidence. Her wedding and engagement rings are missing so I wouldn't be surprised if he's stolen them.'

Terry blew out air. 'Unbelievable.'

'I've left a message on DI Price's answerphone. Hopefully she'll call me back soon.'

I sat at the table while Terry insisted on making me a sandwich even though there wasn't much in and I wasn't hungry. I felt grateful he didn't press me for details or hammer me with questions. He just got on quietly, deep in his own thoughts, giving me some space.

'Thanks,' I said, feeling a bit emotional when he brought it over. A cup of tea and a cheese sandwich didn't mean anything really, but to have someone here to make it for me and be with me... it meant the world.

We'd had lots of happy years together as a family and then just a couple of years ago, everything changed, almost overnight. At least that's what I told myself and other people, that we were the perfect family until an attractive young waitress came on the scene and Terry's brain dropped into his trousers.

It had helped me to deal with it, to convince myself that's what had really happened. But him being here now made me realise we had lost the care and mutual respect a long time before our relationship failed. It wasn't just the fact he'd met the younger woman that had caused our break-up. I'd felt so humiliated and just hadn't felt strong enough to handle the truth.

Terry sat down opposite me and, even though he'd looked tired at the door, I saw the sun had caught his face. His nose looked burnt and had started peeling. 'What have you been up to?'

'I've been stuck in the flat mostly. Keeping a low profile.'

'Really? Looks like you've been out in the sun quite a bit.'

'Oh, that?' He flicked the end of his nose. 'I did go out a bit, I went to the print shop on the High Street. A mate works there and he did me some flyers for free. I was out on the streets, pushing these through letterboxes. I'd only been home half an hour when the police came.' He reached over and opened his rucksack, pulling out a stack of paper. Ivy's face shone out at me, making my heart squeeze in on itself.

MISSING: IVY, EIGHT YEARS OLD
IF YOU HAVE ANYTHING AT ALL THAT
MIGHT HELP US FIND OUR DAUGHTER,
NO MATTER HOW SMALL...

Underneath he'd put his mobile number and email address for contacts.

'I hope you don't mind, Josie,' he said, watching my reaction carefully. 'I just felt so hopeless and you weren't around to ask, so I—'

'It's amazing you've done this,' I said, putting down my cup and reaching for his hand.

He pushed the wedge of posters back in his bag. 'It's nothing, really, but you never know what might come of it. I wish I could do more.' He stopped talking and studied my face. 'You look so tired.'

'I'm exhausted, but there's no way I can sleep. The doctor's given me sleeping pills but I won't take them. They won't let me help with the search but I still need to keep my wits about me.'

I watched the digital numbers on the bedside clock click through the minutes and hours.

My head whirred, wavered between whether my decision to speak with Maggie Barlow was the right or wrong thing to do. Maggie Barlow, my mother?

I thought about her hair, nose, eyes, mouth... I couldn't see myself. My birth certificate stated my parents' names, not hers and Reg Barlow's. If Maggie and Reg were my parents, then Samuel was my brother... and Jimmy hadn't been my brother at all.

My head thumped with the awful possibility of it all. It changed everything, and yet it changed nothing at all because Ivy was still missing. I really didn't want it to be true. A simple DNA test would either prove Maggie's truth or expose her lies. But I hadn't got time for DNA tests. My only priority was to find my daughter.

And how could I trust a woman who'd already lied to the police to try and save her son?

The police had no solid leads at all. Despite my girl being missing, it seemed they would not go after Samuel Barlow without the solid evidence that just didn't seem to exist yet.

I thought about Maggie's final words and shivered. I couldn't put it off any longer; I was going to have to ask her to arrange a meeting with Samuel.

FORTY-TWO

MAGGIE

1990

In the years that followed Reg's death, the gossip about Samuel's violent tendencies had finally faded. Maggie got herself a job at the local schools. The infant, junior and comprehensive all shared the same campus. She was assigned to look after the younger children and she loved being a midday supervisor – or dinner lady, as everyone called it – and enjoyed the camaraderie that came from working among the other women.

'Samuel seems to have shot up,' one of her colleagues said as they stood together on duty in the playground. 'He's taller than most of the other boys in school. It's a shame he's always on his own.'

It was a fair observation. At nearly sixteen, Samuel was still a growing lad and Maggie always made sure he got a bigger portion of his favourite dishes in the dinner hall. But he hadn't got any real friends his own age and seemed to spend any free time he had in school shadowing Josie Bennett.

Maggie would watch as he'd wolf down his food at lunchtime and then head straight outside to find her. During breaktime, he'd stand against the wall and watch her almost proprietorially as she played with friends her own age.

'I don't mind,' Josie had said sweetly when Maggie had gently probed how she felt having Samuel around a lot. 'I feel safe when Samuel's watching me. I never get bullied.'

By this time, little Jimmy Bennett was now five years old and the apple of Pauline Bennett's eye. Pauline's husband was stricken with cancer and lost his job. The family had moved on to Sherwood Hall Road, just a couple of houses down from Maggie and Samuel. They had no choice in the matter; the council always placed people in need on this, the longest road. On her way backwards and forwards to various neighbours' houses and the local shop, Maggie had often noticed Josie hanging around the streets after school. She'd raise a hand in greeting but looked pale and thin, a shadow of her former self. She didn't seem interested in making friends or joining in with the other children's games. When the other kids went in for their tea, eleven-year-old Josie would walk around, as if she was trying to find someone to talk to.

Then one day, Maggie spotted her walking past the house in the pouring rain. She called her inside and asked her why she never went home like the other kids.

'Mum wants me out of her way,' she said. 'Otherwise, it disturbs her and Jimmy's time together.'

Maggie's blood boiled at Pauline's obvious cruelty and neglect. She placed her hands on Josie's narrow shoulders and looked into her eyes. 'You listen to me, Josie Bennett. *This* can be your home whenever you need it. Me and our Samuel, we're your family too, if you want us that is. You're never to stand out on your own again in all weathers, you hear me?'

Josie looked down at her hands and nodded.

'And another thing—' Maggie was on a roll '—you're welcome to have tea with us every single day if you'd like.'

'Thanks, Maggie,' Josie said in a small voice. 'I would like that.'

'Good, that's sorted then. Let's get you dried off because tonight it's chips, egg and beans and a slice of bread and butter. How's that sound?'

'Sounds lovely.' Josie beamed.

Since then, Josie had come over to the house most days after school. During the holidays, she was there every single day without fail. Maggie had never known Samuel so content. They sat for hours playing board games; sometimes even Maggie played too.

The happy days didn't last. When they started the new school year in September, there was a serious incident at school. Maggie was in the playground at lunchtime when another midday supervisor rushed over.

'Maggie, you'd best come quick, love. Your Samuel has hold of another lad and he's bashing his face into the wall.'

Maggie raced to the rear playground and, as the first member of staff to arrive, wrestled her way through the large group of students that had gathered to watch the show.

'Sammy, enough!' Maggie shrieked and grabbed her son's collar. She pulled hard to separate him from the terrified younger boy underneath him. Samuel turned and raised his fist, only stopping the punch when he realised it was his mother. Maggie had staggered back, shaken by the dreadful look on his face. Like a wild beast baying for blood… it hadn't seemed like her Sammy at all.

A couple of male teachers arrived and carted Samuel and the hapless Year 8 lad to the headteacher's office.

Maggie was asked to return to her post but, before she got her bag and coat from the staffroom, she too was summoned to the head's office.

'I'm afraid Samuel made quite a mess of the other boy's face,' he said gravely. 'I have the boy's parents coming in after school. I'll encourage them to leave it to us to dish out a suitable punishment, but there's always a chance they might involve the police, Maggie.'

'What? That's a bit unnecessary for what amounts to a scuffle, isn't it?' Maggie said, aghast.

'Samuel's a good few years older than him and about a foot taller. It wasn't a fair match.'

Maggie felt herself turn on the defensive. 'Did you find out why Sammy flipped? What did the other lad do to him? It must have been something bad.'

'There were plenty of witnesses. Seems the lad is sweet on Josie Bennett. The Year Eight boy had walked over and asked her for an early Christmas kiss. Samuel told him to back off and, when the lad resisted, Samuel wrestled him to the ground.'

Maggie's blood had run cold. She recalled Reg's warning from years ago as though he were taunting her from the grave.

That lad's soft on her... he's got an unhealthy obsession...

When Maggie got back home, she sat down, still in her coat and shoes. When she looked down at her hands, she saw they were trembling.

She waited until the noise in her head had quietened, until she could hear the tick-ticking of the clock above the mantlepiece and the faint buzz of the fridge from the kitchen.

What would become of her boy? Surely he couldn't keep getting himself in trouble like this... otherwise, where might it all end?

FORTY-THREE

NOTTINGHAMSHIRE POLICE

2019

After Helena and Brewster left Terry Gleed's flat they had arrived back at the station thirty minutes before her meeting with Detective Superintendent Grey at 12.30.

Brewster got straight on the phone when they walked into the large, open-plan office. Helena slipped off her jacket and sat down at the desk, and, ignoring the messages and various new pieces of paperwork that had been placed there, she reached for Samuel Barlow's file. This file was the most comprehensive resource she had in reviewing the murder of Jimmy Bennett.

She flipped the paperwork right back to the beginning, read the first sheet that briefly detailed juvenile offences that Barlow had committed in childhood and his teens, together with some background information that was relevant but hadn't officially been reported to the police.

Helena immediately focused on a paragraph an officer previously working on the case had highlighted at the top of the page.

Samuel allegedly assaulted Jimmy Bennett when he was a baby. The incident was not reported to police and caused minor injury but was widely talked about in the community, resulting in the Barlow family being temporarily shunned by neighbours and the wider community.

Brewster approached her desk and nodded at the file. 'Straight down to it, eh?'

'Look at this.' She pointed out the paragraph, and he moved to her side to read it. 'Josie Bennett has never mentioned that Barlow assaulted Jimmy when he was a baby.'

Brewster pursed his lips and frowned. 'She would've only been about five herself though, wouldn't she? Maybe she doesn't know about the incident.'

'I can't imagine her mother wouldn't have told her though,' Helena said. 'Or someone else. It says here the community knew about it.'

'You might want to ask her yourself,' Brewster said, popping another sticky note on her desk. 'I just picked up a message on our direct line. Josie Bennett ranting that Barlow had faked a letter and visited her mother at her care home. She finished by saying she'll only discuss it with you.'

Helena checked the wall clock: 12.10. 'Right. We need to know what's happened here. You never know, what she has to say might help me out a bit when the super's got her foot on my neck at our meeting.'

Helena picked up her desk phone and tapped in Josie Bennett's number. She picked up almost immediately.

'Hello?' Josie's voice sounded haunted.

'Hi, Josie, DI Price. I got a message to—'

'Oh, thank God you've called back. I found out this morning that Samuel Barlow has been to visit my mum at her care home, Magnolia Fields, in Warsop,' she said breathlessly. 'He took a letter with him, supposedly signed by me but I haven't authorised anyone else to visit her. He can't do this, can he? He can't just turn up to see my mum.'

'OK, let's start again,' Helena said, keeping her voice level and speaking slowly to try and calm Josie down. 'You're saying that Samuel Barlow is at your mother's care home now?'

'No! This was six days ago, so it would be the day after he got out. I only just found out though.'

'Didn't the staff contact you at the time?'

'No. They said they did the customary checks, basically that he showed the office a letter, supposedly from me. I demanded to see the CCTV but she said it's not in working order. I told them I'd be reporting it to the police because it's a very serious matter.'

'Was your mother hurt?' Helena asked.

'No, but that's hardly the point! She might well have been and her rings are missing which has never happened before. Barlow must have stolen them. He can't go around faking my signature like that.'

'I'll follow this up with the care home if you can give me the details,' Helena said, picking up a pen.

'That's it? That's all you're going to do?' Josie sounded outraged.

'We're putting all our resources into finding Ivy, as you know. I have a meeting with the detective superintendent in fifteen minutes so I'll be in touch again later today with what we plan to do next, but before you go, there is one thing I wanted to ask.' Josie was silent. 'I've been reviewing the case file of your brother's death. There's a note on there about an incident. It says Barlow assaulted Jimmy as a baby?'

'I was very young but Samuel attacked Jimmy when he was left alone with him in a room for a matter of seconds. Jimmy was about six months old, I think,' Josie said quietly. 'Samuel injured his face with something sharp but my mum never found out what. Maggie denied it, tried to say the baby had scratched himself but it was too deep for that. In the right light you could still see the scar on Jimmy's lower cheek.'

'Right, and no police report was ever made?'

'Mum told me she couldn't prove it. But she told everyone: all the neighbours and parents at school. After that, nobody let their kids play with Samuel. They say his dad lost his job over it... I can't remember anything about it.'

'I see,' Helena murmured.

'You can see the kind of person he is... he was hurting people even as a boy! He hated anyone who came near me at school. He was so jealous of Jimmy and now... well, now he's taken my daughter to get revenge, or because he's jealous of her, too. Who knows. But nobody – not even you – will believe me.'

'It's not a case of that, Josie,' Helena said. 'The fact is that simply because Barlow has been released from prison, it isn't enough to bring him in. We need solid evidence to link him with events and we will keep trying.'

'Well, now we know he's visited my mother fraudulently in her care home,' Josie said icily. 'I'm sure you don't need me to tell you, DI Price, that your investigation is starting to look a shambles. That's what the local newspaper is saying.'

'I do understand your concerns, Josie. Our utmost priority is to get Ivy home safely and I'll be in touch later today to give you an update.' When Helena put down the phone, Josie's words replayed in her head: *Your investigation is starting to look a shambles.*

Helena shivered. She got the feeling that Detective Superintendent Della Grey would be saying something rather similar in a few minutes' time.

FORTY-FOUR

Helena tapped at Detective Superintendent Grey's door and waited. 'Come in,' Grey called.

'Ma'am,' Helena said, stepping inside and closing the door. Seeing Grey sitting behind her desk with her usual impeccably erect posture never failed to get Helena subconsciously pushing her shoulders back and standing a little taller.

Helena brushed down her dreary black trousers as she took in the expensive-looking sapphire blue jacket that offset Grey's striking cropped silver hair perfectly.

'Helena.' Grey trained her searching dark eyes on her. 'I'm hoping you're bringing me good news. Almost twenty-four hours now and no sign of Ivy Gleed. What have you got for me?'

One thing about Grey, she didn't waste time on small talk, Helena thought as she opened the folder containing her notes. 'It's been a frustrating case so far. We've had no sightings and despite an extensive door-to-door and a comprehensive search of the area, we're getting few new leads.'

Grey's expression darkened. Clearly not what she'd wanted to hear.

'And Samuel Barlow?'

'We interviewed Barlow last night, but we had to release him without charge. Save for a damaged photograph and a taunting, arrogant attitude, we've nothing concrete. We've also spoken to his mother, Maggie. Again, nothing useful to report. It goes without saying that Josie Bennett is convinced Barlow has her daughter and has accused him of lots of things we have no evidence for as yet.'

'Anyone else in the frame, apart from Barlow that is, for Ivy's suspected abduction?' Grey tapped her pen on the desk and Helena's nerves jangled in response.

'Not yet. But we are looking closely at Terry Gleed, Ivy's father, who's got himself tangled up with some unpleasant characters courtesy of his illegal gambling habit.'

'You're suspicious Terry Gleed might be involved himself?'

Helena shook her head. 'He seems just as shocked as the mother, but he's still in denial that his gambling activities might have anything to do with what's happened to his daughter.'

'Naturally.' Grey raised one corner of her mouth cynically. 'I'm sure it'll come as no surprise that I've had it on good authority the local community are getting restless with the lack of progress on this case. I don't need to remind you it's essential the public have complete faith in our ability to manage this investigation, Helena.'

'Yes, of course. I do realise that.'

She checked her watch. 12.35. 'We're fast approaching that crucial twenty-four-hour deadline without any arrests or leads on the whereabouts of the missing child. It's far from ideal. We can't be seen to be sitting on our laurels when a child's life is at risk.'

'Ma'am.'

It wasn't a veiled threat exactly, but Helena knew what she was getting at. Grey had flagged up that perhaps a fresh perspective – and a new senior investigating officer – may be required unless something changed, and soon.

It would be difficult for someone of Helena's rank to shrug off the stigma of being removed from an ineffectual investigation. Still, she wasn't panicking... yet. She prayed new information would soon come in that led to a new drive in the investigation. Often in these serious cases, things could turn around in a matter of hours.

'Was that it for now, Helena?' Grey said briskly.

'There was just one other thing.' Helena took a deep breath and crossed her fingers under the lip of the desk. 'I'd like to put surveillance on Barlow. Just for a short while.'

Grey sniffed and laced her fingers on the desk in front of her. 'A few moments ago you told me we had nothing on Barlow. Nothing to tie him to the area on that day, no sightings elsewhere, no hard evidence.'

'That's true, but we've reason to believe he may have faked a letter of authority to visit Josie Bennett's mother in her care home. It's one heck of a coincidence Barlow is released after twenty-five years and, within a week, another child in the Bennett family goes missing.' She played her ace card. 'According to DS Brewster, who's been keeping a close eye on the social media channels, that's the crux of the concern in the local community.'

Grey picked up her paperwork and tapped it into a neat stack. 'Right-o, well, bearing in mind the time-sensitive nature of this case, I'll say yes, temporarily. I want a full report each day.' She sighed as if Helena was testing her patience. 'Sort out the paperwork and I'll sign it before I leave the office today.'

'Thank you, ma'am.' Helena stood up, feeling lighter in herself. 'Let's hope I have better news for you very soon.'

'Indeed, DI Price,' Grey murmured, looking down at her papers. 'Indeed.'

FORTY-FIVE

JOSIE

After speaking to DI Price about Mum's unauthorised visitor, I sat in the cold, empty kitchen. It was late May, but the weather was cool and dull for the time of year. It seemed to reflect the hopelessness I felt inside. I couldn't cry, couldn't speak... I felt like an empty shell. I had nothing left to give.

I'd ranted and raved, reported the Magnolia Fields imposter to the police, but it was the same old story: leave it with them to check out. I'd wanted them to send marked police cars with screaming sirens around to Barlow's house so everyone knew to be aware he was involved in Ivy's disappearance. Instead it felt like they were holding back yet again.

I closed my eyes. With the thoughts of Ivy never coming home came dark imaginings I knew better than to linger on. Yet at the same time, I knew I'd pushed this stuff away for long enough and it had festered and burrowed deep. Instinctively, I now recognised that nothing would change until I forced the pain back to the surface.

Back in the days after Jimmy's death, I couldn't eat, sleep and I didn't know what to do with myself when I was awake.

When Mum insisted I had to go back to school, I ran away time and time again until she just gave up on me. She barely noticed I'd gone, so lost was she in the fog of grief that had swallowed her up after Jimmy's death.

I could feel myself slipping that way again. Like I was standing at the top of an icy slope and feeling one foot give way and start to slide. I knew from experience there was almost no way of stopping it once it started.

A sharp tap-tapping sounded from the front room window. Then a fist banging on the door. Terry's trademark knock. He'd only left the house a short time ago.

I ran into the hall and opened the door. 'Let me in. Let me in,' he hissed, pushing past me.

'What is it? What's wrong?' I closed the door.

He stood, his head down. 'Terry?' He wouldn't look up to meet my eyes.

'Josie, please. I beg you. Just let me in and I'll explain everything.'

Something about his desperation made me feel sick. I double-locked the door. 'Come through to the living room.'

I shivered when he responded. 'Can we pull the blinds?'

'What's going off? Who's out there?' I led him into the living room and turned to face him. Finally, he looked up and I saw his face. 'My God, what's happened to you?'

His right eye was swollen closed. His cheek was also puffed and bleeding. When he opened his mouth to speak, I saw he had a front tooth missing. 'They found me, Josie,' he croaked. 'The man I owe the cash to caught me as you can see but I managed to get away again. He chased me here.'

'What?' I rushed over to the window. 'What's his name? Surely you can describe him to the police!' There was nobody on the street but I closed the blind. 'What if he's followed you here, to the house?'

'I didn't know where else to go,' he said, hopelessly. 'I don't think he saw me turn into the street. I hid behind a wall until he'd passed.'

He looked wretched. He had on a long-sleeved sweatshirt, but I could see his bony wrists and thin, red fingers. The man I'd married had been well-built and groomed. He was a shadow of his former self, and I hadn't even noticed it happening.

Part of me wanted to push him back out on the street, but when he looked at me like that, sort of pleadingly, I saw my daughter in him. I saw my beautiful Ivy.

'I'll make you a coffee,' I said.

'No, I... I'll get going. I just needed somewhere to run, to hide for a while. I'll figure out a way of getting back to the flat once it gets dark.'

I pulled my phone out of my jeans pocket. 'We need to call the police.'

'What? No!'

'Are you crazy? These people who are after you, they might have Ivy!'

'They haven't, Josie. I know they haven't. They just want their money, they're not child snatchers.'

'You don't know that for certain! We can't risk Ivy's life because you don't want to face up to the fact they might have her.'

'Is there... is there any news about Ivy?'

'No,' I said quietly. 'There never seems to be any news.'

'We'll get her back, and when we do, I'm going to be a better dad, take her—'

'Terry, don't,' I said quietly.

He hung his head. 'I've made such a mess of things and I'm so, so sorry I wasn't a better husband and father.' He looked at me strangely. 'I can't bear to be this man, Josie. I detest myself.'

'Hey,' I said softly. I didn't know what else to say. I'd never seen Terry this low. But then I'd never felt so down in myself, either.

Slowly but surely, it felt like we were both crumbling into little pieces. If we didn't get Ivy back soon, we might just fade away.

FORTY-SIX

MAGGIE

Samuel sat at the small wooden kitchen table, reading the same dog-eared paperback he carried everywhere with him. When Maggie got back from the police station last night, he'd fallen asleep and hadn't even registered she'd been out.

Maggie pulled out a chair and sat down opposite, but he didn't look up.

'I thought you ought to know something,' she said. 'I've told Josie she's one of us.'

His head jerked up. 'She knows?'

Maggie nodded.

'And?' he said. 'What did she say?'

'It was a shock, as you can imagine.'

'Did she ask about me, her brother? Did you tell her you knew—'

'No,' Maggie said. 'I didn't get into any of that because she's got to get used to the idea. What she did say was that she'd like a chat with you, soon, if you can.'

Samuel narrowed his eyes, instantly suspicious. 'A chat about what?'

'She's in a bad way, what with her little girl missing, Sammy. I think she wonders if you might help her.'

'She hates my guts.' His mouth twisted like he'd chewed on something sour. 'She probably thinks I've got something to do with it. Like everybody does. Even you.'

'I never said that,' Maggie said calmly. 'The only way you'd take that girl is if you wanted to go back to prison because they'd have you there faster than you could say "not guilty". I assume you don't want to go back there?'

His cold eyes regarded her. 'You think I took the kid. Josie thinks I took the kid. The police think I did it too.' He closed his book and laid a hand on top of it like a bible. 'Nice to feel popular for a change.'

'I've told the police you've got nothing to do with little Ivy's disappearance.'

'When?' He scowled.

'While you were asleep yesterday. DI Price rang and asked if I could go in. It's only a fifteen-minute bus—'

'What did they ask you?'

'If I knew anything about where Ivy was. You'd told them quite a bit about me, it seems.'

'Like what?'

'That I followed Josie everywhere and took photographs without her consent.'

'I never said all that. I told 'em you gave me that picture. That was it.'

Maggie kept her face impassive, determined not to show she was rattled. She didn't want to go down the finger-pointing route. There was something more important at stake. 'Shall I tell Josie you'll talk to her? She can come here. Josie, here at the house again.'

'How cosy.' Samuel grinned wolfishly. 'Just like the old days.'

'Is that a yes?'

He nodded slowly. 'I'd quite like a civilised chat with my sister. The three of us will certainly have a lot to talk about.'

Maggie went upstairs and texted Josie.

Samuel willing to talk. Can you come over here to speak to him? Text back soon.

She slipped the phone back into her knitting bag. Was it too late to hope for a future of sorts? For Maggie to get to know Josie again, and to spend time with her only granddaughter.

She couldn't help thinking that it was Samuel who held the key.

FORTY-SEVEN

JOSIE

I replied to Maggie's text.

I'm coming over to speak to Samuel. Leaving now.

I wanted to appear strong and determined, even though I felt sick with nerves. This felt like my last chance.

Samuel gone out. But come over, shouldn't be long before he's back.

It wasn't Maggie I wanted to talk to. I had to speak to Samuel. I believed he was the only one who could help me get Ivy back.

I drove over to Ravensdale. The place had barely changed in all this time. The derelict pub on the corner with boarded windows, a burned-out car on a back road... I missed this area like a hole in the head.

I pulled up outside Maggie's house but didn't get out. I stared at the house two doors down. The house I'd lived in with Mum and Jimmy after we'd had to downsize. It had a different coloured door now, no front gate and paving stones instead of grass.

I looked at the upstairs window. Imagined myself standing there and looking down, watching Jimmy get to the gate on that last morning. The day he took his picnic up to the old railway. I'd seen Samuel talking to him down there. I could have stopped him going alone, asked him to wait for me.

I shook the memories from my mind, grabbed my handbag and locked the car.

I'd only taken a few steps towards the Barlows' gate when I heard feet scuffling behind me.

'Josie?'

I turned around. Samuel stood there. We looked at each other. His eyes, nose, long face. In seconds I'd compared them to my own... I couldn't help myself.

'Mum says you want to talk to me.' He walked forward and we were close. Closer than at the café. I could smell him. Strong, earthy... he made me want to retch.

My knees started to quiver but I dug deep for the strength to speak. I did it for my girl. When my voice emerged, by some miracle, it came out steady and assertive. 'Samuel. Do you know where Ivy is?'

He smiled. 'Ahh, now I see. You don't really want a conversation with me at all, do you, Josie? You just want to know where your daughter is. My niece, I understand.'

She's nothing to do with you, I wanted to spit back at him. Instead, I said, 'How long have you known?'

'Years. Before Dad died. I heard them talking one day. Course, they denied it, but I knew. In my heart, I knew.' He looked around, nodded to the top of the street where there was a small park and a few wooden benches. 'Shall we walk a little?'

Wordlessly I started to walk. I was walking up the street with my *brother*. Was I? It didn't feel true. It revolted me to be anywhere near him.

I had to focus on not becoming breathless. My chest was so tight I couldn't draw enough air in. Did he know where Ivy was, at this precise moment? *Of course he did.* People had refused to listen, refused to believe me. All this time.

Samuel had abducted Ivy and this was my chance to save her.

Walking up the road, he was doing the 'ordinary' thing. That knack he had of appearing just like a normal person, so your eye just grazed past him but never noticed him.

The man walking at my side was a child killer.

He'd killed Jimmy, he'd visited Mum – for reasons unknown – and now he had my daughter. I'd finally realised he'd always hated anyone close to me. If I could just say the right things, agree to whatever he wanted, I might, just might, get Ivy back. It was possible.

That filled me with so much relief and sickening anticipation, I had to fight not to throw myself at his feet, right here on the street. I wanted to beg for his mercy. Beg for him to spare the only thing that mattered to me in life: my daughter.

We got to the small park where we'd often played as children. Samuel stood still, watching a little boy climbing to the top of the highest frame. I shivered and walked over to the bench on the other side. The young mother, chatting animatedly on her phone, was completely oblivious to who was watching her boy.

Samuel saw I'd sat down on the bench and tore himself away. I watched as he loped across the park. He looked too tall, his arms hanging too long. Hooked fingers and thin hands trailing loosely at the ends of them. I felt hot, cold. I could hardly bear it.

Mummy's going to get you back, beautiful girl. I promise.

Samuel sat down on the bench. Too close. Like the time he was nineteen and I was thirteen and we sat on the broken bench at the park that day and he whispered poison in my ear. That smell... earthy, ripe... a lump rose in my throat.

'Please, just tell me where she is,' I cried out before I could stop myself. 'I can't stand this any more. I know you have her and I'll do anything. Anything you want, I'll—'

He held up a bank of long, pale fingers in front of me. 'Josie, Josie, calm down. Please don't embarrass yourself like this. Screeching in a public place? This isn't the girl I've dreamed about for all these years.'

Dreamed about? I was his *sister*! Was I? He was so disturbed. The sickness rolled off him in waves.

I watched as the little boy on the climbing frame took a tumble from the rope wall. He didn't fall very far and landed on the play bark, but he cried out in distress. His mother ran to him, still clutching her phone, talking, helping him up with one hand.

'I have to know Ivy's OK. Where is she?'

'We're civilised people, Josie, and I'll be honest. I'm not going to give you what you want. Not here, on a nasty little park bench in a rundown park. That's not what I want to happen at all.' He smiled widely and his incisors looked dull and yellow.

I felt a wet warmth on my cheeks and brushed it away with the back of my hand.

'Don't cry. We're a proper family now. You and me.'

'Where is she?' I wailed. 'I can't go through another day without her. I can't get through, I can't.'

'Hey.' I froze as his hand gripped mine. His fingers felt cool and clammy. I tried to pull away, but he gripped harder, leaned in towards me. 'We're family, remember? You, me, little Ivy.'

'Don't!' I snatched my hand away. 'Don't you dare even say her name!'

He coughed hard, directly into my face. Droplets of spittle showered my cheeks. Choking, I turned my back to him, used the cuff of my long-sleeved T-shirt to wipe my face clean.

He leaned into me, his chest touching my back and the side of my arm.

'If you want to see *our little Ivy* again, listen up, sister dear. We'll meet here tomorrow afternoon. Pick me up in the car, and we'll have an honest chat about lots of things that have bothered me while I've been away. And when we've had our chat, I'll take you to Ivy and this will all be over. Involve the police and you'll never see her again. Deal?'

I turned, shrinking away to try, in vain, to put some space between us. I looked at him and found that, for a moment, I couldn't speak.

This was an admission. Samuel had admitted he had her.

And while we sat here talking, he had my daughter locked away somewhere, crying and alone.

'Where is she?' I stood up and the park seemed to wobble around me. I heard my own wail like something outside of myself. 'What have you done with her?'

He looked around the park and I followed his eyes. The young mother and the little boy had left the play area now. A dog walker strolled close to the cluster of straggly trees that bordered the road, soon to walk out of the park. He didn't so much as glance our way.

In a moment or two I'd be completely alone here with Samuel.

'I'll tell you this. The police will never find her, so if you go to them, you're as good as sealing her fate. It will be like little Jimmy all over again. Left for dead.' He gripped my upper arm tightly and I let out a yelp. 'You have two options. You either meet me tomorrow as I've planned, or I can guarantee, you'll never see your precious Ivy again.' He released the pressure. 'You choose.'

FORTY-EIGHT

MAGGIE

She watched the scene from the other side of the hedge and, when she heard Samuel's words, she left the park and walked quickly back into the house. She slipped off her jacket and trainers and put daytime television on. When Samuel got back, possibly in only few minutes' time, Maggie planned to be sitting on the sofa, leafing through a magazine as if she hadn't moved.

She peeked through the net curtain to ensure Samuel and Josie were not on their way back from the park yet. When she'd satisfied herself the coast was clear for now, she went into the kitchen. She reached to the back of the cleaning products under the sink and pulled out an old half-bottle of brandy. She felt unsettled and fearful. This wasn't how she'd envisaged life.

The fantasy went like this: Samuel would be released and he'd want to turn his life around. Once he got back home, his underlying aggression would disappear and he'd be back to the son she loved. Maggie would help him get his own place and he'd get a job. He'd come round every Sunday for a proper roast dinner and then he'd watch the football while Maggie sat with her knitting. They'd look after each other.

A simple, honest life. That's all she wanted.

All the years she'd indulged in the dream, she knew it was nothing but a silly fantasy. Yet what was there to live for, without it? She'd watched Samuel change – for the worst – inside prison. And since his release, far from reverting to his old self, she'd realised he was an even worse person than she'd ever imagined.

All was lost in more ways than one and Maggie realised it was finally time for her to decide where her loyalties lay.

She'd watched Josie pull up and then Samuel arrived outside the house earlier. Samuel had spoken to her in the street. Then they'd walked off up the road together. Maggie had hastily shrugged on a light jacket and her trainers and, after waiting a couple of minutes until they were safely up the road, she'd followed them to the park. They'd sat on a bench and Maggie had hidden behind the hedge, watching and listening.

There they'd sat together, talking. It was a sight she thought she'd never see – her son and daughter, together after his release. But far from warm the cockles of her heart, the sight of it made Maggie's blood run cold.

She'd seen Josie getting distressed. Samuel getting creepily close, and she knew her son well enough to know his taunting face. It had taken all her resolve not to charge over there and intervene.

Maggie now realised her worst fears were true: Samuel had taken Ivy. He'd left the house early on the day Ivy disappeared – supposedly to go walking at Sherwood Pines – and on his return he'd looked dishevelled and shifty. He'd told Maggie, if anyone asked, she should say he'd been at home all day. Since then, whenever she'd tried to broach the subject, he'd sent mixed messages. 'I don't know what you're talking about,' he'd snap and then one side of his mouth would curl in a smirk.

Yes, she'd told the police she knew nothing about the child's disappearance... and that was true. Not the kind of information they wanted: facts and hard evidence tied in a bow. They'd interviewed Samuel and had come up with nothing. She was beginning to think nothing could stop him, this monster she'd helped to create.

Maggie poured a generous measure of the brandy into a heavy cut-glass goblet that had belonged to her father. She downed the drink in a couple of gulps and poured another measure then leaned against the sink and looked out on to the scruffy back yard.

She'd let this situation go on too long. It was time for her to stand up and be counted, to go to the police and tell them what she knew about the day Ivy went missing, no matter how sketchy the information.

Maggie knocked back the brandy and savoured the burn as it trickled down her throat, first warming her chest and then her whole body. She'd just rinsed the glass and shoved the bottle back under the sink cupboard when she heard the front door open and slam again.

'Where have you been?' She stood in the kitchen doorway, staring as Samuel walked into the hall.

'Who wants to know?' Samuel leered.

'I do. This is my house and I've every right to ask the question.' Emboldened by the alcohol, Maggie threw her shoulders back and marched forward. 'If you don't tell me what you've done with that little girl, I'm going to... I'm going to...'

'You're going to what?' Samuel's mouth split wide, and she stared up at him as he towered over her. Her son, over six foot tall and evil all the way through to his bones. She should have found him the help he needed as a kid, instead of making excuses for his violent behaviour.

Maggie dashed out from his shadow and ran into the living room. Samuel followed, his face dark and malevolent.

'You're to blame for the car crash my life has turned out to be. *You!*' He reached inside his jacket inner pocket and pulled out a paperback. 'This book taught me what you are. A manipulative witch who controlled my life like I was a possession, not a person.'

'I did my best for you, but I was wrong,' Maggie cried out. 'I protected you when I should have got you some help. Should have sent you to an institution to get you straightened out. That's my only crime... that I stood by you.'

'Stood by me until it really mattered. Then you let me go to prison for twenty-five years. *Twenty-five years!* Can you even imagine what that does to a person? You call yourself a mother, but you stitched me up good and proper. Sacrificed me and we both know why.'

Maggie rubbed her forehead. 'Sammy, come on. Let's talk about this. It's all got out of hand.' She looked up at him, her eyes pleading. 'If you've got that girl, you need to tell me where she is. She's my granddaughter... your niece! We have to all stick together, don't you see that?'

His mouth creased into a sneer. 'Even now, your loyalties are elsewhere. I wish you'd hurry up and die, so I can sell this house and live my life in peace.'

'It's time for this to stop,' Maggie said. 'I'm going to do what I should've done years ago.'

Samuel gave a bitter, harsh laugh. 'What can you do? Nothing!'

'I'm going to ring the police myself,' she said, delving into her knitting bag for her phone. Her fingers closed around something else and she gathered confidence when his face dropped. 'Enough is enough. I won't stand by and watch you hurt a hair on that innocent child's head.'

He pressed his face so close to hers she could smell his sour breath.

'You're already too late for that,' he said, his large fist grabbing her hair and causing her to scream out. 'And now it's your turn to disappear.'

He dragged her head back hard. She screamed out in pain

but he did not let go. Instead, he pulled her upright, slamming her face into the wall. Maggie's head exploded in a bright flash. She gasped for air, wriggling against his grasp but she couldn't break free. She was so weak and ineffectual against him. She winced as his other hand came up, fist clenched and she lunged forward... once, twice... and then he cried out, stumbled and fell on top of her, pinning her under his weight.

She cried out feebly, her hand sticky and warm. The pain in her head began to fade.

As she lost consciousness, she said a silent prayer for the grandchild she would never now get to know.

FORTY-NINE

JOSIE

Since meeting Samuel in the park, I'd showered twice, trying in vain to erase the sour stench of him from my skin. My nose was full of it; no matter how hard I scrubbed, I couldn't seem to get rid of it.

I was so close to getting Ivy back now, I felt sick with excitement, anxiety and relief. I was so, so close to holding her in my arms. I could smell her hair, feel her smooth cheek against mine... I'd do anything. *Anything*, to get her back.

My phone rang. I stepped out of the shower, dripping wet, and reached for it from the windowsill. My heart lurched.

'Josie? DI Price. There's been a development. We're on our way over.'

'Wait... what's happened? Have you...'

'We'll explain when we get there.'

'I can come to the police station. I can—'

'We're already en route to your house. We'll be about ten minutes.'

I paced around the house. Them coming here could ruin everything I had planned with Samuel. Surely to God, she'd have told me if they'd found Ivy. It must be something else.

I couldn't let anything interfere with my meeting with Samuel. That was the only way I was going to get her back. He was a liar, a killer but... I'd seen a softening of his face when I played along, told him I cared. It nearly killed me, but I thought I'd done a convincing job and it had done the trick. I was so close. So close to getting Ivy back! I couldn't let anything interfere with that, even the police.

I grabbed a towel and quickly dried myself, trying to think it through.

An hour ago, I'd seen Samuel and he'd told me he would take me to Ivy tomorrow. Did I believe him? Yes. I had to. Without it, I had nothing else.

Involve the police and you'll never see her again.

It could ruin everything, them coming here... but what if they'd found her? Despite Barlow claiming they never would, it was possible. They could have found another clue, be much closer to rescuing her. They might want to take me with them, to be there when they located her...

I combed back my damp hair and got dressed quickly, running downstairs and standing by the window, watching for the car. I was torturing myself, I knew it, but I couldn't help dreaming of the possibility of their car pulling up and the door flying open and Ivy running out, up the path and into my outstretched arms at the front door.

I knew deep down the police don't play games like that. 'Surprise! Here she is, we didn't want to tell you on the phone.'

No. Something else must have happened.

An unmarked silver car parked up outside and a well-built man with red hair and a grey suit got out. I rushed to the door, feeling sick. The world seemed to slow down as he and a woman in a black trouser suit walked up to the small front gate. They both spotted me at the door, said something to each other before opening the gate and walking up the path with sombre expressions.

The woman held up a warrant card. 'Hello, Josie. I'm DI Helena Price and this is DS Kane Brewster. It's nice to meet you at last.'

Panic rose in me like a storm. 'Oh God, no! Have you found her?' I fell against the doorframe. 'Please...'

'I'm afraid we have no news on Ivy yet.' She held her hands up in a stop sign. 'That's not why we're here.'

I stood there, arms folded, hugging myself. Telling myself everything was going to be OK but not believing it. I needed to get rid of them and quick. I couldn't have this interfering with my meeting with Samuel.

'What is it?' I said, my heart banging hard against my chest. I led them inside, my damp hair sticking to my face and neck. 'What's happened? I was in the shower and—'

'You've just showered?' Price said. 'Have you been out?'

'Yes, I... I went for a walk to clear my head.' Frustrated, I looked from one to the other. 'Why are you here? It sounded urgent.'

'We have some important news,' Price said, watching me. 'News that could change everything.'

'Samuel Barlow has been found dead at his home,' Brewster said. 'He's been stabbed. Maggie Barlow is also injured, but not seriously.'

The room seemed to tip. I sat down heavily, my head swimming.

Samuel, dead?

'It must be a mistake,' I said faintly. 'I was...' I couldn't say I was just with him.

'You were what, Josie?' Price said.

'I can't believe it.' And then the enormity of the news hit me. 'If he's dead, and he took Ivy, then...' I started to tremble. My hands, legs. I stood up, sat down, began to walk out of the room. Then suddenly, DI Price was between me and the door.

'Come and sit down,' she said, laying a hand on my arm. 'Come on.'

I followed her blindly. When she pressed down on my shoulder, I sat obediently.

Brewster shuffled to the edge of his seat and leaned forward. 'Josie, we know you're out of your mind with worry about Ivy, but we need to ask you a few questions.'

I nodded. I couldn't take any of it in. How could Barlow be dead? If he'd told me the truth, he was the only person who knew where Ivy was.

Price said, 'Josie, when was the last time you saw Samuel and Maggie?'

'I don't know,' I said. I couldn't tell them the truth. 'He came to the café two days ago.'

'What about yesterday, when Ivy went missing?' Brewster said. 'You said you thought you'd seen him outside the child-minder's house. Is that right?'

It was just yesterday. Ivy had been there, at Fiona's. Playing in the garden. Perfectly safe and now... now the only person who knew where she was was dead.

'Oh no,' I whispered, my cheeks suddenly wet. 'Please God, no.'

'Josie?' Price said firmly. 'We need to know the truth. When did you last see Samuel Barlow?'

'Outside Fiona's house,' I said blankly. If he'd hidden Ivy away... somewhere like the refrigerated unit Jimmy died in... she could be in terrible, terrible trouble.

The detectives looked at each other.

'I don't need to remind you that Ivy is still missing, Josie,' Brewster said. 'It's imperative you're truthful with us. There isn't time for us to try and untangle truth and lies here. I'm going to ask you once more. When did you last see Samuel Barlow?'

I dropped my head and covered my face with my hands. 'I

just need her home, we have to find her,' I wailed. 'I can't stand it. I can't...'

Price said. 'Josie, we're having to press you about this because we know you were with Samuel this afternoon. Just over an hour ago you were with him at the park just around the corner from Sherwood Hall Road.'

I sniffed, looked up. Wiped my eyes.

'You walked up from his mother's house to the park. You both sat together. What were you talking about?'

'I... I just asked him if he knew where Ivy was. How do you know all this?'

'We had Barlow under surveillance,' Brewster said, and Helena looked away.

They were disappointed in me for lying, but what did I care?

'My daughter is still missing!' I stood up. My whole body felt alight with heat and rage. 'That's all you should be worried about.'

Helena walked over to the sofa. She sat down, her body angled towards me.

'Josie,' she said, 'I'm afraid we're going to have to ask you to accompany us to the police station.'

I jumped up. 'What, you think I killed him? He had Ivy, that's why I met him... he was going to take me to her tomorrow... she could be trapped somewhere like Jimmy was. We have to find her!'

FIFTY

1993

We had a very small garden at home. It was just a square of grass and a couple of stringy bushes, but Jimmy loved to be outside.

'The garden's too little for us all to be out,' Mum said to me one day in the summer holidays when the sun was high in the sky and hot even before ten. 'Why don't you take a book to the park while I sit out with Jimmy?'

I spent an awful lot of time at the park in the school holidays. I'd sit well back, near the trees around the edge, and watch the families with their picnics and games. I liked being near the big groups. Parents and kids, grandmas and grandads, all sitting and talking together. Nobody was made to sit out on the edges. They brought big cool boxes full of sandwiches, pop and cake – enough for everyone – and played badminton and threw frisbees. It was easy to pretend I was with them too, that I belonged.

Sometimes, I managed to get talking to one of the children and when it was time to eat, if I was lucky, their mum would offer me a bit of the picnic. Mostly though, the mummy would call the kid back and I'd go and sit back near the trees and watch them laughing, eating and drinking and my tummy would rumble so loud I felt like I might die of starvation. But I never did die because even when hunger hurts really, really bad, it still goes away eventually.

'If you go now then Jimmy won't make a fuss,' Mum said. My brother liked me around. He always wanted to come with me when Mum sent me out and when she said no, he usually kicked off.

I loved Jimmy so much. Even though he was Mum's favourite, even though he got all her affection, I never blamed him. It was just the way things were in our house. I suppose, deep down, I knew there was something wrong with me. I wasn't loveable. I ruined everything just by being around. I never thought it was Mum's fault that she loved Jimmy more. I loved Jimmy too, far more than I liked myself.

The beautiful thing was that no matter how many times Mum said I was bad, unreliable, selfish... so many things... Jimmy loved me for who I was. He saw the loveable side of me. When I got sad, he'd comfort me. He'd ask me to explain stuff and he'd listen to what I had to say, as if he thought I was clever. He saw me as his big sister and that was that.

But that day, I didn't feel like going to the park. I wanted to stay at home with my own family, and besides, I happened to know that, yesterday, Mum had bought a box of choc ices that she'd hidden at the back of the tiny freezer compartment of the fridge.

'I'm staying here today,' I said.

Mum turned on me, her eyes blazing. 'That's you all over. Selfish. Well, I'll tell you now, don't try ruining it for us. I don't want to see or hear you. As far as I'm concerned, you're invisible.'

I went outside and sat on the grass with my back up against

the trunk of the tree against the fence. I watched Mum fill an old plastic sandpit with water for Jimmy to play in.

I wanted to change everything about myself. I tried to be better, prettier, cleverer but none of it worked.

She set her deckchair up next to him and sat down with a magazine and a cup of tea. She'd washed her hair and had put it into rollers to make it curly. She only did that when she had a new boyfriend, but nobody had been to the house for a while. She put her bare feet into the water and Jimmy tickled her toes and she laughed, a pretty sound I didn't hear very often.

'I'm going in to take my rollers out,' she called. 'Watch our Jimmy and don't set him off.'

Jimmy getting excited or a bit boisterous was what Mum called 'setting him off'. Lots of people at school had little brothers and sisters; I'd seen them in the playground and so I knew it was normal for kids to run around and shout and pull faces.

When she'd gone inside, I ran over to the sandpit and Jimmy splashed me, squealing with laughter as I pretended to fall over every time the cool droplets hit my skin. The sandpit was small, and I didn't own a cossie, but I wondered if Mum would mind me stripping down to my pants and T-shirt and squeezing in there, too.

'Get in, Josie. Get in!' Jimmy laughed, splashing up deliciously cool water on to my hot face. I rolled up my trousers, took off my socks and stepped into the sandpit. I picked some stones out of the soil and Jimmy washed each stone carefully, lining them up on the grass. I felt the hot sun on the back of my neck, and I closed my eyes, listening to the splashes of water and the birds singing.

Mum came out with two choc ices. 'Get out of there now,' she said sharply. 'You're too big and I told you before, there's not enough room.'

She unwrapped a choc ice and gave it to Jimmy then sat

down in her chair. She opened the other and took a bite. She'd taken out the rollers and her hair bounced around her face.

'Can I have a choc ice please?'

'None left,' she said, leafing through her magazine.

'That's a lie.' I felt the rumble of heat building in my chest. 'There were six in that box you bought. So there must be four of them left.'

'You little...' Her eyes narrowed to slits. 'Get out of my sight. And don't come back until after tea.'

The heat exploded in my chest, my legs thrashed around and Mum screamed as I drenched her in water. I stood for a moment, drank in the sopping newly curled hair. When I turned around, Jimmy stared up at me, non-plussed.

I grabbed my socks and trousers and, without looking back, I ran in the house.

'Where's Josie going? I want to go!' Jimmy started to wail. I heard Mum's voice drop as she tried to soothe him.

I had nobody to fight for me. Nobody to say to Mum, 'Pauline, she's just a kid. She's not a nuisance. She just wants to be part of the family.'

I shoved my feet into my too-tight trainers and ran out of the house.

FIFTY-ONE

I insisted on following the detectives in my car so I could get back home straight after.

The journey to the police station was a blur. I couldn't process the facts DI Price had told me. All I kept turning over in my head was that Samuel Barlow had been found dead and he was the only person who knew where Ivy was. The only thing that mattered now, the only thing I could do for my daughter, was to tell them the truth about everything I knew.

They took me into an interview room and I was vaguely aware of DS Brewster talking about recording the interview.

'I was there, at the house,' I blurted out. 'I saw Maggie last night and she arranged for me to speak to Samuel. She told me that she hadn't got cast-iron proof but that she thought Samuel knew where Ivy was. She said the only way to get information was if I spoke to him.'

'This is because Samuel had a thing for you?' Brewster said.

'It wasn't a "thing"; it was because... it was...'

'You need to tell us everything you know,' Helena said firmly.

'According to Maggie, she's my biological mother and Samuel is my brother. She told me my parents paid her and Reg, her husband, to have a baby because they couldn't.' The detectives looked at each other. 'My parents were quite well-off in those days and it was a business agreement. The two women worked out how to cover up the secret and my birth was registered in my adoptive parents' names.'

'So there is no document trail stating that Maggie was your biological mother?'

I shook my head. 'DNA testing is the only way, but, as you can imagine, that's been the last thing I've been worried about checking out.'

'So, let me get this straight.' Brewster frowned. 'That would make Samuel Barlow your brother and Ivy... his niece?'

I nodded. 'Which I can't even get my head around. Maggie told me Samuel has known for years that I'm his sister. But that's not the most important thing. Samuel confessed to me that he has taken Ivy. He said, if I didn't involve the police, he'd take me to her tomorrow.'

'Did he give you any proof he had Ivy?' Price said.

'No, but he doesn't need to. I know he took her. I always have. It was you who refused to listen and to take me at my word.'

'It's not the case we don't listen, Josie,' Helena said. 'We have to follow all leads through. It would be a mistake to focus exclusively on Samuel.'

'Who else would take her?' I cried out, too loud, and bit back. 'And now he's dead and my daughter is somewhere he said nobody would ever find her. Please can you speak to Maggie? Threaten her, make her tell you if she knows anything...'

'Why do you think Samuel wanted to abduct Ivy when he knew she was family?' Brewster ventured.

'Who knows? He had some kind of weird obsession with me. I just found out he knew I was his sister and so he hated anyone I got close to. Whether that was a boy at school, Jimmy, or now, my daughter.'

I was finding it hard to breathe. This room was so stuffy, I felt like I was reaching overload in my head about where Ivy could be. The sense of impending doom was so strong, I honestly felt like I might just keel over. I forced a deep breath and pushed away the dark thoughts. The only way I could help Ivy was to keep going and never give up.

FIFTY-TWO

1993

After I'd drenched Mum in water in the garden and run out of the house, I went to the park. I sat on the broken bench everyone avoided that was partly covered by an overgrown bush. It felt like something heavy and hard was pressing down on my chest.

Up above me, the sky was blue and seemed never-ending. All the small clouds were fluffy and white like Jimmy always painted them in his school pictures. Everything felt as if it had been set just so, behind a sheet of Perspex. The sky, the traffic noise from the road, the dogwalkers and mums with their babies... even the blackbird singing in a tree behind me didn't feel quite real.

I imagined I was the only person in the world.

I saw how other families worked. Going to my best friend's house and seeing she was treated the same as her sister. Seeing how her parents loved and respected her. They weren't always trying to get rid. They wanted her around.

Mum didn't want me around. She just wanted it to be her and Jimmy.

I could only take little breaths of air. I heard something rustling then a deep voice said, 'Fancy a cheese sandwich?'

I looked up and saw Samuel Barlow standing there. He held up a see-through sandwich bag. 'Made 'em myself this morning.'

I caught sight of his grubby fingernails. 'OK,' I said, when my stomach rumbled. 'Thanks.'

He sat down next to me. It felt like he was too close as a third of the bench had splintered wood that you couldn't sit on. He pulled out half a sandwich and gave it to me. I took a bite and chewed. It was warm and the cheese smelled too strong, but I had to stop myself snatching the bag off him and stuffing the whole lot into my mouth.

'What's up with you?' he said, his mouth full.

'What?' I took another bite of sandwich.

'Somebody must've upset you. You look proper fed up.'

I shrugged. 'I'm not. I just wanted to get out of the house.'

He lit a cigarette and took a drag. 'I know how that feels.'

I gave him a sideways glance. I didn't know if he was joking or not.

'Your mum is nice,' I said. 'She doesn't kick you out all the time.'

'No. She wants to keep me tied to her apron strings twenty-four-seven, like I'm still a little kid. That's just as bad, trust me.' I supposed he had a point but I'd like to try it, to see what it felt like. 'Why'd you get kicked out?'

'She's just in a mood with me. Told me to go to the park and not go back until after tea.'

Samuel nodded slowly. 'So, what's your plans then, for today, I mean?'

'I'll just sit here for a bit, I suppose,' I said. I looked at my hands and realised the sandwich had gone.

'You shouldn't let your mum dictate your life, you know,' he said and offered me the remainder of his own one. 'She can't make you do stuff. You should try sticking up for yourself. Shock her a bit.'

'Shock her how?' I took a bite of the sandwich and chewed.

'She tells you to go to the park and you go to the park. She tells you be back after tea and you do it. Right?'

'What choice have I got? I'm not an adult like you, I'm just thirteen.' I popped the rest of the sandwich in my mouth.

'That's just it. You're a kid, so you can get away with practically everything. I found that out years ago. But see, I've got an idea.'

He began to whisper next to my ear and the words trickled in like poison. Back then, I thought he was just trying to help.

FIFTY-THREE

NOTTINGHAMSHIRE POLICE

2019

Helena had just reached the top of the stairs on the detective superintendent's floor when she heard someone shout her name. She stopped and turned to find Brewster haring upstairs behind her, pausing at the bottom of the final short flight of stairs to take a breather.

'Boss, something's just come up. Barlow's probation officer's been on the blower. Something about the guy he shared a cell with inside.'

Helena frowned. 'What, this guy knows something about Barlow?'

'That's what it sounded like. She's on her way into her office. She's going to call and speak with you in about thirty minutes' time. I gave her your direct number.'

Helena couldn't help but feel a wash of relief. This nugget of hope was just what she'd hoped to take in to the super. Maybe the fresh lead they were so desperate for. 'Thanks, Brewster; it's all bit vague but maybe Barlow and his ex-cellmate are still in touch. He might know something about where Ivy Gleed is.'

'Well, let's hope it leads to us finding her because time's ticking on. We've just passed the first twenty-four hours,' Brewster said grimly. 'I'll brief the team so we're ready to go when you know more.'

Detective Superintendent Grey was on the phone when she got up there, so Helena stood outside in the corridor for a couple of minutes and looked out of the window.

From this, the highest floor of the station, you could see right across Bestwood on a clear day like today. Over the Top Valley and Rise Park housing estates, towards the lush woodland of Bestwood Country Park in the distance.

She jumped as the door behind her whipped open. 'Come through, Helena,' Grey barked. 'Just speaking to the area commander about your investigation.'

Helena swallowed and followed her in, closing the door behind her.

'I hadn't much to tell him apart from the main suspect now being dead,' Grey said, fixing her dark eyes on Helena. 'Hopefully, you're about to give me more. We've arrested Maggie Barlow in connection with her son's death, is that right?'

'Yes, ma'am. We'd already got Josie here when information came through that Maggie Barlow had confessed to killing her son. Seems there was a struggle and she stabbed Barlow in the stomach with a knife she'd kept concealed for reasons currently unknown. She claims he fell on top of her and bled out before she was finally able to wriggle free and call for an ambulance. She has superficial injuries, mainly to her hands. She's out of hospital now and we're due to interview her at home at five o'clock.'

Grey nodded gravely. 'Any other developments?'

'There have been some developments, ma'am, but sadly, we're no closer to finding Ivy Gleed at this precise moment. However,' Helena added hastily, 'an interesting phone call came in literally minutes before I came up here that could mean a new lead.'

'Go on.'

'I'm due to speak to a probation officer in about half an hour's time regarding a former cellmate of Samuel Barlow. We've very few details at this stage but, if they were still in touch, we're sincerely hopeful this guy could have information he's willing to share. Now Barlow is dead, there'll be no repercussions for him.'

'Sounds promising. Tell me about the circumstances of Samuel Barlow's death.'

'When the call came through that Barlow was dead, we brought Josie Bennett in, as you know. The surveillance team had already reported she'd met Barlow in the park earlier today.'

Grey nodded. Helena had spoken to her briefly after the surveillance tip-off to get the all-clear to pull Josie in. 'You thought there was a possibility she was responsible for his death?'

'Yes. At that point, Maggie Barlow had not confessed. Josie has been obsessed with Samuel's involvement since her daughter went missing, and with the history of her brother in the mix, it seemed like a reasonable scenario,' Helena said. 'But it soon became apparent that Josie had no idea Barlow was dead. She panicked because he'd promised her that if she met up with him tomorrow, he'd take her to Ivy.'

Grey raised an eyebrow. 'Did he give her any clue where the child is, or why he'd taken her?'

'Nothing like that. As you can imagine, Josie is now in a terrible state, worrying that Barlow has Ivy locked up somewhere nobody will find her. It's like a nightmare replay of her brother's death all those years ago and she's begging us to force Maggie Barlow to tell us what she knows.'

'It feels very much like we've been going round in circles for a while now, Helena.' Grey sighed and looked at her from under hooded brows. 'The clock is ticking and Ivy Gleed has been missing for over a day now. I'm going to need something solid today, or I'm afraid the structure of the team will be out of my hands.'

Helena nodded and stared ahead. What was there to say?

Detective Superintendent Grey had just told her, in polite top-brass speak, that if she didn't come up with something worthwhile in the next few hours, she was off the job.

Fifty minutes later, in the team's incident room, Brewster called over, 'Here's your call, boss. Candice Bowman, probation officer.'

Helena snatched up her phone. 'DI Helena Price speaking. Thanks so much for getting in touch, Candice.'

'Hi there. I don't know if it will be of any use or not, but since I've seen details about the missing girl and Barlow's possible involvement, it's kept niggling me. When we heard about his death, I spoke to my line manager and he said to give you a call.'

'We're happy for any detail that might help, however small,' Helena said, holding her breath.

'OK, well, I spoke to the probation officer for a man who was Barlow's cellmate for eighteen months of his sentence. His name is Colin Saunders.'

'OK,' Helena said, writing down the name. 'Did Barlow confide in him?'

'No,' Candice said. 'Nothing like that.'

Helena's shoulders dropped like a lead weight. Seemed like their best chance of getting a solid breakthrough had just evaporated. Brewster caught her downbeat expression and raised his eyebrow in an 'any good?' gesture. Helena shook her head and his face clouded over.

'Like I said, I don't know how much help it'll be if anything. But Barlow and this guy, Saunders, they had a couple of disagreements during their time inside. The first one was over something silly like who slept on which bunk. But the second one was far more serious.'

'Go on.'

'Saunders was dealing on the inside. Sometimes it's a bent screw who's supplying, but rumour had it he was getting drugs through a visitor who was never identified. Anyway, Barlow did a deal with the prison management for information. For the remainder of his sentence, he was given a job in the library and a cell on his own, in exchange for squealing on Saunders. As you know, he was also successful in his parole application.'

'Sounds like Barlow negotiated himself a very nice deal there,' Helena remarked. At least they had an answer as to why this latest parole bid was successful.

'Not so good for Saunders, who got another year lumped on to his sentence,' Candice said. 'Anyway, he still got out six months before Barlow. When Barlow moved to his own cell, Saunders shared a cell with another man. That man's still inside but when he heard about Barlow's possible involvement in the child abduction, he informed the prison authorities that Colin Saunders told him when he got out, he was going after Samuel Barlow to get even.'

'That's very interesting,' Helena said. 'I'm not sure how this all fits in with our investigation but it's certainly something to bear in mind.'

Helena thanked her and ended the call.

'No good?' Brewster sat on the edge of her desk.

She shook her head. 'Disappointing, really. But there you go. You never know what you're going to get until you take the call.'

She might as well start packing up her desk now, she thought morosely.

FIFTY-FOUR

JOSIE

When I left the police station, I got in my car and drove around the area, through all the streets closest to Fiona's house.

I felt utterly exhausted. My head pounded, my legs felt shaky... I knew I was in no fit state to be driving but what else could I do? Sitting at home waiting for the police to come up with something felt like pulling my fingernails out one by one. I had no other option.

I turned into Fiona's street and hit the brakes. There she was, up ahead of me walking towards her house. From the back I could see her arm raised, her phone pressed against her head. The other arm was flapping around as she talked animatedly.

I crawled forward and saw Darcy skipping ahead in front of her with another girl... her hair a dark bob, wearing a coat I hadn't seen before but... it looked like Ivy... it was her. I was certain!

I put my foot to the floor and zoomed up alongside Fiona. I jumped out of the car, wildly shouting, 'Ivy! Ivy!' They all turned around, the phone fell from Fiona's hand and the car started rolling forwards at the same time the girl stopped skipping and turned and... my heart dropped into my boots. It wasn't Ivy. It wasn't her.

I wrenched open the car door and jumped in, slammed on the handbrake.

The passenger door opened and Fiona bent forward. 'Josie! What are you doing?' She glanced at the two girls, both standing staring with wide eyes.

'Sorry, I... I thought...'

Fiona shook her head sadly. 'You thought it was Ivy?' she said softly. 'It's Amara from school, love. I can see she's got similar hair from the back but... oh, Josie, you look terrible. Were you coming to see me? Have you heard anything from the police?'

I shook my head. 'I was just driving round, looking for her. I don't know what to do, Fiona. Samuel Barlow is dead.'

'Dead?' Her mouth dropped open. 'Oh my God... how? I mean...'

'He admitted taking her. He was going to take me to her tomorrow and now... now, he's dead and nobody knows where she is.'

'What? Have you told the police all this?'

I nodded.

'Look, come inside, I'll make us a drink.'

'No, I can't. I have to get home in case there's any news.'

'Let me know if you hear anything, OK? Darcy's really missing Ivy, we all are.'

I nodded. Watched as Fiona walked up to her front gate and followed the girls to the door. Darcy didn't look like she was missing Ivy, skipping along with her new friend. Fiona had been chatting on the phone when I pulled up. It looked to me like they were getting along just fine without my daughter.

I drove past the house and didn't look back. I felt crushed inside, like the very core of me was dissolving.

. . .

Back at the house, there was more press outside the front gate. They called out to me, shouting over each other. I ignored them all.

'Miss Bennett, is there any news on Ivy?'

'Josie, have you thought about making an appeal? It could help!'

'Is it true that Samuel Barlow is dead? Was he a suspect in Ivy's disappearance?'

I rushed up the path, keys in my hand. I unlocked the door and slammed it behind me, leaning against it to get my breath. I felt bruised and inadequate, like an injured bird in a fast-moving river. I didn't know what to do.

I went into the kitchen and got myself a glass of water. I felt flat inside. Hollow. Samuel was dead and nobody knew where he'd put Ivy but him.

I jumped up, startled at a loud knock on the front door. Surely the press interest hadn't turned to harassment? I didn't go to the door; I walked into the living room and peered through the window, my legs feeling wobbly. There was a marked police car outside and a uniformed officer standing at the side of it. Another unmarked car I didn't recognise was parked in front of it.

Another flurry of banging on the door.

'Hang on!' I called out. 'I'm coming.'

I put on the chain and opened the door slightly. It was the two detectives.

'Hi, Josie,' said DI Helena Price. 'Can we come in?'

Quickly, I unlatched the chain and opened the door. 'What's happened?'

'There's no news about Ivy yet,' she said and I sagged, leaning against the wall.

They came inside and I led them into the living room.

DS Brewster said, 'Josie, do you know anyone called Colin Saunders?'

I thought for a moment and something buzzed at the back of my head... and then nothing. I shook my head. 'Who is he?'

'He shared a cell for eighteen months with Samuel Barlow in HMP Wakefield,' Brewster provided.

'I... no, I don't know that name.'

'You seem unsure,' Brewster said. 'Take your time to think, it's fine.'

Silently, I repeated the name again and again to myself. *Colin Saunders...* but there was nothing. 'Sorry,' I said. 'I'm sure I don't know him.'

DI Price shook her head in frustration, her face falling and I knew yet another lead had come to nothing. I tried and failed to smother darker thoughts that the police were just clutching at straws. The terrible reality was that with Samuel now dead, it was already too late to find my missing girl.

I paced around the house, trying to escape myself. Trying to silence the terrible thoughts. I picked up my phone and called Sheena.

'Is everything OK at the café?' I said weakly.

I didn't care about the café at all. I didn't care about anything but Ivy. I just needed someone to listen. To understand.

'Everything is fine.' She sighed. 'Josie, you sound terrible. What's happening?'

'Samuel Barlow is dead,' I said blankly. 'He confessed to me he had Ivy. The only person who can tell me where she is has gone.'

'What?' She fell into stunned silence. 'When did this happen? Did you tell the police he confessed?'

'Yes. He...' My voice cracked. 'He was going to take me to her tomorrow. I was so, so close to getting my baby back.'

'Oh, Josie. I'm so sorry.' She hesitated. 'I'm going to close the café and I'm coming over to see you, make sure you're OK. You shouldn't be on your own at a time like this.'

'I'm fine. I'm—'

'You are not fine. You sound devastated and understandably so. I'll be there as soon as I can. Warren will run me over.'

I ended the call and sat staring at the wall. I felt blank and cold inside.

Without Ivy, I had nothing.

FIFTY-FIVE

I got more and more agitated waiting for Sheena to arrive. I was really regretting calling her. I didn't want company... and yet I was also desperate for it.

I called her number in frustration, but it went to answerphone. 'Sheena, listen, thanks for offering to come over but... it's OK. I'm not much company and... well, don't take this the wrong way, but I'd rather just be on my own right now. Hope you understand.'

Fifteen minutes later, she was at the front door. I opened it and looked down at the weekend bag she carried.

'Didn't you get my message?' I said stiffly. She turned and waved as a black car drove off.

'I did. But here I am.' She stepped forward and I moved aside. 'Being alone isn't good for you, Josie... I'm honestly worried sick about you.' She put the bag down and I closed the door. When I turned around, she wrapped her arms around me. 'I'm so, so sorry you're having to go through this. Have you heard anything from Fiona?'

I shook my head. 'I saw her earlier. Darcy was with another girl from school who... I thought... I thought it was Ivy.'

I melted. Dissolved. I howled and shook with rage. Sheena held me tight and strong and I leaned into her. And afterwards, I felt lighter. Lighter and ready to fight again.

I took a step back and looked at her, feeling a determination spark again.

'I can't stop thinking, she's *somewhere*. She's out there. She can be found! We just have to look in the right place.' Sheena nodded, and I could see she was pitying me. 'It's simplifying things, I know, but the kernel of truth is there. Samuel was taking me to her tomorrow and that means she is out there. Somewhere.'

We didn't talk much during the evening. We left the television on in the background, and mostly, we sat in companionable silence. I found it felt reassuring to have someone there, who I knew well enough I didn't have to put on an act.

We went to bed about ten o'clock.

'Try to get some rest,' Sheena said as we parted ways at the top of the stairs. 'Tomorrow is another day.'

I didn't take a sedative and at midnight, I was still awake. I lay in bed staring at the ceiling in the near-dark, the room slightly lit by the moon.

My optimism had evaporated. All the time Ivy had been missing I'd felt a tiny spark deep inside. Despite all the anxiety, panic, fear and grief, when I sat quietly, I'd felt that spark of hope.

I could no longer feel it. I closed my eyes, breathed deeply, visualised Ivy's face, her smile, her soulful eyes... but the spark didn't appear.

Was this it? Was this the darkest hour before the final curtain fell? Had my daughter, alone and terrified, crying for me to save her, taken her last breath? Was that what had happened to the spark?

Tears spilled silently from the corners of my eyes, ran into my ears and down on to my neck. A quietness settled over me. If my daughter had already slipped away from this world then I truly had nothing. I had nothing to live for.

5.35 a.m. My phone rang, shrill and harsh in the first light of dawn. I jumped up out of bed and snatched it up. My screen displayed: Fiona.

'What's wrong?' I cried out into the phone. 'Fiona, is that you?'

'Josie? She's... she's...' She couldn't get her breath.

A fumbling noise and the phone was snatched from her. 'Josie? It's Dave. Ivy's here. She's sleepy and confused but she's here, back in the garden.'

'What?' I whispered and moved the phone away from my ear. Stared at the screen.

My bedroom door opened and a flood of bright light from the hallway filled the space. Sheena padded in with bare feet, in her pyjamas. 'Josie? Is everything...' She saw my shocked expression, looked at the name on the illuminated phone screen and took it gently from my hand.

'Hello, Fiona? This is Sheena, Josie's friend. What's happening?'

I heard Dave's deep voice again. Sheena's mouth opened into a big 'O' shape. 'Are you sure? I mean... is it definitely her?'

She listened, and I watched her face. Her eyes darted to me and away again. She nodded, touched her fingers to her lips.

'Right, and she seems OK? She's... yes, course.'

Her mouth closed, her eyes brightened.

I can't think.

I can't hope.

I can't breathe.

'You're calling the police right now? Good. We're on our way.'

She ended the call, threw the phone down on to the bed. She grasped my shoulders and pressed her face close to mine, staring into my eyes.

'Get dressed, Josie. Ivy's back.' She jiggled my shoulders gently, her eyes glistening, bright and wide. 'Do you understand what I'm saying? Ivy is *back!*'

FIFTY-SIX

'I'll drive,' Sheena said, grabbing my keys and ushering me out of the door. 'You can tell me the way to Fiona's house.'

'I don't understand,' I said faintly, looking up at the tangerine and violet split sky. 'Samuel took her. He admitted it... so who brought her back?'

'I can't understand why you blindly trusted everything Samuel said. He's a liar and a murderer.'

She was right. But... Samuel was dead, so who had brought her back? Who had known where Ivy was?

In the car, my arms and legs felt like jelly. Sheena fastened my seatbelt like I was a child. She started the engine and pulled away.

Within minutes, the colours changed and a beautiful pink sunrise stretched across the sky, casting us in a heavenly glow. I closed my eyes and saw Ivy's face.

Sheena said, 'So, Dave told me on the phone that he couldn't sleep and got up so he didn't disturb Fiona. He peeked out of the curtains before going downstairs and saw what he thought was a big heap of clothing and material in the garden.' She gripped the steering wheel hard, her voice trembling with emotion. 'He went out to have a look and it was a sleeping bag and blankets and wrapped up inside was Ivy!'

I stared at her. Repeated her words to myself.

'Is this going in, Josie, do you understand what I'm saying? Ivy is back!' She looked at the road again, shaking her head in wonder. 'Dave said she's sleepy, like she's been drugged. But she's fine. She's inside now, and from what they can see, she's OK. No marks on her, just very groggy. He said it's like she's waking up from a deep sleep.'

'I'm scared to believe it,' I said at last. 'I thought... I honestly thought she'd gone. Slipped away from this world.'

Sheena looked at me, shocked. 'Oh Josie, no. Don't say that. But... this has got to raise questions for the police about Fiona. Ivy disappeared from her house and reappeared there, all without Fiona seeing a thing, apparently.'

'I should call DI Price.' I patted my pocket for my phone. 'And Terry! I have to call Terry.'

'You can do that when we get there. Dave was calling the police after we spoke. He said they just wanted to tell you first.' She fell quiet for a few moments. 'I know this is awful, but I'm going to say it. You don't think Fiona and Dave have anything to do with Ivy's disappearance, do you?'

I took a breath to defend my friend and her husband but found I couldn't do it. I didn't know anything for sure any more. Nothing was real.

I managed to gather enough sense to navigate Sheena to Fiona's house. When we turned into the road, I saw immediately every light in the house was on.

'Looks like the police haven't arrived yet,' Sheena said.

We got out of the car and Dave appeared at the door. 'She's fine, Josie,' he called, sounding close to tears. 'She's OK.'

'Ivy?' My voice was so faint. I tried again. 'Ivy?' It felt like one of those dreams, where someone is chasing you and you run for your life, except you can't. You can't run, can't gather any speed or strength. I wanted to shout, to scream out my daughter's name but my voice was hollow. As if I'd ceased to exist at all.

We got to the door and Fiona appeared, her face tearstained and puffy. Wordlessly, she wrapped her arms around me. 'Darcy's still upstairs asleep,' she said. 'We're trying to keep it quiet down here. We think Ivy has been drugged; she's in and out of sleep.'

She led me down the hallway into the living room.

Fiona stopped walking and pushed open a door already ajar. And there, lying on the sofa with a blanket draped over her, was my daughter. Her face was deathly pale, her hair stuck to her clammy skin. She had on a dirty, oversized fleece top that didn't belong to her.

I let out a whimper, stumbled forward. Sheena pressed close to my side and steadied me. 'It's me, darling. It's Mummy.'

Ivy's eyes flickered and I sat on the floor next to her and slid my arm around the top of her chest and shoulder, laid my head on her. Sheena moved to the end of the sofa, and stroked her hair back from her cheek before bending forward and kissing her forehead.

I heard Dave and Fiona whispering behind me. Fiona walked over. 'Josie, Dave has just made a really good point. It's best you try not to touch her until the police get here. There might be... I don't know, clues.'

I squeezed my eyes closed but I didn't move away from her. I couldn't ever imagine letting go again.

Nothing mattered except Ivy. Nothing. Not the café, or a better future, or a life far away from here.

Every single thing in life that mattered was right there. All wrapped up in my beautiful Ivy.

FIFTY-SEVEN

Brewster parked the car behind the stretch of marked police cars and the ambulance. Inside, the house was in organised chaos. Uniformed officers were taking statements from the childminder and her husband. The SOCO team and police photographer were in the garden.

Helena walked to the front of the house, ignoring calls from the gaggle of press that had gathered on the pavement,

'The child and her mother are in here, ma'am.' A young constable pointed to a door off the hallway.

There were two paramedics attending to a child and Josie Bennett sat on the floor next to her, holding her hand. Another woman, younger than Josie, sat in an armchair, texting on her phone.

Everyone looked round as Helena and Brewster entered the room.

'She's OK, DI Price,' Josie said faintly, looking back at her daughter, who had her eyes closed. 'They say she's going to be OK.'

'That's fantastic news,' Helena said, swallowing down a lump in her throat.

Brewster addressed one of the paramedics. 'She looks unhurt?'

'Seems that way. We're just monitoring her vital signs then we'll be taking her to hospital for the thorough checks.' He glanced at Josie. 'It appears the child has been sedated.'

'Probably to avoid her recognising her abductor or the location she was taken,' Brewster said grimly.

'She keeps opening her eyes, right, Josie?' the other woman said. 'She's coming round.'

Helena turned to her. 'Can I ask who you are?'

'My name is Sheena. I work for Josie at the café.'

'Sheena brought me over here when Fiona rang,' Josie confirmed.

'Right, well. It's wonderful Ivy is back, Josie,' Helena said warmly. 'We'll let you get on and catch up later.'

Back outside, they stood at the front door. Helena sighed. 'If Samuel Barlow did abduct Ivy, then someone else returned her to this garden. That means there's definitely someone else involved.'

'Could be Maggie Barlow.' Brewster pursed his lips.

'Not likely. She's in her late sixties now; it's a hefty job to lift a child and carry her around the back of a house.'

'Plus we know her hands are quite badly injured,' Brewster added.

'Now, if Samuel was in cahoots with an old cellmate, that might make sense. Once he found out Samuel was dead, the only way out – save a terrible ending – would be to return Ivy and hope he was never caught.'

'Aside from the mystery of how the child came to be returned to her mother, he might hope the blame falls squarely on to Barlow,' Brewster remarked.

'Just wait here a moment,' Helena said. 'I'll just check something with Josie Bennett again.'

She returned to the living room and addressed Sheena. 'Would you mind waiting outside while I have a quick word with Josie, please?'

'Course! No problem.' Sheena stood up and left the room.

Josie looked up but Helena could see she was just a distraction, that Josie's attention was, quite understandably, firmly on her daughter.

The paramedics walked across the room. 'Ready to take her in now. Just let us know.'

'Thank you,' Helena said. 'I'll be just two minutes.'

When they were alone, Helena sat in the chair and Josie turned to look at her.

'I'm so delighted for you, Josie. There's lots to sort out and the priority has to be Ivy's health checks, but I just want to run something by you again,' Helena said. 'We've done some preliminary checks and we can't find Colin Saunders' whereabouts. He was released about a year ago so is no longer on probation, but we've put in a query with his ex-probation officer and she's going to send us more details over this morning.'

'I've racked my brains and I don't know anyone by that name.' Josie frowned. 'But somebody brought Ivy back, and it wasn't Samuel Barlow. And... I honestly don't think Maggie Barlow knew nothing about Ivy's whereabouts.'

Helena nodded. 'We think a woman of Maggie's age and frame would struggle to bring Ivy back here.'

'So you think for some reason, Saunders and Barlow were working together?' Josie's face darkened. 'It makes me shudder. I can't rest until I know she's OK.'

'Of course,' Helena said. She understood completely. Until they got the all-clear that Ivy was uninjured, it made her shudder, too. She stood up. 'If anything occurs to you, anything at all, give me a ring. And I'll keep you fully informed.'

FIFTY-EIGHT

I'd called Terry before we left Fiona's house for the hospital. It went straight to answerphone, and I left him a garbled message.

As Ivy was still under the influence of whatever substance she'd been given and still sleeping, instead of travelling in the ambulance, I followed so I'd have my car.

'Don't worry about me,' Sheena said. 'I'll make my own way back. I'll go straight to the café to open up for the weekend staff. Let me know how Ivy is when she wakes up.'

'Thank you so much,' I said. 'I don't know what I'd have done without you this morning.'

She gripped my hands. 'Please let me know if there are any developments, Josie, or if you need anything. Anything at all.'

At the hospital I remained present while the doctors ran a full roster of tests on Ivy. After a thorough physical examination, the female doctor said, 'The test results will take a couple of days but I'm confident your daughter is physically unharmed. If you want to get some lunch, take a break, now's a good time. She's still lightly sedated but we're hoping she'll come out of it in a couple of hours or so.'

I promptly burst into tears. 'I can't thank you enough.'

Terry arrived at the hospital at 9.45 just as a text came through from DI Price. I left the doctor to explain Ivy's condition to Terry so far and opened the message.

Attached is photo of Colin Saunders, provided by probation service. Let me know if it rings any bells.

I opened the photograph and stared at the image of a man I'd never seen before. He looked big and burly but not rough. He was younger than I'd imagined.

'This is like a miracle,' Terry said, walking over to me, smiling with relief. 'Sorry I missed your call, I overslept. I've been awake half the night worrying and – what's that?'

His face paled as he stared down at my phone, the photograph of Colin Saunders still displayed on the screen.

I looked at him. 'His name is Colin Saunders; he shared a cell with Samuel Barlow for a while. Do you recognise him?'

'He's one of the guys involved in the gambling ring before the coppers closed it down. He's the one who gave me a good hiding yesterday.' Terry frowned. 'He's not one of the top guys but he's important to them. I found out he runs a delivery company which is a front for moving various illegal goods around the country.'

I clamped my hand over my mouth, ready to throw up. 'We need to call DI Price and tell her. He must have been involved in Ivy's abduction.'

Terry frowned. 'But Colin isn't his name,' he said.

FIFTY-NINE

I made an excuse to Terry and left the ward.

Outside the hospital, I paced back and forth, repeating the name in my head. *Saunders. Saunders.* I'd racked my brains since the detectives said the name. I'd repeated it so many times I'd begun to think that's why it sounded vaguely familiar. There was something there, so close now... but, if Terry was right – and he couldn't remember his first name – we needed to tell the police.

I felt so exhausted my mind had stopped working. I felt like, if I lay down, I'd be able to sleep for a whole day. But Ivy wouldn't be awake for a couple of hours and I couldn't stop my mind racing. And then something popped into my head. Something random but... I felt an overwhelming need to check it out.

I called DI Price on her direct line. There was no answer, so I left a message.

'It's Josie Bennett. I'm heading over to the café now. Can you come as soon as you can? I think I might have some information on Colin Saunders.'

I jumped into my car, my head spinning so hard I forced myself to sit and take a breath before pulling away. The ten-minute journey felt like an eternity. I quickly lost count of the number of horn blasts I received as I headed for the main road out of town.

I shouted at vehicles who were turning to get out of the way; I ran through two amber traffic lights, glimpsing red before I sped through. I felt terrified at the suspicion I had but, at the same time, exhilarated that Ivy was safe.

Calm down. Calm down. If I had an accident, that would only slow me down.

I parked up at the back of the café and ran to the door. It was locked, as I'd asked the staff to keep it since Barlow turned up the day before Ivy went missing. It was a waste of time hammering, probably, as the staff would most likely be out front. I pulled out my keys then thought better of it. It was easier to dash around the side and through the customer door on the street.

As I ran, I realised the café would be busy with Saturday morning breakfasts, one of our most popular times. I didn't want customers to see me in this state, but if they did, then so be it.

I immediately knew there was something strange, just by the look of the glass, and then I realised the blinds were half-down. The sign in the door had been turned to: 'Sorry we're closed'. The fact the blinds weren't fully down meant someone was probably in there. I brought my hands up either side of my face and pressed my nose to the glass. The door to the kitchen was closed and there was nobody at all out front.

Rather than start banging on the glass, I took out my key and opened the door. I closed it behind me. 'Hello?' I called out. Nothing. Perhaps Sheena had been forced to close up shop for some kind of emergency, had had to dash off somewhere.

I walked across the café floor. The chairs had been put under the tables as we did before opening up each morning. At night we left them on top so we could mop the floor and leave it to dry.

I opened the kitchen door just as Sheena came running over to it.

'Oh God, it's you!' Her hand flew to her throat. 'You frightened me to death!' She'd changed back into her normal uniform of black trousers and a white T-shirt, her black apron halved and tied around the back. She held up her phone. 'I was just about to call you. Is everything OK? Is Ivy alright?'

'Why is the café closed?' I said distractedly, walking across the kitchen, noting the tidy worktops and lack of oven noise. I didn't really want to talk at all. I just needed to find out if my sliver of a memory had any grain of hope in it.

Sheena began babbling about some minor catastrophe involving a power cut. I wasn't really listening. The lights worked now, I thought, as I snapped them on in the tiny office that used to be a store cupboard until I'd shoved a miniscule square table, chair and laptop in there. A shelf ran across one wall and that was stacked with box files marked for different aspects of accounts paperwork. I ignored the files and began to rummage around in the overflowing wire tray at the side of the laptop.

'It should be here somewhere,' I murmured, rifling through the till receipts, bank statements and supplier advice notes, among a ton of other stuff I'd neglected to deal with over the past few weeks.

'What is it you're looking for, Josie?' Sheena hovered around the door, craning her neck over my shoulder. 'Maybe I can help.'

'I'm OK, I'll know when I see it...' I knew I wasn't making much sense, turning up like this, not listening to the problems she'd obviously had in trying to open up. Then, I saw it. A crumpled green duplicate sheet with my signature on the bottom. 'It's here! I knew it! I knew it!'

I waved the paper above my head, almost crying in relief.

'What is it?' Sheena looked wary, as if she suspected I might have lost my mind.

I held the delivery note in front of me, facing her. 'C.W. Saunders. The supplies delivery company for our chilled goods.' I pushed the sheet higher, directly under the light. I looked at her. 'Colin Saunders! I knew I'd seen that name!'

Sheena shook her head, threw her hands in the air. 'Josie, I haven't a clue what you're on about. Why don't I make us a drink and we can sit down and talk about—'

'No time,' I said, snapping off the light. 'I have to ring the police again.' I patted my pockets for my phone and cursed. I'd left it in the car in my haste to get in here. I thought about using Sheena's phone, but I had DI Price's direct number in mine.

I reached for my bunch of keys to open the back door. I had butterfingers as I tried to extract the key with the green fob.

Sheena touched my arm. 'Explain, Josie. Who's Colin Saunders?'

I couldn't even remember what DI Price had said in full. Her words were just a jumble. 'He was in prison with Samuel Barlow for a while,' I said. 'The detective asked me if I knew the name and I said no. Terry recognised the picture the police gave me of Saunders and he said he was a crook but Colin was not the name he was known by on the street. I thought and thought and... I had seen the surname.' I waved the paper. 'Most suppliers use an electronic signature device but this one is old-fashioned. They still give you a duplicate copy.'

'I think Saunders is probably a popular surname, Josie,' Sheena said dismissively. 'I can understand your desperation to—'

'Here... look!' I pushed the paper toward her and pointed to the names along the bottom. 'Director: Colin W. Saunders.' I jangled the keys at her. 'Open the door, will you? I can't function. I need to let DI Price know I've found him. There's a connection with me, with Ivy, with Terry.'

Sheena took the keys. 'But how could this guy be running a delivery company if he's been in prison?'

I stood still for a moment. 'Companies can be run by other people, right? If I was in prison, you could run the café on my behalf. It might not be him delivering the goods. He's just the guy behind it.'

'Right,' Sheena said, sounding unconvinced. Her phone pinged with a text notification, and she tapped on it, sending a message back.

My heart was racing. Saunders had been involved in taking Ivy. He had some kind of link to Samuel Barlow and he'd been delivering to the café. It was the one thing that made sense; Barlow had paid him to abduct her to keep his own hands clean while carrying out his revenge on me.

'The keys!' I snapped, irritated by Sheena's preoccupation with her phone. 'Open the door, I've got to get out to the car.'

The colour drained from her face. 'Josie, I need to tell you something. Please, I—'

'What is it? What's wrong?' She was scaring me now.

She'd turned grey. She pressed her mouth closed and her lips disappeared, and an awful idea dawned.

'Sheena, do you know Saunders?'

She did, I could see it on her face. Come to think of it, she'd dealt with all the deliveries from the off, including which company we used.

I grabbed her, my eyes filling. 'Sheena, if you know anything about this man, you have to tell me right now.' My voice sounded so pleading, so hopeless. 'Ivy might be back, but we need to find out exactly what happened to her. He can't get away with this.'

'I don't know him! I swear, I don't.' She shrugged herself free, stumbled back from me as her eyes searched the walls, as if looking for an escape.

'I know you're lying,' I said, my voice breaking. 'I'm going to ask you once more; do you know him?'

'No! Look, I—'

Her phone pinged and she read it.

'I'll open the door now.' She pushed the green-tabbed key into the lock and twisted. As I headed for the door, it flew open and hit me on the side of my arm. I cried out in pain as a tall, well-built man with dark hair and wild black eyes thundered through, into the kitchen. I recognised him as the man in the photo DI Price had sent to me.

'Warren,' Sheena gasped. 'She knows!'

Warren? Her boyfriend! C.W. Saunders.

'Did you take my daughter?' I screamed, launching my whole body at him. It was useless; he batted me off with minimal effort. I went for him again and the next thing I knew, my back hit the stainless-steel worktop surface and I cried out and crumpled in a heap.

Sheena rushed forward, but Saunders growled, 'Leave her alone.' She faltered, stepping back.

'Why did you take my daughter?' I cried out, wincing as I tried to get up, the pain sharp and incisive. 'Why did you do that?'

'I'm sorry, Josie.' Sheena started to cry. 'It all got out of hand. I never meant—'

'Shut it,' Saunders instructed Sheena. He took two long strides and grabbed me. I cried out in agony as he wrenched my arms roughly, pulling me to a standing position.

The kitchen, Sheena, Saunders, they all felt like they were fading away. I had to keep my wits about me. I turned to my right and fell forward and pushed the mixer tap on, splashing cool water on my face.

I turned to them both. Saw Sheena's shadowed expression, wide frightened eyes. Saunders stared at me, his face devoid of emotion.

SIXTY

NOTTINGHAMSHIRE POLICE

Helena and Brewster had just returned to the station. They had parked the car and entered via the rear of the building. Helena sat down at her desk and her phone immediately rang.

'Visitor just turned up for you, Helena,' the desk clerk said in a low voice. 'He's demanding to see you now. Very agitated about something. Says his name is Terry Gleed and it's urgent.'

'Brewster?' She put down the phone and called over to her colleague, who was heading out of the door. 'Where are you off to?'

'Vending machine, boss,' he mumbled guiltily. Helena had noticed Brewster's boasts about the gym had dropped off recently, coinciding with more frequent trips to the 'naughty cabinet', as the team called the station's popular chocolate store. 'Is there a problem?'

'I'm afraid your Twix will have to wait, Brewster.' She stood up and shrugged her jacket back on. 'Terry Gleed is downstairs. He wants to speak to us.'

. . .

Helena found an empty interview room and Brewster went through to reception to collect their impromptu visitor.

A few minutes later, Brewster led Terry through. Helena was struck by how dishevelled he looked. Even worse than he'd been at the flat. Greasy hair, clearly several days unshaven, his red-rimmed eyes underscored by dark shadows. He was twitchy, too, Helena noticed. Kept scratching at his arms and neck like a man who didn't want to be in his own skin.

'I saw Josie at the hospital about twenty minutes ago,' he said breathlessly. 'She showed me that photo you'd sent her of Colin Saunders. I recognised him as the guy who's running the illegal betting ring at the Hare and Hounds pub and he's known as Warren, not Colin. He's the guy who gave me a good hiding.'

'Where's Josie now?' Helena asked as Brewster scribbled down some details. 'Is she still at the hospital?'

Terry shook his head. 'No, Ivy is sleeping. She took off somewhere without telling me, that's why I came straight here. She said she was going to call you, but I'm worried what she might do.'

'One second.' Helena took out her phone and pressed the key to access the answerphone messages left on her direct number. The second recording was from Josie.

'Hi, DI Price, it's Josie Bennett. I'm heading for the café. There's something about that name... Saunders. I think it might be the name of the delivery service we use. Terry just recognised the guy in your photo and... look, could you come to the café as soon as you get this message? I'll explain everything to you then.'

The message ended and Helena played it for the others on the phone's loudspeaker. When it had finished, she stood up.

'Fetch the car, Brewster, we need to get over to the café,' she said, looking at Terry's haunted face. 'You'd better come with us, too.'

SIXTY-ONE

JOSIE

Saunders pressed his face closer to mine until I could feel the trace of his breath on my face.

'If you know what's good for you, you'll get back to your daughter and forget we ever had this conversation.'

The café kitchen felt so strange. Cool and echoing rather than buzzing with the noise of the ovens and their heat. Waiting staff running in and out to fulfil our Saturday customers' requests.

'Why? That's all I want to know,' I said, meeting Saunders' malevolent stare and ignoring his advice. He didn't scare me and Ivy was safe now. I had to battle the urge to lunge at him again. 'Why choose *our* lives to try and ruin? We've never done a thing to you.'

'It wasn't personal, so don't flatter yourself.' He gave me a sly smile. 'It was Barlow I wanted to ruin. You and your kid were just collateral damage. You were never important.'

'Barlow caused a lot of problems for Warren in prison,' Sheena offered hastily, earning herself a warning glare from Saunders.

She shuffled her weight from one foot to the other. Her eyes darted from Saunders to me and back again. He stared at me with his fists clenched, as if he was deciding whether to wipe me out or answer me.

'Look, we were never going to hurt the kid. The quickest way to get Barlow banged up again was for him to be found messing with another child. That was the situation I provided. The fact you and him had previous with your brother was icing on the cake.' The corners of his mouth curled up into a sickening smirk. 'You should look on the bright side. Getting vermin like him off the street can only be a good thing. I like to think I was performing a public service.'

'And what about my daughter? She'll probably be traumatised for the rest of her life thanks to your sick plan.'

'That's why we sedated her, Josie,' Sheena said, as if it made everything OK. 'She was never aware of what was happening.'

'The kid will be OK.' Saunders flippantly waved away my concern. 'She was only gone for just over a day and she never even saw me. Sheena looked after her.'

Sheena took a step forward and looked at me imploringly. 'Josie, please believe me. I took good care of her. I made sure she was—'

'You snatched her away! He couldn't have got her without your help,' I yelled at her. 'Don't you see, you made it all possible? You used Ivy's trust of you as a weapon against her... I will never forgive you for that!'

Tears rolled down her face and she looked away. What did she expect me to do? Take her into my arms and tell her everything was good again between us?

'What were you going to do if your plan worked? If the police had arrested Barlow for Ivy's abduction and took him into custody, then what?' I snapped at Saunders. 'If you'd returned Ivy to the garden, the police would have released him anyway as it would have been obvious someone else was involved.'

'We'd got plans to arrange her to be found. A note from Barlow, some of his belongings around her,' Sheena said. 'Like that fleece top we brought her back in.'

'Enough,' Saunders growled at her. 'You've said too much already. We're in this mess because of you panicking.'

She took a couple more steps towards me so she was nearly at my side. She turned to face Saunders. 'He means because I threatened to go to the police unless he brought Ivy back to Fiona's house,' she said, looking at him with fear but also with disdain. 'I reminded him if anything happened to Ivy, *he'd* be the one back in prison with blood on his hands.'

'I said enough!'

'You couldn't just keep drugging her, Warren. I was scared what you might do, I was—'

He moved quickly. Darted forward and slapped Sheena hard across the face. She cried out as he turned and pushed me hard, sending me flying back into the corner of the steel kitchen worktop, cutting my face. I cried out in pain and slid down to the floor.

He stood astride me, jabbing his finger into my face as he yelled at me, his unshaven face pressed too close.

'You keep your mouth shut, or else. I swear, if you go to the police, I'll pay you back no matter how long I have to wait.'

I flinched and held up my hands in a feeble attempt to protect myself as he pulled back his fist ready to punch me. I caught a blur of movement behind his head and a flash of metal as Sheena cried out in rage, bringing one of our biggest steel-bottomed saucepans down across the back of his head.

SIXTY-TWO

Terry directed Brewster to park around the back of the café.

'Strange it's closed, and yet it's Saturday, which she told me is one of her busiest trading days,' Terry said as they passed the front of the café and turned left down a side street. 'She said Sheena was opening up today... they must be in the back.'

The blinds were all lowered and it looked to Helena like there was nobody in there. Perhaps Josie had already been and gone again, but they'd need to check now they were here.

Brewster parked up and Terry jumped out the car.

'Terry, wait!' Helena called as she and Brewster followed closely behind.

Terry rushed ahead and flung open the back door to the café. Helena heard a woman crying out and then the scene before her revealed itself. The man in the photo – Saunders – on the floor with a head injury, groaning. Josie Bennett – and the woman who'd been with her at Fiona's house – Sheena. Both women were also bleeding from the head.

Helena whipped out her phone. 'I'll call for an ambulance and assistance.'

. . .

While they waited, Josie explained some of what she'd been told to Helena.

'They were both in it together. Saunders and Sheena. He was her boyfriend – went by the name of Warren. I knew of him but had never met him.'

'I didn't know his second name,' Terry provided, staring with hatred at a groaning Saunders. 'When I spotted his photograph on Josie's phone at the hospital, I just recognised him as the main player in the illegal gambling ring and the guy who'd attacked me. I didn't realise he had anything to do with what happened to Ivy.'

'So Ivy was taken in revenge for your gambling debt, Terry?' Brewster said, frowning. 'Seems like—'

'The gambling debt was nothing to do with it,' Josie interrupted. 'Saunders wanted revenge on Samuel Barlow for an old grudge that had its roots in the prison time they'd served together.'

Sheena, silent until now, took a breath and began to speak. 'Warren knew about Barlow killing Josie's brother and when he was released he tracked her down to the café. He engineered a meeting with me and we started a relationship. I knew nothing about his plan at that stage, I was just swept off my feet by him. Now I know I was only ever a way into formulating a plan to take Ivy. I never meant anything to him.'

'He tracked Josie down because of her link with Jimmy Bennett all those years ago?' Helena said.

Sheena nodded. 'It was a readymade plan. Warren said, originally, he'd planned to abduct Josie herself but when he found out – through me – she had a child who was the same age Jimmy had been when he died, he said it was the perfect scenario.'

'And how does Terry fit into all this?' Brewster said.

'Terry was already involved in the gambling ring but Warren recognised Terry's surname being the same as Ivy's,'

Sheena said miserably. 'He saw him as another way of getting insider information about the police investigation.'

'His main aim was getting his money out of me,' Terry mumbled.

'He figured the coppers would automatically suspect Barlow, so half the hard work was already done.' Sheena looked down at Saunders. 'All he cared about was getting his revenge and he didn't care who got hurt in the process. He used people like chess pieces.'

She screwed up her face, stepped back and before Brewster could restrain her, she sank a kick into Saunders' side.

SIXTY-THREE

JOSIE

The hospital treated Sheena and I in adjoining cubicles. A uniformed police officer stood nearby but I seized my chance and pulled back the side curtain separating us.

She lay on her side, her face pale and miserable. When she saw me, she squeezed her eyes closed. It wasn't going to be that easy to shut me out this time.

'Sheena, you owe me. I need to know exactly what happened or I might never sleep a full night again.' She opened her eyes. 'Please... tell me everything.'

She sat up and leaned on her elbow, facing me.

'When Warren turned up at the café, supposedly looking for work for his delivery business, I thought I'd finally done it. I'd met that special someone. Things got serious within a short time and soon, we were saving for a deposit together. At least I believed we were.' Her expression darkened. 'Turns out that was just something Warren told me to keep me sweet.'

'You told me you'd met a guy who'd been living and working abroad,' I reminded her.

'Yes. Warren said he wanted to tell me the truth, that he'd been in prison for a financial crime. But he swore he was innocent of the crime, that he'd had no part in it and been framed by an acquaintance.' Sheena shook her head at her own naivety. 'He seemed so embarrassed and ashamed and he begged me not to tell a soul. That's when he gave me the readymade excuse about him working abroad if anyone asked.'

'I find it staggering you'd ever get involved with anyone like that,' I said. I'd always assumed she'd led a quiet life, been completely law-abiding.

Sheena looked down at her hands. 'I can only explain it by describing how Warren made me feel. He said he'd been searching for his special someone and I was the only girl in the world for him. Finally, I had everything to look forward to. Buying a house together, the prospect of having a child together. It sounds pathetic, I know. But it was truly all I wanted and I did really trust him.'

A nurse came into Sheena's cubicle. She looked at us both and smiled. 'Shouldn't be too long before someone's with you, ladies,' she said, before disappearing again.

'I assume he asked you questions about me and Ivy? After all, that's what he was interested in. Finding out how he could use us to get at Barlow.'

She nodded, her face long and drained. 'It all seems so obvious now, but he'd ask me stuff when we were out, or at home after we'd had a couple of drinks. I just thought he was interested in where I worked and the people I knew.' She sighed. 'I was an idiot, I know that now. It's just... I don't know, infatuation just got in the way. It was such a strong pull... stronger than anything else I've experienced. I made decisions I would normally have never done. It felt like true love.'

'So how did he get you to buy in to his plan to abduct the eight-year-old daughter of your friend and employer?' I said shortly.

'This won't make any sense... but somehow, he made it sound almost acceptable,' Sheena said simply.

I stared at her. 'You're saying he made the prospect of abducting a child acceptable?'

'No, that would never be acceptable. But you must understand, I was so tangled up with him by then. We were buying a house together, talking about getting married... he explained Samuel Barlow was out to get him and that unless he stopped him, he could ruin all our plans. Warren said he might be the one who ended up back in prison for a few years.'

'Let's hope he's right about that one,' I said icily.

'He assured me Ivy would be gone for just a few hours, no more. Then she would be returned.' She hesitated before adding, 'Warren made it sound like he was doing it all for *us*. So we could enjoy our life together.'

It sounded too ludicrous to even comment on. Lovesick wasn't the word for it. I'd expected far, far more from Sheena. I had trusted her implicitly, even above Fiona.

'One thing has been playing on my mind,' I said. 'If his plan had worked, what was he planning to do with Ivy when Barlow had been arrested for her abduction and he'd achieved his goal of getting him arrested?'

I shuddered at the possibilities. Had he been prepared to go the whole way and kill my daughter? It was a question I had to ask.

'Oh, nothing terrible would have happened, I promise!' Sheena took in my expression of dread. 'That's why we kept Ivy sedated, so there would be no problems. She was always going to be coming home.'

The way Sheena repeatedly tried to normalise what had happened was so disturbing. I couldn't and wouldn't excuse her part in it, but it seemed Saunders had effectively brainwashed her. Judging by what she'd told me, she had bought in to everything he'd said, barely questioning him at all.

'Like I said, if his plan to frame Barlow for the abduction succeeded, Warren was planning to fake an anonymous note that would be found by Maggie after Barlow's arrest. Something to tell the police where she was.'

'And where did you keep her?'

She hesitated. 'Warren had this place... a sort of converted farmhouse building in the countryside surrounding Newark. He'd have moved her from there, of course.'

Newark was a market town on the River Trent, just off the A1. It was around twelve miles away from Hucknall. About a thirty-minute drive away. The police would have no reason to search that far afield unless they'd had the information to warrant it.

'How was Saunders planning to get this note about Ivy's location into Maggie's hands?'

Sheena swallowed. 'I don't know. I mean, I don't think he'd thought it through that far.'

'When he heard about Barlow's death, Saunders must have panicked.'

'He did, but in a dark way. His whole personality changed just like that.' She snapped her fingers. 'I got very scared he wasn't going to let Ivy go. I'd seen glimpses of some of the people he was involved with by this time. Thuggish types turning up at the door, whispered phone calls about sorting people out.' She looked at me, imploring me to empathise with her so-called dilemma. 'I tried to discuss it all with him but he cut me off. Said I should keep my nose out and that's when I realised I was seeing the real Warren. He just wasn't caring towards me at all. I started to feel he'd used me to get his revenge on Barlow and now that he was dead, Warren had no use for me any more.'

Sheena had always been so caring with Ivy. The thought she could be part of this was still so hard for me to grasp and accept.

'When I knew it was all but finished between us, I threatened Warren I'd go to the police if he didn't just return her to you. I was getting worried about Ivy's health – being drugged-up for so long couldn't be good for her. I slept there in the building, but I constantly worried she'd choke when I left her for periods during the day. Warren became threatening towards me but when he found out Barlow was dead, he was satisfied his enemy had got his come-uppance. Then he just wanted rid of the problem that remained – Ivy – and I came up with the suggestion he just return her from where she was taken.'

'So when you came over to the house, so concerned about me, and insisted on staying over... you already knew we'd get the call from Fiona in the middle of the night to say Ivy had been returned?'

Sheena nodded and looked away, unwilling to go into details. But I wasn't going to let her off the hook so easily.

'You kept asking me how well I knew Fiona. You got me wondering if she'd had something to do with Ivy going missing.'

'Warren told me to try and get you to suspect other people and to make you feel more anxious,' she said. 'The tablets I said I'd found on the café floor, the window you'd supposedly left open... I fabricated all that stuff. Whipped the tablets out of your bag, reopened the window when you'd already closed it. I'm sorry, Josie.' When I didn't answer, she continued. 'Warren dressed in a hoodie and dark clothing, concealing his face when you came outside of Fiona's house to watch the search for Ivy. That wasn't Samuel Barlow, it was Warren. But you were so convinced, it could have been anyone. You'd made up your mind and looked for any clues to make it fit.'

I remembered my utter belief it was Barlow outside the house that day, despite Fiona and the police trying to reason with me.

I looked away from Sheena and around the ward as it bustled with people coming and going. Young people, older people, children, babies... a snapshot of humanity. A lady pushing a refreshments trolley rolled it past us without stopping.

Sheena shrugged. 'Fiona made it all so easy, I have to say. I followed her and the two girls from the school to the house while Warren waited in a van parked down the road. Fiona never even looked behind her. I just walked up the path and down the side to the small gate, which I unbolted. I could hear the girls squealing and laughing in the back garden. I stood behind the corner of the house and watched. They were out there for what seemed like ages with no sign of Fiona.'

'Then Darcy went to look for the water gun and Ivy was alone in the garden,' I murmured, picturing my daughter seating the soft toys around the small plastic table I'd seen when I first heard she was missing.

Sheena nodded. 'I just called out to Ivy from the gate. When she saw it was me, she came running over immediately, happy to see me. I told her I had something exciting to show her, that it would only take a couple of minutes.'

I felt horrified that someone Ivy trusted and loved had tricked her so callously... and that this person was talking so casually about it. I wanted to scream at Sheena but, more than that, I wanted to find out the truth of what happened while Sheena was willing to talk so freely. So I bit back my vitriol.

'I'm surprised she just left with you like that,' I said carefully. 'That she didn't let Fiona know she was leaving the garden.'

'She was a little hesitant but I made it sound exciting and told her she'd be back in two minutes with a surprise for her friend, too.'

'And then what? Warren bundled her into a van?' The thought of Ivy, terrified and upset, made me want to slide my hands around Sheena's throat.

'She didn't suffer, Josie. It happened in seconds. When we began to walk past the van, he jumped out the back of it with a chloroform cloth he'd prepared to put her to sleep for a short time.'

My eyes filled up. I couldn't bear the way she reeled it all off, talking about Ivy as if she was just an object to help them achieve their twisted aim. Not a human being at all.

'Can you find it in your heart to forgive me, Josie?' A single tear ran unchecked down her face. 'Please... just think about it. I made sure no harm came to her. I would have gone to the police if Warren hadn't agreed to return her, I swear to God it's the truth.'

But Saunders could not have carried out his plan without Sheena. Ivy trusted her implicitly and Sheena had insider knowledge about our lives that had enabled her to take Ivy away from Fiona's house completely undetected.

Their plan could have failed so easily. If Fiona had come outside and seen Ivy leaving, or if a neighbour had looked out of the window and seen a young girl walking past with a woman. But thanks to Sheena, the plan had worked brilliantly for Saunders.

She had betrayed both mine and Ivy's trust for the sake of someone she hadn't known very long and I knew in my heart I could never let her near my daughter again.

I would never ever forgive Sheena for what she'd done.

SIXTY-FOUR

One week later

I sat opposite Maggie in my living room. She looked in a sorry state. Her hands were still bandaged from injuries sustained from the violent incident with her son. Her face seemed thinner, more drawn than the last time I'd seen her, the day she'd turned up at my house.

'I asked you to come here today to say I'm sorry for your loss,' I said. 'I know how much you loved Samuel, even if I disagreed with the things you did to protect him.'

The funeral, I'd heard, had been quick and minimal, with Maggie the only attendee.

'Thank you, Josie,' she said. 'I appreciate that more than you can know.'

'If there's one thing all this has taught me, it's that our whole lives can change in a heartbeat. We make assumptions about people, about what we believe happened but don't know for sure... it will probably take years for me to get my head around it all.'

'You live life, you learn,' Maggie said. 'Sometimes it takes a long time to gather the courage to face the awful truth. I know I've done a lot of things I'm not proud of over the years. Making excuses for Samuel as a child, defending him when I knew he was clearly in the wrong. It was all done in the spirit of hoping desperately for things to turn out well, but in the end, I got the exact opposite of that. He died blaming me for the way he'd turned out. He shrugged off responsibility for his actions right until the very end. All on the strength of some book he'd read in prison.'

She wanted me to reassure her she'd done the best she could. But I couldn't do that.

'Things could have been very different in all our lives if you'd realised that before,' I said and waited. I wanted to hear her to say it... not just acknowledge, but to apologise for what she'd done. The way she'd lied to the police and obstructed the investigation into Jimmy's death.

'Things would undoubtedly have been very different, Josie,' she said. Her voice sounded curiously calm. As if we were discussing the weather. I felt the familiar spike of anger that was indelibly linked to my brother's death.

'If by things being different you mean Jimmy would probably be alive, then yes. You're right,' I said sharply.

'Well, I'm not sure about that, love,' Maggie responded gently. 'Because you see, the one person who could have saved Jimmy's life got knocked over by a car about ten minutes after he was shut away in the airtight unit. That person was you, Josie. That's right, isn't it?'

The walls of the room seemed to wobble around me. I took a deep breath and collected myself.

'I got knocked over and so I couldn't rescue him from Samuel.'

'You were the one who locked Jimmy in the refrigeration unit in the first place to teach your mum a lesson. That's right, isn't it?'

'What?' My mouth felt so dry, my throat tight. The room began to spin slightly.

'I know, Josie. I've always known what happened that day.'

I felt something rush through my body, leaving me weak and shaking.

Maggie leaned forward and said earnestly, 'I didn't lie to the police to save Samuel, Josie. I lied for *you*.'

I stood up, intending to leave the room, but Maggie's face and the stuff around me seemed to fade out and I sat down again. I had to keep my truth at all costs. I had to defend the story I'd told myself for so, so long because without it... I would slide into oblivion.

I turned on her. 'You told the police Samuel was home all day and that was a bare-faced lie. I know that because I saw him talking to Jimmy outside the gate when he left home. I saw him follow Jimmy up the road, lagging behind so he wasn't seen. I saw him up near the railway. He wanted to harm Jimmy. He'd harmed others, lots of people. That was just Samuel, how he was.'

'That's as may be. But I do know what happened that day, Josie. You followed Jimmy into that warehouse.'

'That's rubbish,' I whispered. 'I went up to the old railway to join him for our picnic. That's all.'

'No. You found him in the warehouse and saw your chance. You shut him in the old freezer room, probably told him you'd be back soon. Or maybe you didn't say anything. Maybe you even wanted him to believe it was Samuel so you wouldn't be blamed afterwards.'

A cramping pain shot through my neck and right shoulder. 'I was always going to let him out!' I blurted out. 'After I'd run home and told Mum I couldn't find him...'

'To teach her a lesson. To have her in tears and position yourself as the hero when you went back and found him safe and sound,' Maggie said quietly. 'But rushing back home to tell your mother that Jimmy had disappeared made you reckless, and you got knocked over on the main road.'

'I never saw the car. I... I just woke up in hospital and at first I couldn't remember anything at all.'

'Everybody was still looking for Jimmy.'

I nodded.

'Samuel told me about that day at the park he'd whispered to you about giving your mum a scare. To pay her back for the way she'd treated you.'

I nodded, thinking back. 'I was so fed up that day. Jimmy had the paddling pool out and she forced me out of the garden one time too many. I felt angrier than I'd ever been. That's when I got the idea.'

Maggie nodded. 'You did everything you could to get Pauline to notice you, I understand that. Punishment is almost as good as affection to a child starved of love from her own mother.'

'I just wanted to feel part of our little family,' I said. 'Instead of always being the outsider, the one she didn't want around.'

'Little did you know back then, you were with your real family most of the time. You were with us.'

I looked up sharply. 'A simple DNA test will show the truth of that matter.'

'That's right,' Maggie said softly. 'It will.'

She didn't seem in the least bit perturbed about having a test. I twisted my fingers together and said nothing.

'I let Samuel take the rap for Jimmy's death. I told the police I'd seen him around the area Jimmy went missing.' Tears welled in my eyes. 'The police totally believed me, they never really questioned my story.'

Maggie nodded sadly. 'When they found Jimmy's hairs on Samuel's hoodie from when he'd larked around with him at the gate and a soil match on his trainers from previous times he'd been up there, it was enough for them. Especially with Samuel's track record.'

Larking around. There it was again, the blatant absolving of the bullying, intimidating behaviour Samuel used constantly on others younger and weaker than him. The ability we have to make excuses for ourselves and hold on to that through years, decades even…

'I'm not sure I'd call it larking around. When I looked down from Mum's bedroom window, I saw them at the gate. Samuel trapped him in a headlock,' I said.

Maggie said steadily, 'But he didn't lock him in that refrigeration unit and leave him for dead.'

I felt so sick. 'Stop it, please. I can't stand it…'

Maggie reached for me. She held my cold hand in her two injured ones. 'It's painful, Josie, I know. All this time you've run away from that day because you couldn't handle the truth. I know how that feels, believe me. But it's time to face it, Josie. It's time to tell me everything that happened that day. It's the only way you can ever be free.'

SIXTY-FIVE

1993

Mum had been in a terrible mood. She spent more and more days in bed or lying on the sofa, out of it. Some days she didn't even know we were there.

I suppose, in a way, I kind of became a replacement mum to Jimmy. I'd get his breakfast, make sure he washed his face and hands before getting dressed. But Mum didn't care about any of that. She hated me, told me so all the time. Then one day, I don't know what got into me. I thought about what Samuel had whispered in my ear at the park, about hiding Jimmy away somewhere to jolt Mum out of her drunken or drugged state. I just snapped.

She'd seemed brighter that morning, as though she hadn't been drinking or taken any medication. She was all over Jimmy.

'I've got us a special tea for later,' she cooed, kissing and hugging him. 'Your favourite, macaroni cheese and there's Mr Kipling cakes for afterwards.'

Jimmy had looked at me over Mum's shoulder. 'Can Josie come to the party too?' he said.

'What? No, Jimmy. It's a special party just for you and me.'
Her voice dropped lower but not low enough for me not to hear.
'We don't want her spoiling it.'

I walked out of the room, tears prickling at my eyes. You'd
have thought I'd be used to it by now, but it never got any easier.

But something was different this time. A strength of feeling
surging up inside me. It scared me, but I couldn't stop it.

Mum had looked at me, her eyes cold. 'You can take him out
until then, so I can get some rest.'

I packed us up a little picnic and sent Jimmy up to the
grassy banks near the old railway. He thought he was so grown-
up walking there on his own. 'I'll be right behind you,' I said. 'I
won't be long.'

About half an hour later I set off. It was about a twenty-
minute walk from home. Jimmy wasn't on the banks of the railway. I looked around and saw the old warehouse. I'd been in as
a kid but it was creepy and there were local stories about it
being haunted.

Anyway, I couldn't see him anywhere so I went inside and
realised what a great place it would be to hide Jimmy away in.
Perhaps in a cupboard or in a little side room, just for a short
time to scare Mum. Then I'd 'find' him and she'd realise that I
was a good person to have around after all.

I heard him shuffling about over in the far corner and I crept
up there. I heard him call out and I shut the door. I didn't want
Jimmy to see me because he might tell that I was the one who'd
shut him away. There was nothing on the door to say it was
effectively a fridge and therefore airtight.

I left the warehouse and started running home. I planned to
tell Mum Jimmy had got lost and when she was crying and
begging me for help to find him, I'd come back here and be the
hero for once. She'd realise I was worth having around and we
could all have tea together.

I don't remember much about the accident. Just a red blur

and the sound of a car engine revving. I can't remember any pain because I must have been knocked unconscious immediately on impact.

I woke up in hospital. 'You've been here for two days,' the nurse told me, pressing a glass of water to my lips. For a while I couldn't remember anything about what happened before the accident and then, within a few hours, it started flooding back.

'Jimmy,' I croaked. 'We've got to find Jimmy.'

The police came to speak to me while I was still in there a day later. They told me Jimmy's body had been found. That's when I found out it hadn't been a side room at all. It had been a meat freezer. Airtight and no way out.

I remembered Samuel's words at the park and how it had all gone wrong. I remembered how I'd spotted Samuel playing rough with Jimmy and I told the police officers I'd seen him up near the old railway.

The story had all seemed so real in my head, like I'd actually seen him up there. Every fibre of me believed it and I clung to my story for dear life.

A few days later, they arrested Samuel for murder.

I stopped thinking back and looked at Maggie, expecting her to be furious. But her eyes were kind, as if she understood.

I felt raw inside. I hadn't meant to hurt Jimmy. I'd loved my brother so much. Somehow, I'd got so used to blocking out the truth of what I'd done, and Barlow had been such a perfect candidate for blame.

He wasn't a good person and so it had seemed poetic justice for all the people he'd hurt over the years. Even Jimmy as a baby.

'I've carried the truth of who you really are with me all these years,' Maggie said. 'I protected you when I could have told the police about your conversation at the park with Samuel.

And he never forgave me for that. He'd tried to tell the police himself but, of course, they wouldn't believe a word he said. He came out of prison hating me.

'So you see, when I told the police Samuel stayed home the day Jimmy went missing, it wasn't a lie, not really. I knew he wasn't responsible.'

'I never meant to hurt him,' I whispered, tears tipping from my eyes. 'I'd rather I'd died than hurt Jimmy.'

'I know that, Josie. I do. You convinced yourself that Samuel killed your brother so you could cope with what happened. And Samuel served half his life in prison for something he never did.'

I looked at her. 'Why didn't you tell the police? You could have got him out.'

'Just like I lied for Samuel, I protected you, too. You're my daughter, Josie, my own flesh and blood. I'd do anything for you.' Maggie sighed and looked down at her hands. 'Right or wrong, I made a judgement: you were the better person. Samuel has always been troubled, from the day he slashed Jimmy's face as a baby. But you were a good girl, I knew you'd do well for yourself, and Samuel, well, foolishly I saw prison as a chance for him to change his path.'

SIXTY-SIX

NOTTINGHAMSHIRE POLICE

One week later

Helena sat opposite Detective Superintendent Della Grey and waited for her to finish her phone call.

'One has a pink collar, the other has the blue, yes,' Grey said with a frown. 'Last time you got them the wrong way round but I'm sure you don't need me to tell you the difference between a boy and a girl. And can you make sure to trim all of Pixie's claws please, last time I recall one or two were missed.'

Helena stared straight ahead, focusing on keeping her face straight. Wait until Brewster heard about this.

'Sorry about that,' Grey said when the call had ended. 'My pugs are at the grooming parlour this afternoon. I have to watch them like a hawk.' She trained her cool stare on her detective inspector. 'Congratulations on a very successful conclusion to your case, Helena. Confessions from Saunders and his accomplice, Sheena, and both safely in custody awaiting trial.'

'Thank you, ma'am.'

'Quite a tangled riddle in the end, I understand?' Grey leaned back in her chair and unbuttoned her pink and blue tweed jacket with neat fringing around the collar and cuffs. 'Samuel Barlow was involved but not in the sense we'd suspected.'

'That's right. Samuel was a compulsive liar. When he met Josie Bennett on Friday, he promised her he'd take her to Ivy the next day.'

'But he died on Friday afternoon after the altercation with his mother,' Grey provided.

'Exactly. Samuel had nothing to do with Ivy's abduction. He knew nothing of what had happened, but had no problem lying to Josie for his own ends.'

Grey nodded. 'So this man, Colin Saunders, or – as I believe his alias is – Warren Saunders. He's the one who abducted Ivy.'

Helena nodded. 'Saunders shared a cell with Samuel inside, ma'am. The two men hated each other and Samuel grassed him up for insider dealing. We didn't know much about him; he's always managed to fly under the radar outside of prison. Travels a lot with his work, uses cash and burner phones, usually gets others to do his dirty work.'

'He's in the business of delivering drugs and stolen goods.'

'Yes. He's got a catering delivery business on the surface, but it's a front.' Helena paused. 'That's where the next twist occurs.'

'I'm listening.'

'Turns out Warren Saunders is the partner of Sheena Smith, who works at Josie's café.'

'Sheena Smith knew Josie and her daughter, Ivy, well.'

'She knows them *very* well,' Helena agreed. 'Saunders got out of prison about six months before Barlow and swore revenge. He did his research, knew about Josie Bennett's link to Samuel. He located her café and engineered a relationship with Sheena solely because she worked there.'

'Sheena took Ivy from the childminder's garden?'

'Yes, of her own admission she just called to her and, knowing her well, Ivy came running out. Sheena was virtually invisible to neighbours as they were used to seeing women go in and out of the property to drop off and pick up their kids.'

'They drugged the child and kept her at a remote location, waiting for Samuel Barlow to get arrested.'

'But when he died, they needed to get rid of Ivy, quick, and on Sheena's insistence, Saunders dropped her back into the childminder's garden in the early hours of the morning.'

'It's a sobering thought what might have happened if Sheena hadn't insisted Saunders brought her back.'

'Agreed,' Helena said. 'None of us want to think about that. And now for the final twist.'

Grey raised a perfectly pencilled-in eyebrow. 'I can hardly wait.'

'Samuel Barlow didn't murder Jimmy Bennett. Josie confessed that she'd locked her brother in the refrigeration room as a prank all those years ago, not realising it was a sealed unit because the sign had fallen off the door.'

Grey's eyes widened. 'Now that is a turn-up for the books. Josie was never questioned at the time?'

Helena shook her head. 'She was involved in a car accident as she ran home to tell her mum Jimmy was missing. She was emotionally abused by her mother and, on Samuel Barlow's suggestion, she locked Jimmy away so she could position herself as the hero who found him.'

'Goodness me,' Grey said.

'Josie was knocked over in the hit-and-run incident and woke up with amnesia in hospital. By the time she began to recall what had happened, Jimmy had already perished and Barlow was in the frame for his murder. Seems Josie had convinced herself of Barlow's guilt. Psychologically, at thirteen years of age, she just couldn't handle the fact she'd inadvertently killed the little brother she adored.'

'I see,' Grey murmured. 'Well, the CPS will have their work cut out deciding what to do about that one. A psychological evaluation of Josie Bennett is imminent, I expect.'

'Yes, ma'am.' Helena nodded, thinking how unfair it would be if, finally having her daughter safely back home again, Josie was sent to prison herself.

SIXTY-SEVEN

JOSIE

Three months later

Terry sat in the armchair, cradling the mug of coffee I'd made him. He stared into the depths of it, his foot tapping relentlessly on the floor.

'I attend a meeting once a week, on a Wednesday night,' he said without looking up. 'It's hard to open up, to trust total strangers with your shame. But I'm getting there. They're helping me sort out my gambling debts, my whole life really.'

'And you're working again?' I said.

'Yeah. I'm registered with three agencies now so there are plenty of temporary labouring jobs on building sites to tide me over.' He took a sip of his drink. 'A few more weeks and I'm hoping I'll have enough saved to put a deposit on a new flat.'

I stood up and walked over to the window. I could feel the waves of tension rolling off him like invisible mist. 'When you rang, you said you had something important you needed to tell me, Terry.'

'Yes.' Carefully, he placed his mug down on the floor next to him. 'It's hard to know where to start, Josie. You've been so patient, so supportive of me getting help. I can't tell you how grateful I am for that. I don't deserve your—'

'Don't, Terry,' I said, still standing with my back to him. Outside, it had started to rain. Just spitting for now but the darkening sky promised worse to come. 'You're Ivy's dad and we had many happy years together. Just say whatever it is you need to get off your chest. I don't think anything could shock me now after everything that's happened.'

He took a deep breath in. 'Remember how angry you were that Samuel Barlow forged a letter and visited your mum at Magnolia Fields?'

I turned around to look at him. 'Yes.'

'Well, it wasn't Samuel Barlow who visited her. It was me.'

We stared at each other. 'You? Why would you want to visit her?'

He shook his head and looked down at the floor. 'Because I was desperate. Because I was a piece of... I went to ask her for money, Josie. I... I didn't know how bad she was. It was a shock. I—'

'What did you expect after everything I'd told you about my visits? You knew she had advanced dementia!'

'Yes, but I've never seen anyone like that. Never spoken to them. She looked normal but she didn't even have a clue who I was.' He pinched the top of his nose. 'When I realised it was hopeless, I came over to ask you for help instead.'

I remembered the night he came late to the house. Ivy had been in bed and Terry had looked a bit wild and had asked for money.

'But...' I tried to make sense of it. 'Why would you pretend to be Samuel Barlow, of all people?'

Terry shrugged. 'You were obsessed with him being released. Nobody would believe him if he denied it. I... I don't know. There's no good reason for it.'

'The letter... it had my signature, but I never wrote it.'

'Remember that guy I know at the print shop who did the leaflets when Ivy was missing? Well, he did me another favour. I got your signature from some old paperwork and he worked his magic. It looked genuine, you couldn't tell it was a cut-and-paste photocopy.' Terry sighed. 'I told him it was to help you out, that you were in no fit state to write a letter. I said I just wanted to relieve the burden of you having to visit your mum, that you felt too guilty to let someone else help.'

'I see,' I said. Back then, blaming Samuel Barlow for everything that was wrong in my life had expanded to mammoth proportions. I'd become paranoid and fearful. I'd believed there was no area of my life he couldn't touch.

'I was going to tell you, I swear. I wanted to own up to it but... I didn't expect you to visit Pauline in the midst of Ivy going missing. I couldn't believe my luck when you said the care home CCTV cameras were offline. I thought, why not let Barlow take the rap?'

I said nothing. By telling me the truth now, Terry thought he'd set things straight, but what he'd done had damaged me. The thought that Barlow had been to Magnolia Fields had been another thing to infuse me with terror at the time. Another piece of evidence – in my head – that signalled he had Ivy.

When he next spoke, his voice sounded strange: shaky and too high. 'I've hated myself. I...' He paused and then the words tumbled out in a big fast lump. 'Christ, I'm so, so sorry. I took her rings to sell, Josie. I slipped them off her finger right there in the communal lounge and she never said a word. She never even gave her hand a second glance.'

'Oh no,' I said, shock and sadness mingling to completely disarm me. Then anger. 'I can't believe you did that.'

He put his hand into his pocket and pulled out a tiny plastic self-sealing bag. He held it out to me. 'I'm returning them to you now. I couldn't bring myself to sell them... I was going to just throw them away, but I couldn't do that either.'

'I never realised you'd sunk so low.' I felt like crying. I wanted to throw something at the wall.

'I'm so sorry, Josie. I wanted to tell you, honestly I did, but I was too much of a coward. It's only through attending the Gamblers Anonymous meetings I've forced myself to face the bad things I've done to support my addiction.' He shook his head and wiped tears away with the back of his hand. 'It was a form of madness, that's the only way I can describe it. I'm so very ashamed.'

I walked over and took the tiny ring bag from him. This man I'd used to love, who had been so proud and principled and then... I didn't know what had happened to him. He'd fallen by the wayside. But I couldn't hold him, couldn't offer him any solace by telling him what he'd done didn't matter.

I wanted to scream at him, to give him a piece of my mind, but when I looked into his eyes, I saw my own dilemma reflected back. Terry had done something terrible and now he was owning it. He was trying to gather the pieces of himself and stick them back together again.

I knew how that felt. I knew how hard it was to face your demons after running from them for so long.

'Thank you,' I said, looking at the dull, worn rings in my hand. 'I'll make sure Pauline gets them back.'

EPILOGUE

JOSIE

Eighteen months later

'Let's get you an ice cream,' Maggie said, and we stopped at a kiosk on the promenade.

'But it's windy and raining,' Ivy said, her face brightening as if it was a dare. She looked around. 'Nobody else has ice cream.'

'Well, we can be trailblazers.' I laughed, studying the board. 'I'm going to have mint and chocolate chip. Maggie?'

'Strawberry please, love.' Maggie regarded me warmly before turning to Ivy. 'What about you, sweetheart?'

'I'll have strawberry too, please, Gran,' she said, grinning. 'Do they do ice cream for dogs?' She looked down at Pip, our rescue whippet. We'd got her just a few months ago and she was still a little nervous but coming on leaps and bounds. Like the rest of us.

'I'll ask,' I said, joining the queue as Maggie and Ivy walked to the barrier with Pip and stood side by side, looking at the sea.

We'd come to Filey, once a small fishing village and now a popular seaside town in the borough of Scarborough on the North Yorkshire coast. Ivy had loved it here since being very small. With its beautiful wide, sweeping beach and kids' open-air paddling pool, it had a lot on offer.

'Next time we're coming with you,' Fiona had said when she learned of our plans for today, but she'd had a family event arranged she couldn't get out of. 'We've waited long enough for you to finally stop compulsively baking biscuits twenty-four-seven!'

'OK, it's a deal.' I'd laughed, happy our friendship was stronger than ever after everything we'd all been through.

Fiona was right about the biscuits, though. My problem had always been finding the time to make daytrips like this. But no more. A year ago, the lease on the café came up for renewal and I made the decision to close the business. The final day when the place was emptied of all the furniture and equipment I'd sold, I felt no sadness, no regrets.

I realised I'd never really wanted the commitment of a growing business. I'd started it all for the wrong reasons... to be financially successful enough that I could take Ivy and run even further from my past.

Virtually every big decision I'd made in life could be traced back to the deeply buried fear of having to finally face the truth of what had happened that day in 1993. By forever running, I'd effectively trapped myself in a nightmare that would never go away until I stopped, turned around and faced my monsters.

Her hands now fully healed, Maggie pointed, showing Ivy the whipping waves. Then they both turned and looked towards Filey Brigg, a long, narrow peninsula with steep cliffs to the north that protected Filey from the northerly gales.

After we'd got Ivy home from hospital and managed to return to some normality a few months later, Maggie had contacted me.

'Can we keep in touch, Josie?' she'd said. 'You and Ivy are all I've got. I don't expect much, maybe a chat now and then. I'd really like to show you photos of your dad, tell you a bit about him. And I'd love to see Ivy from time to time, even at a distance. I could sit on a bench at the park when you take her if you don't want her knowing who I am. I wouldn't say a word, I swear.'

Something about her pleading tone had pulled at my heart-strings, but I was still on medication for anxiety and what had happened had taken its toll. I couldn't put more pressure on myself. 'Work your way back to a normal life,' my GP had said when I'd visited again after Ivy came home. 'Easy does it. No more drama for a while.'

'Let me think about it,' I'd told Maggie. 'I promise you I will give it some consideration.'

I had, too. I'd spent weeks soul-searching, just not knowing what to do for the best. In the meantime, the police had gathered evidence and liaised with the CPS and it had been decided not to prosecute Maggie for Samuel's death. She'd clearly acted in self-defence and, as much as she knew she'd had no choice or Samuel would have killed her with the knife she'd kept to protect herself, she had been devastated her son had gone. Despite everything, I could understand that. Any mother would.

During that time, there were developments. I had a DNA test and the results showed a parental-level match with Maggie and a sibling match with Samuel. I wanted to instantly forget about my link to him, but Maggie was a different matter. Maggie was my mum and not just on paper. She had shown me such care and love as a child. Not Pauline, who'd decided coldly she didn't want me after all and nearly destroyed my self-confidence.

Reversing your thinking on something as fundamental as knowing who your parents are is stressful and takes an enormous amount of energy to process. For months I had a feeling of being untethered, like I didn't know where I belonged. But knowing the truth about my biological parents also brought relief. It gave me a reason why Pauline had despised me so, other than what I used to think: that I simply wasn't good enough.

After all the debating with myself, I realised, when it came down to it, Maggie had always loved me. The knowledge of that simple fact had begun, at long last, to thaw the core of ice inside me that nothing had previously been able to reach.

When Ivy first came home from the hospital, I was ill for days. Shivering, then feverish, as if I was trying to sweat something bad out of me. I ached from top to toe as if I'd been opened up and rearranged inside. Everything felt wrong, unfamiliar, but with it came a new clarity.

Fiona was a lifesaver. She made sure Ivy was safe and looked after in her family home and gave me the time and space to recover.

When I felt better, I'd sat Ivy down and explained, simply. 'I found out Maggie is my real mum. I didn't know until now,' I'd said.

'Why didn't you know who your mum was?'

'Because someone told a lot of lies when I was a little girl, like you, and I only just found out the truth. Do you understand?' She nodded solemnly. 'And that means that Maggie is also your gran.'

Her face lit up. 'I have a *gran?*' she'd said in awe.

I could have cried. No questions about how this could be, just astonishment and delight. Grandparents had always been a mystery to Ivy. I'd decided long ago she'd never meet Pauline, and Terry's parents had both passed when he was a teenager. When we were out, I'd notice Ivy watching other children interacting with their grandparents in that way kids were often fascinated by what they didn't have.

We arranged for Maggie to come over to the house and Ivy had an instant childlike acceptance of her. She asked no questions and insisted on calling her Gran from the off.

Watching Maggie's face the first time Ivy had shyly used the term had choked me. Her face had instantly bloomed so she looked ten years younger, and the effect had lasted. Slowly, over the last twelve months, they'd seen more and more of each other and now it felt natural to have Maggie around.

A year ago, I'd also come to the difficult decision not to see Pauline any longer. I returned her jewellery and appointed a solicitor on her behalf, turning all legal powers over to them. I had the chance to build myself up from the ground again and there was no place for a wicked, cruel woman in there any longer. I felt a stone lighter when I'd decided to cut myself free from her. For a time, I was brand new, felt like I could conquer the world.

I paid for the ice creams and carried them over. 'Nothing for Pip here, I'm afraid, but we'll give her this.' I pulled out a few grains of kibble from my pocket, which Pip accepted gratefully.

We walked along the seafront, the wind whipping our hair into wild shapes and making us laugh. The sea was a mass of raging froth, but we stood our ground and ate our treats there on the promenade.

I watched my daughter, her face bright, chattering and happy. She'd been surprisingly unscathed by what had happened. After the doctor had checked her over, she suggested Ivy should see a counsellor at school, which I thought was a good idea.

I knew stuff could come up later in her life, just when we thought it had gone away. I should know, after all. I was also seeing a therapist after the CPS reviewed my confession and thankfully decided it was not in the public interest to proceed with any charges against me. They said my good character and obvious remorse went in my favour and the fact I was still a child when it happened.

Their decision was an enormous relief, but the sentence I have given myself will never be served. I will miss Jimmy and blame myself for his death until I take my dying breath and that will never change.

Following their trials, Saunders was sentenced to eight years in prison and Sheena to three years. The world can only be a better place with the two of them off the streets.

Terry was now financially solvent and living in a new apartment in a nice part of town. He'd given evidence about the illegal gambling ring in court and, with a representative from his ongoing affiliation with Gamblers Anonymous to speak up for him, he had escaped any penalty himself. He'd asked me for a complete overhaul of his visits with Ivy, so we'd sat down together and devised what we thought would be a workable schedule where Terry saw Ivy for a day weekly and we'd agreed he could keep her overnight, starting once a month.

As Maggie and Ivy walked ahead with Pip, happily chattering and laughing together, I stood still for a few moments and stared at the wild, untamed beauty of the North Sea. After everything that had happened, I'd finally realised it was normal for life to have its ups and downs. You couldn't escape your troubles. Not by becoming obsessed with the future, and certainly not by running from the past.

By facing the truth and having faith in my own strength, I now believed it was possible to bounce back even from the darkest times.

I watched as the waves frothed and whipped up a frenzy at the shoreline. Yet when I took in the whole picture, I could see calmer waters were on their way.

'I miss you so much, Jimmy. I know you're watching over us,' I whispered into the salty sea air. 'I will always love you, little brother.'

A LETTER FROM K.L. SLATER

Thank you so much for reading *Missing*, and I really hope you enjoyed the book. If you did and would like to keep up to date with all my latest releases, just sign up at the following link. Your email address will never be shared and you can unsubscribe at any time.

www.bookouture.com/kl-slater

Missing children are a popular trope for psychological thrillers. I've previously written stories about this subject in *Blink* and *Finding Grace*. There must surely be few worse scenarios for a parent. As readers, one of the reveals we keep turning the pages for, is to learn the identity of the person who has taken the child.

I had the spark of an idea about a missing child. I wanted to follow the story of a mother who already KNOWS the identity of the person who has taken her child. I began to wonder how it might feel to have this certainty and yet nobody will believe you. The panic, the frantic sense that time is running out... surely you would consider anything or anyone who offered to help?

In *Missing*, when Josie's daughter, Ivy, is snatched from a childminder's garden, Josie knows with every fibre of her being that Samuel Barlow, recently released and the man who twenty-six years earlier murdered her younger brother, is the culprit.

Yet nobody will believe Josie in the absence of solid

evidence. So when Maggie Barlow – Samuel's mother – offers her assistance, Josie feels she cannot refuse despite the fact she despises Maggie for providing Samuel with a false alibi all those years ago.

I put my initial thoughts down and discussed the outline of the story with my editor. We brainstormed a few details and *Missing* was born!

As always, once I began the writing process, the characters took on a life of their own. Maggie, who I'd originally intended to appear conniving and manipulative, turned out to be a vulnerable and lonely woman, racked with regrets. *Missing* explores parenthood and how most of us try to do our best in a very difficult job that – as those of us who are parents know – doesn't come with a failsafe manual! We might not always realise it, but the influence of a parent can have such a marked effect on how we live our lives, and relate to other people, in adulthood. Our strengths and weaknesses can often be attributed to how we were raised. Equally, we may hold on to outdated values that have been instilled in us but are not helpful in the way we now wish to live our lives.

Josie discovers this and finds the strength to face the past at last. Maggie, as a mother who made constant excuses for her son, finally understands that she inadvertently caused long-term damage that permanently impacted the lives of other people.

This book is set in Nottinghamshire, the place I was born and have lived in all my life. Local readers should be aware I sometimes take the liberty of changing street names or geographical details to suit the story.

I do hope you enjoyed reading *Missing* and getting to know the characters. If so, I would be very grateful if you could take a few minutes to write a review. I'd love to hear what you think, and it makes such a difference helping new readers to discover one of my books for the first time.

I love hearing from my readers – you can get in touch on my Facebook page, through Twitter, Goodreads or my website.

Thank you to all my wonderful readers... until next time,

Kim x

https://klslaterauthor.com/

facebook.com/KimLSlaterAuthor

twitter.com/KimLSlater

instagram.com/klslaterauthor

ACKNOWLEDGEMENTS

Every day I sit at my desk and write stories but I'm lucky enough to be surrounded by a whole team of talented and supportive people.

Huge thanks to my amazing editor at Bookouture, Lydia Vassar-Smith, for her enthusiasm for my work and for her first-class editorial support.

Thanks to ALL the Bookouture team for everything they do – which is so much more than I can document here. Special thanks to Alexandra Holmes for her expert handling of the editing process.

Thanks, as always, to my wonderful literary agent, Camilla Bolton, who is always there with expert advice and unwavering support at the end of a text, an email, a phone call. Thanks also to Camilla's assistant, Jade Kavanagh, who works so hard on my behalf. Thanks also to the rest of the hardworking team at Darley Anderson Literary, TV and Film Agency, especially Rosanna Bellingham.

Thank you to eagle-eyed Donna Hillyer and Becca Allen for their excellent copyediting and proofreading skills.

Thanks as always to my writing buddy, Angela Marsons, who has been a brilliant support and inspiration to me for many years now. Our writing careers have grown and flourished together from the early days when we'd keep each other's spirits up on the long road to becoming published authors, both dealing with disappointments and rejections. Now, we remain thankful for being able to do a job we love every day.

Massive thanks as always go to my husband, Mac, for his love, support and patience with my schedule! Also, I'm so grateful to my wonderful daughter, Francesca, who has believed in me from the very beginning of my writing journey.

Special thanks to Henry Steadman, who works so hard on my striking covers.

Thank you to the bloggers and reviewers who do so much to support authors and thank you to everyone who has taken the time to post a positive review online or has taken part in my blog tour. It is always noticed and much appreciated.

Last but not least, thank you SO much to my wonderful readers. I love receiving all your wonderful comments and messages and I am truly grateful for each and every one of your support.

Made in United States
Orlando, FL
01 June 2022